The
Empress
of Idaho

D0110967

The
Empress
of Idaho

Todd Babiak

McCLELLAND & STEWART

McClelland & Stewart and colophon are registered trademarks of
Penguin Random House Canada Limited.

Library and Archives Canada Cataloguing in Publication is available
upon request

ISBN: 978-0-7710-0984-6
ebook ISBN: 978-0-7710-0985-3

This is a work of fiction. Names, characters, places, and incidents either are the
product of the author's imagination or are used fictitiously. Any resemblance to
actual persons, living or dead, events or locales is entirely coincidental.

The author acknowledges the support of the Canada Council for the Arts
and the Alberta Foundation for the Arts.

Book design by Terri Nimmo
Cover image © Ilka & Franz/The Image Bank/Getty Images
Typeset in Bembo by M&S, Toronto

Printed and bound in Canada

McClelland & Stewart,
a division of Penguin Random House Canada Limited,
a Penguin Random House Company
www.penguinrandomhouse.com

1 2 3 4 5   23 22 21 20 19

Penguin
Random House
McCLELLAND & STEWART

The
Empress
of Idaho

PART ONE

one

the woman lowered herself from Marv's pickup truck wearing the first pair of high-heeled shoes I'd ever seen touch Jefferson Street. At contact she lifted one from the gravel like she had stepped into a colony of snails and looked up the sunburned lawn at me.

I was pulling weeds along the front of our bungalow next door to Marv's. Every year at Christmastime our insurance agent stapled a pouch of flower seeds to a desk calendar and hired a girl to put it in the mailbox. With a shaky hand he wrote a passage from the Bible, the same one every year, and included it in the envelope. I remember how it ended: *the time of the singing of birds is come, and the voice of the turtledove is heard in our land.* In 1988, his gift had been a packet of sweet williams.

In the spring I had followed the instructions on the pouch and planted the seeds. I'd checked the patch on my way to and from school and I watered it even though a drought was on and the mayor had discouraged it. By early July only dandelions had come up.

The haze had cleared off Mount Herman and already it was hot. I needed suntan lotion on the back of my neck. Two doors down, the bikers were playing Black Sabbath. Between songs, grasshoppers hissed.

In his senior year, 1951, Marv got in a car accident hazing some freshmen. He ended up with a lumbar spinal cord injury that ruined his prospects. That was why he lived on Jefferson Street instead of New York City or Miami Beach, and why he sometimes drank too much and shot his gun in the air when the train passed and why he spent the odd night in jail. Some days he used a cane, but not that day. The day he brought a woman with red high heels to town he forced himself to walk with his shoulders back and his belly in, his chin up. Though he was mostly bald and everyone knew it, Marv grew his hair long on the right side and glued it on top with a musky cream.

"Adam, my boy."

I rubbed my hands so the dusty soil would fall away. "Yes, sir?"

"How're them sweet williams coming along?"

They were not coming along and he knew it. We had discussed them a week earlier, when he had encouraged me to take up a more manly and useful pursuit like carpentry. He'd offered to show me how to use his band saw anytime I wanted, but the notion frightened and bored me at the same time. The back of his truck had furniture and boxes in it. I realized he was not asking about the flowers for himself, but for this woman. She wore a short white dress with two red stripes, like a stewardess in the movies.

When she looked at me I saw what I had not seen. Our house was little more than a trailer. The blue vinyl siding was faded by the sun and carried years of dust. The front lawn was really a collection of weeds, but still it needed cutting. There was a filthy red chair with broken springs on our front porch. Weeks ago my mother had asked me to carry it to the corner so the garbage men could pick it up.

Now that the woman was looking at me I understood what Marv had said, that a man does not concern himself with gardening. I was too nervous and too ashamed to answer about the sweet williams. It did not matter because she had already turned and walked up his driveway. From a distance she seemed to float over the gravel. Marv raised his eyebrows and pointed in her direction with both his thumbs, took a step closer and whispered at me. He told me her name, *Beatrice*—like in poetry, he said. What poetry? It would come to him. Then: "Get this. We just got married."

"You *married* her?"

"I goddamn married that woman."

"Did you know her from somewhere before?"

"We met at O'Grady's three nights ago." He reached into the back pocket of his jeans and pulled out his thick, oily leather wallet. "How you set up for cash? I'll give you a five if you'll help me unload her things."

I hopped into the bed of the old truck and lifted the only heavy piece of furniture, a solid wood coffee table with a sticker on the leg that said "$9." Marv grabbed a garbage bag full of clothes.

"How's your mom?"

"She's good."

There was no sidewalk on Jefferson Street. We stood on the meeting place of weed and gravel. Marv looked at the front of our house. There was a constellation of wet spots where his breasts had pressed against his shirt. Now that Beatrice was not watching he let himself go crooked.

"I'll cut the lawn." The hard edges of the coffee table dug into my palms. "And get rid of that chair."

"If you get a chance. A lady only gets one first impression."

Inside, his house smelled of cigarette smoke and chemical peaches. An aerosol can of room deodorant, with an old English orchard on the front, had fallen over on the kitchen counter. The morning sun shone through Marv's beige curtains and turned his living room the colour of weak tea. It was tidier than usual.

"Where would you like the table, ma'am?"

She wore big gold rings and bracelets. She was thin like a boy and tanned. The garbage bag of clothes leaked. Marv struggled to contain it. Three panties and a sock fell on the green shag carpet and Marv laughed and cussed as he kneeled to pick them up. Then the bag tipped and a fur coat fell out.

I tried to right the bag. It was hot and melty. Beatrice bent and rushed me like a dainty ram. "Jesus Christ, child. That floor isn't clean. Pick up that coat."

"Yes, ma'am."

"Now Beatrice, a boy like this never seen one of those before."

She turned to Marv and he took a step back. Then she brought the coat to her nose and inhaled deeply, closed her eyes. By the time she looked at me again she was smiling. "You are?"

"Adam, ma'am, from next door."

"Charmed. Beatrice Cyr. *Walker*-Cyr, I suppose, right, Marv?"

"Damn right."

"This is a Valentino, Adam. *Sable*, it's called." She enunciated as though I were either six years old or from Honduras. "You can touch it to your face."

"No, that's okay, ma'am."

"Touch it to your face."

I touched it to my face.

"Soft, isn't it? Softer than a dream. This coat was ten thousand dollars once. Can you imagine?"

I tried to imagine how a woman with a ten-thousand-dollar coat had a nine-dollar coffee table. When would she wear something like this on Jefferson Street?

There wasn't so much in the bed of the truck: three more garbage bags of clothes and linens, a suitcase, an old lamp whose dust had survived the trip, two boxes of jewellery, a stuffed bunny with one eye, and a set of books about real estate and sales.

When I was finished unloading I waited in the kitchen. I did not want to go into the living room because everything was quiet and I was worried they might be kissing. The wallpaper had drawings of horses and buggies on it. Marv had found it at an auction in Denver. I had helped paste it up and there were a few bubbles and lines from where I had been hasty. It had been a fun day with Marv. We listened to Led Zep and drank root beer. Whenever I smelled commercial glue I thought of us that day, buzzed on sugar and fumes. A cloud of fruit flies hovered over a bowl of bruised bananas. She had a few cassette tapes: *Out of the Cellar* by Ratt, *W.A.S.P.* by W.A.S.P., and *Songs from Des Knaben Wunderhorn* by Gustav Mahler. I peeked inside a faded Converse shoebox and I did not understand what was in it apart from a black leather mask and a silver chain.

"Adam."

I put the broken lid back on the box. "Ma'am."

"Are you snooping?"

"No."

She took a step toward me and crossed her bare arms. They had visible muscles and tendons in them. I did not look into her eyes but I could not look at her arms or her chest or her legs either so I looked at the fruit flies and the bananas.

Marv hobbled in. His shirt was undone and his cheeks were plummy.

"All done?"

"Yes sir."

Beatrice turned and left us there in the kitchen. Marv watched her go and then he raised his eyebrows at me. "We meet at O'Grady's and next thing you know we got a suite at the Brown Palace."

"In Denver?"

"You bet." He fished around in his wallet, which was a wreckage of receipts and scratch tickets and credit cards.

"But your house is right here."

"Hotels are for romance, Adam." Marv peeked around the corner. "She's different from other ladies. This one's been all over the world. She's met industrialists, queens, the whole thing."

"What was she doing at O'Grady's?"

"Tell your mom I'll be there tonight. With my bride."

Marv did not have kids, and his first marriage had ended like my parents' had ended, with someone running. My dad ran. His wife ran. This is how I imagined the 1970s: people alone in convertibles with pink nylon scarves, crying good-byes into the wind and driving to Los Angeles.

There was a spray of blood on my mother's scrubs. I knew not to ask her about it. She euthanized sick animals and strays, the unloved, and it devilled her. One week earlier, when she was finished drinking and we had done cleaning the bottles and cans from the deck, I heard her tell my uncle on the phone, "All I do is kill. You know what I see as I fall asleep at night, every night, Oscar? Their eyes as I do it."

The animals were in love with her by then, even if they arrived at the humane society vicious and naughty. My mother whispered sweetness to the dogs and cats as she put them to sleep.

I told her about Marv Walker's new wife, her nine-dollar coffee table and her Valentino sable. We were in the kitchen. I had forgotten to close the curtains in the heat of the afternoon. The butter had melted off the plate and onto the mail. She turned the fan to its highest speed and sat at the little round table, clearing flyers and bills away to make room for her elbows. She asked me to mix her a drink. Our dogs, Gary, a white mutt with only three legs, and Maggie, a Yorkshire terrier, jumped at her to be picked up.

"What is it, Mom?"

"You wouldn't understand."

When I was in grade five, something had happened between her and Marv. They whispered to one another and closed doors behind them and then it all stopped and I did not see him for a while. I never liked to think about it but they had been a couple, or tried to be.

I told her Marv was going to bring his new bride over, for Thursday night drinks.

"You and Phoebe can join us too, if you like."

"We'll just go for a bike ride."

"Some night, anyway. We can make her a proper dinner, you and me."

I had eaten at Phoebe's and I would never allow her to eat at our house. It was not only the front, with the dirty siding and the weeds and the old smelly chair. There were cracks in our foundation and mice got in no matter what we did to stop them. I did not want my girlfriend to see a mouse trap while she was eating pasta on our old couch plastered in dog hair. One day in the spring the mice had babies and the blind pink hairless things wandered like little drunks around the living room until we picked them up and drowned them in a bucket of cold water. "The bike ride's already planned, so . . ."

My mother looked down at the blood on her scrubs and scraped at it. Her fingernails were short and unpainted because of the animals at the clinic. The cats and dogs squirmed and she did not want to scratch them. "She's a hell of a girl."

"Is that what's wrong, Mom? Phoebe hasn't come for dinner?"

"Nothing at all's bothering me." She could get angry at a moment like this, shout and stomp off because I was the only person in her life and I did not listen right, but instead she took in a deep breath and exhaled with a smile. "I mean it. This is happy news. Marv's been alone a long while. If he can feel adored in this world it's a godsend." My mother took her Bloody Mary with a squeeze of lemon and a teaspoon of horseradish sauce, celery salt, and whatever picante Uncle Oscar had last brought back from Acapulco. We were out of ice but I knew my mother wouldn't care. She made a silent little prayer over her Bloody Mary, drank a good slug, and wiped her lip. "What did you accomplish today?"

My older brother Jason and I had to do at least one thing every day that advanced our knowledge, our skills, or our humanity. Other kids were allowed to just play video games, read comics, jump on trampolines, fish at the lake, bike to the Rock, watch three movies in a row, skateboard at the half-pipe by the train tracks all day. Not us. "I got some gardening in."

"And?"

"It must be the shade that ruins things. I won't plant flowers in a shady spot again. And at practice I ran wind-sprints on offence and defence even though I didn't have to."

"When does Coach make the call on starters for the fall?"

"Soon."

"What are you thinking?"

"I'm running hard, trying not to think about it."

"Good boy."

I realized what was bothering her. She was lonely—despite Jason and me and the dogs, and the neighbours every Thursday night. She could have divorced my father years earlier by filling out some papers at the county clerk's office and putting an advertisement in the newspaper, but she never stopped believing he would return. Before July of 1989, the main worries in my life were whether Soviets would vaporize my town with a nuclear bomb and whether my father would come home.

I swept the dead bugs and dried leaves from the back deck. I dragged the rotten chair out to the street, next to the mailbox, but it looked worse there. So then I shoved it two blocks along the gravel. It slid so nicely I wished I was sitting on it like a chief and my brother Jason was pushing. I left it next to the dumpster behind Big Red, the old brick school that was now an abandoned building. It had the ghost of a hanged outlaw telling kids he was thirsty.

When you walked through our yard grasshoppers rose up and hopped in front of you. I cut the lawn and hoped the bugs were smart enough not to get themselves killed. In our part of town we always cut the lawn with our shirts off, wearing Broncos hats, with a can of something cold. There were two ponderosa pines that had grown too big but filled the whole backyard with butterscotch. A good one could live for five hundred years. The smell of the afternoon, of what heat did to a dry town, was promising.

My arms were tanned. I was too bashful to say it to my mother but I was sure I would be a starter, though it was nearly impossible for a sophomore. Phoebe and I had plans to ride our bicycles to the far side of the lake and kiss in the moonlight.

My mother liked me to spend time with adults, when they were over, to better understand their world and to learn how to speak to them. The first guests to arrive were Geraldine and Don, a couple from England who owned a tanning salon in Monument, two in The Springs, and a La Petite Boulangerie franchise in Denver. They lived in the oldest and finest house on the street, the white one on the corner with a wraparound front porch and a garage so big and so empty of crap you could actually park a car in it. They were the only ones to bring imported beer. A snack, to Geraldine and Don, was a cheese plate that did not include cheddar. Both of them had come from a far poorer town than Monument and neither of them had gone to university. Their eyes had a juicy film over them, they walked gingerly through the broken chairs I had set up, and they slurred their words. "We enjoyed a gin cocktail or two this aft, a minty bit of warm-up." Geraldine dropped their beer into the cooler.

Don always wore a pressed button-up shirt, a cardigan sweater, and chinos he cinched much higher than his waist with a blue fabric belt. Geraldine wore almost the same outfit. They reminded me of a cartoon I had seen about storks who were doctors.

The biker couple from across the street came next, with a case of twenty-four Budweiser. Shirley was the woman's name and the man was Hubert but he insisted everyone call him Brother H. He almost never said a word. They had three Doberman pinschers who dug massive holes in the backyard and barked at the passing trains, but no children. They rode loud Harleys with a bunch of other men and women who wore jean jackets with the arms cut off and patches on the back, but the patches had crucifixes on them instead of skulls and crossbones. Every September the gang would raise money with a ride to the Crystal Cathedral in California, and at Christmastime they gave a big cheque to St. Peter Catholic Church. My mother suspected Brother H had done something terrible, that he had hurt someone, and that Shirley and Jesus had saved him.

There was time for everyone to have two or three cans of beer before Marv and his new wife walked up the steps. I was hammering errant nails down because they were rusty and Don had said one of us could end up with tetanus. The adults stood and clapped. Marv took a bow and then he thanked the Academy and Jesus Christ.

Beatrice gently slapped him. "I'd have to verify, Marvin, but that's probably blaspheming."

Everyone laughed at Marv and then they laughed differently

at Beatrice. She wore a diamond necklace, an ironed white dress, and hard-plastic polka-dot shoes. In the soft dusk light she made eye contact with each one of us. She had a dimple on one side of her mouth as she smiled. There was a line of sweat at the place where her forehead met her black hair, pulled back in a bun.

"I am just delighted to be among you, my new friends." She spoke like the winner of an award, like she had been practicing in front of a mirror. "My name is Beatrice Cyr. Hold on now. *Walker*-Cyr, I am proud to say."

No one said "delighted" except the host of *Mouseterpiece Theater* on the Disney Channel, the gentleman who introduced Chip 'n' Dale like they were in Shakespeare.

Marv lifted two beer bottles out of the box he had carried in and popped them open. He slid off his chair and presented one to Beatrice, on his knees. "You deserve Dom Pérignon, darling. We'll get you a bottle of that later."

"Péri . . ." Don snorted. "Oh, please, Marv. Do you have any idea how much a bottle of *haute* champagne costs?"

No one said anything for a while. Marv looked down at his beer. Beatrice sat up straight and put a hand over his. I knocked the last few nails down. Grasshoppers and the distant hum of trucks replaced the kid-shout and lawn mowers of daytime on Jefferson Street. My mother tore the label off her beer bottle and handed it to me, a wet secret.

Shirley said, "Okay, people!" and began introductions. There were no more nails to hammer, Phoebe would not come for a while, so I went down to my room to get the portable stereo and a few cassettes. There was some music old

15

people liked that I appreciated, cassettes my mother bought at Second Glance like Bob Marley and Simon & Garfunkel and Joni Mitchell and Steely Dan. I plugged in the machine next to Marv's chair and put in *Pretzel Logic*. When I stood up, Beatrice was looking at me like mule deer do when they learn to trust people.

Beatrice moved along to "Rikki Don't Lose That Number."

My mother touched people when she spoke, their arms and hands. While she did not enjoy euthanizing animals it had done something to her, telling so many people the bad news. She grabbed Beatrice's tiny wrist. "He's never had trouble with it, hanging around the adults. Jason, his older brother, never wanted a thing to do with us."

There wasn't room enough in the fridge for all the beer on Thursday nights so we kept the bottles and cans in an old orange camping cooler with ice. It smelled like hot garbage in there when it was empty. I transferred Marv's beer to the cooler.

"So you live with two gentlemen, Helen?"

My mother winked at me. "Just one. His older brother's off at college."

"And Adam, how old are you?"

"Turning fifteen."

"So what's that, a . . ."

"I'm a sophomore."

My mother reached for me. "He's a November baby. All his friends are older."

Most Thursday nights, Marv was a monster of energy after a few Coors. He was the man he used to be, back in high

16

school, before his accident. He sang, he danced, he told jokes adults didn't normally tell around boys my age. Marv punched my shoulder. "You'll hear about his brother, Jason. Plays wide receiver for the Oklahoma State Cowboys. But Adam here, boy might be even better."

"Nah."

"You stop it with that modesty, son. He's a hell of a damn fine player *and* he's on the honour roll. He'll get out too."

"As a happy immigrant I dislike the phrase 'get out.'" Don leaned back in his chair and waited for everyone to look at him. "I certainly don't see our lovely town as a place to escape from. Spend a year in the north of England, dear Marvin, and then we'll talk about escape." He turned to me for a moment. "And let's be realistic. There is a vast difference between 'hell of a damn fine player' and what Jason's achieved. Better than *Jason*? Jason is extraordinary. Our Adam here, he's a fine boy, but . . ."

Geraldine laughed. "You've never been to an American football game in your life. You don't even know the rules!"

"Forgive me, but it's dangerous, the way we're raising our children today. 'All your dreams can come true' and such-like. 'When we wish upon a star.'" Don turned to Beatrice for approval before returning to Marv. When he could not think of the next word to say he cleared his throat. This was one of his tics, like yanking up the waist of his pants. I'm not sure he knew he did it. I hated Don.

"In reality, very few of us do much of anything worth crowing about." He shook his head at Marv. "Good God, man. Weren't you supposed to be retired from a career in

Major League Baseball just now? Retired to the islands? Marv
Walker of the—what?—New York bloody Yankees? Yet
here you are, a fat American labourer like all the millions
of other fat American labourers. You do something—what
do you do?—in a medical devices factory that—if my sources
are correct—could shut down any time and move to Mexico
if not China. This is a particularly American disease, wishing
upon a star, and frankly it's below even you."

Marv smiled, like Don had been telling a joke all this time,
and he started to respond but Beatrice whispered to him and
he stopped.

This sort of thing happened at school all the time. No
one teaches us how to react when someone goes after us. If
we're not good at talking, all we can do is fight. But most of
us can't fight. Even if we could fight, we don't. So we laugh
or we say nothing or we choose to speak and give them, the
Dons, more of our hearts to go after. Marv's eyes were puffy
now. I waited for him to respond somehow, to say something
about Don's weak chin or how he pulled his pants up way
too high. Even with his lumbar spinal cord injury, I knew
Marv could pick up Don and crack him in half on top of the
old chain link fence and throw him in a ditch.

"I think it's in us to want the best for ourselves and our
kids." Shirley raised her beer and encouraged everyone to
join her. "I know that's what God wants for us, while we're
here. Otherwise . . ."

It was almost eight o'clock and Phoebe was finished ballet
at seven-thirty. I went inside and did thirty push-ups,
changed into an Ocean Pacific T-shirt warm from the dryer,

checked for new pimples, and splashed water on my face. Then I did twenty more push-ups so the veins in my arms would pop.

Beatrice was talking about the wind. It surprised her, as a newcomer to El Paso County, that it could be soft and warm and fragrant this close to the mountains. While she had lived in many places, here in America and over in Europe, she had never been to Colorado. She had been working in landscape architecture, down in New Mexico—had any of us been to Taos, she asked, and no one responded—and she was really just passing through when she saw a turn-off for Garden of the Gods.

"'Garden of the Gods'! Now what kind of person calls a place that? I had to know. Of course I imagined it would be nothing. A disappointment. Some marketing scheme to get us to pull off the interstate. I pulled off the interstate and *pow*."

"*Pow!*" Marv squeezed an empty beer can. "Her shitty old car dies. And I don't mean it needs a new radiator. I mean her engine block fell out. A good chunk of it anyway. She's looking at a thousand-dollar repair at least."

Beatrice lifted her beer. "On a five-hundred-dollar car, mind."

"I was doing a hot-shot run into The Springs and there she is, leaning over this mess of an old red Mustang."

"It was really quite lovely once."

We were all listening to the story, watching Marv and Beatrice watch one another. She spoke formally and clearly, like she had arrived from another century, but every now and then 1989 would creep in. She would forget to add the

19

g to the end of *passing* or *working*, or she would say *ain't*. I remembered the man's name from *Mouseterpiece Theater*: George Plimpton.

My mother laughed. "And?"

And a bell rang.

I was supposed to meet Phoebe out on the street with my bicycle. I knew she would not want to come up on the deck: her bike's bell dinged every time she hit a bump, and our driveway was an uneven mess of gravel. But my mother called her.

Phoebe took my hand in hers and introduced herself. Some people at school called Phoebe a snob and a preppy but she was neither. Phoebe knew herself. She wore orange shorts with creases ironed into them and a white Polo shirt. Her black shoes were shined and her white socks came up almost to her knees. I knew how she felt about our house, our neighbourhood, our people, but we never talked about it. Phoebe was better than us and sometimes at night it gave me a stomach ache.

"Well, aren't you a gorgeous couple." Only as she said it, Beatrice didn't look at us. She looked at me.

Don mumbled something into his beer. Shirley, who was tiny and muscular and had come to resemble her dogs, clapped her hands again. "All right, Beatrice. Back to the story."

I wanted to hear her story too. Phoebe pulled me and waved with her free hand, wishing everyone on the deck a *really super evening*.

Skateboarding was my preference but Phoebe would not let me teach her. I pumped the back tire of the ten-speed my father had abandoned along with everything else and walked it through the grasshoppers. Phoebe stared at me with a smile that carried no joy.

For all the butterscotch of the pines, it did not smell prosperous on Jefferson Street. There was the beer and the spilled gasoline products, a puff of mothballs from Shirley and Brother H's house, the barbecued wieners, and the cloud of dust from the unpaved street that never had time to settle before another pickup rolled past.

We turned left and then right, along the railroad tracks. At the crossing Phoebe stopped her bicycle. "Why did you make me do that?"

Instead of answering I told her about Don going after Marv right in front of his new bride. We passed my friend Simon's house at the top of the lake. His father, the only Black man in Monument, was inspecting his peonies in the front yard. He wore slacks and a cardigan sweater over a shirt and tie.

It was the last of the light. The sun was on the other side of Mount Herman now but there was enough of it to turn the underside of the clouds soft pink. We parked the bikes by our favourite rock. Monument Lake was stocked with pike and a few of the fishermen remained, their rods set up in tubes in a way that made the whole thing seem boring. They drank beer and spoke softly so they would not spook the fish. Bugs were out but it was not so bad.

Phoebe's hair had feathered in the wind. "Is it hard to fight it off?"

"Fight what off?"

"The caveman thing. That's what the Englishman was doing to Marv. He was snorting and pissing. He was being dominant."

"Me want Phoebe."

We sat on our rock. A bunch of them had stuck around at the end of the last ice age, in random spots along the Front Range. Someone had figured it would be a good idea to pick them up and move them along the lake instead of installing benches. This is what I had been looking forward to all week, an hour or two alone with my girlfriend on an uncomfortable rock. Phoebe was in Denver and The Springs a lot because some of her friends were already sixteen, and their parents had bought them Trans Ams and Jeeps for their birthdays. Then she had ballet and tennis and volunteer activities with the mentally retarded. I had football and my job pumping gas, so it was hard to find nights like these. Though it wouldn't have mattered if she were available every night. Her parents did not like us going on dates too often. There would be plenty of time for that later. We were supposed to be *just kids* a little longer.

The last two fishermen got in their trucks and kicked up a lot of dust. They played country music out their open windows and shouted their goodbyes. One of them said, "Hey, Reg. Maybe tomorrow, hey?"

Reg seemed to think about it a moment and then nodded. "Yap."

When we were alone we slid in close. She hummed when we kissed, so faintly only I could hear. I reached under her shirt and she pushed my hand away and told me to behave, our lips still touching. I wanted to touch her nipple but she was against it. This is all we had done for six months. We kissed so much our lips went dry and our mouths turned bitter. There were frogs and cicadas, and the grasshoppers were at it, and some other bugs whipped along the surface of the lake.

She whispered as the darkness turned complete. "I'm wet down there."

"Can I touch it?"

"No."

Sometimes I asked why we were waiting, but those questions only ruined things between us so I did not press her. Phoebe had red hair and the whitest skin, with freckles around her nose and on her arms. We had been to the pool together a couple of times, so I had seen her in a bikini. The freckles were everywhere. She was older than me, fifteen and a half. She had a few pimples on her forehead and chin and I had to keep telling her I didn't notice.

"What will you wear to the wedding?"

"My dad left some suits."

She palmed herself on the forehead. "Your dad ran off when you were five."

"Four."

"You'll look like John Travolta."

I stood up and performed my interpretation of disco.

"My mom said she'd buy you a suit."

"No way."

"It's our fault you need one—my sister's fault. They're expensive. And there's no other reason to have a suit."

23

"I'll get a stupid suit."

"Don't be mad."

"I'm not a charity."

Phoebe was going to say something else but instead she leaned back on the rock and sighed. There was just enough light from the moon to see half a smile. She was my boss and she liked it. Four ducks bumped into one another near the shore, cooing at us, begging for the stale bread old people tossed in the mornings. A mist came up from the water. Now that we weren't kissing the frogs seemed louder. Our biology teacher, Mr. Bevins, said as long as the frogs are croaking your town is clean. When the frogs stop croaking it's time to pack up and go.

"You have to wonder about that new woman."

"Beatrice."

"I had a doll with that name. Isn't he a bit of a gimp, Marv? How old is he?"

"He's not a gimp. He's fifty-five or so. Maybe sixty."

"And she's, what, twenty-five? Thirty?"

"I don't know. Marv's a great guy."

"He took you to a tractor pull."

"Just once."

"In my crystal ball I see corn liquor and fistfights. But she seems like a . . . I don't know. A cultured woman from the city. I don't know what city, not Denver. Or maybe she's just pretending. '*Gorgeous* couple.'"

I picked up a handful of rocks and threw them into the lake. One of the ducks swam over to see if it was bread. Two fighter jets flew low. People talked so much about war but it never actually happened, unless movies like *Top Gun* told truths we weren't allowed to know. It was there for me, as a backup. If everyone was wrong and I could not get a scholar-ship, either through football or the honour roll, I could become a fighter pilot and fly over Colorado, playing at war.

Other sophomores did not go to the river to kiss. They watched *Dirty Dancing* and *Saturday Night Live* in basements, with all the lights out, and they reached up shirts and touched one another on the nipples and down there. Phoebe said people of good breeding preferred public places.

two

There was a liquor store across from the gas station where I worked, on Old Denver Road. Whenever we needed a bottle of something, we would go over and ask if they could change a fifty. Sometimes they could and sometimes they couldn't, but Dana, one of the cashiers, would always meet Simon or me in the back five minutes later. She had a thin moustache and crooked black hairs that shot out from her chin like the legs of a dead spider. Some nights, at the gas station, we worked through the case of Dana's chin hairs. What kept her from pulling them out?

If we gave her five dollars more than the retail price, Dana would buy us whatever we needed. We almost always needed Jamaican rum.

Eugene's Gas Stop was open until ten o'clock. When new

people came to Monument everyone told them to take Old Denver Road instead of the interstate because it was *so beautiful*. They were not talking about Gene's shack. In our final hour Simon and I had to count the cash and credit-card receipts, sweep and mop the scratched white-tile floor, and drop a long ruler into the tank underneath the pumps to measure the levels. We tried to finish by nine. Gene and his wife often went out of town in the summer, to fish at the Blue Mesa Reservoir. We poured rum into our Dr Pepper and for the last half hour we put Public Enemy in the dirty ghetto blaster and sat on our stools in front of the shack and watched night come to Monument.

There was no movie theatre, the skate park was a single wooden half-pipe, and at night there were rattlesnakes on the hiking trails up Mount Herman. We could stay at home and watch TV or rent movies, but almost no one had air conditioning. If you had a driver's licence either you went to Denver or The Springs or you drove up and down and stopped in at Eugene's for gas and gum and soda. Sometimes a group of guys with restored Camaros and classic trucks would pull up in a group and open their hoods and buy Cokes and talk about their engines: the chrome, the stretchy red hoses, the horsepower. Simon called them all "Brad Chadston," every white man between sixteen and twenty-five who cared about engines.

The day after she moved in, Beatrice drove Marv's truck to the liquor store. She climbed down in a peach dress. My stomach clenched. Simon had been talking about wrestling and he could tell I had checked out.

"Who's that?"

"Beatrice. She married the neighbour."

When I was a bit younger, Marv would take me to Zephyrs games in Denver. He went to St. Peter on Sundays but Mile High Stadium was where he prayed. Simon joined us a couple of times. He and Marv had baseball in common, and they were two of the only people on the Front Range who had any idea what was going on in cricket.

"Who—Marv? No way."

I told him what I knew as we watched Beatrice go into the liquor store. A rusty brown mini-van pulled up with three girls in it, seniors this year, loud girls who dated players. I did not know their names. It was Simon's turn on the pump. The girls had been drinking. They got out of the Caravan, all of them in black with thick eye makeup and dark lipstick.

While they spoke to Simon I watched the liquor store. Beatrice walked out with a bottle in a paper bag and stood next to Marv's old truck and watched me. She just stood there for a moment, like she had figured me out. No one else in Monument stood like her, with her chest out and her chin up. The wind was blowing just enough to move the skirt of her dress.

"Lisinski!"

One of the girls in black was calling out to me, but I ignored her and kept looking at Beatrice. She was still there, next to the truck. There was enough space between us that I could look at a woman looking at me.

When Beatrice opened the door and climbed in I joined the girls and Simon at the pump.

Simon introduced me. The girls knew my name but I didn't know theirs. That's how it was for football players in Monument, but it was especially so for me because I was Jason's little brother. They were Charlene and Melissa and Traci-with-an-I. There was a party at some place between here and Palmer Lake, one of those horse ranches. A goth party. We were invited, if we wanted to go.

"What's a goth party?"

Charlene, the tallest and prettiest of the goth girls, explained about the music and the clothes.

"I don't have enough black."

"You can borrow some of my shit." When we were alone, Simon and I did not speak this way. He was Kenyan, one of the only Black kids on the Front Range. But he wasn't like Black kids on television. We listened to hip hop and we watched *Colors*, and sometimes he tried. He made his Kenyan accent go away and referred to his clothing as "my shit" in front of girls. When he played baseball against teams from Denver and The Springs, teams with real Black kids, he put it on the way these girls put on goth.

At ten o'clock we turned out the lights and locked the door. I had only poured an ounce or so of rum into my Dr Pepper but I knocked over the Castrol display and at first I couldn't remember the combination of the floor safe.

Simon had a yellow 1977 Beetle with a two-thousand-dollar stereo system. We listened to Eric B. & Rakim, and whenever I turned it up too loud he reached over without a word and turned it down. Under the rusted metal Rio Grande train bridge there was a hint of fog. He slowed the Bug and barely sped up as we climbed toward the ranches and Palmer Lake. Simon wanted to drive fast, he sometimes pretended to be the sort of boy who drove fast, but he could not do it. For a while he took Kung Fu lessons in The Springs, and there was a poster on his wall of sweaty, shirtless Bruce Lee with the words "Moving, be like water" at the bottom. But he did not last long in Kung Fu. Simon walked stiffly, and seemed to study each step. He drank weight-loss drinks and, alone on Sunday mornings when his parents went to church, he fried up and ate entire packages of bacon.

The party was in one of the new houses everyone talked about, owned by anonymous city people, hidden from the road by big rocks and ponderosa pines. The girls' brown Caravan and other hand-me-down parents' cars were scattered on the red-gravel driveway, but there were also new BMWs and a Mercedes. Horses peered at us over the fence and shivered. Simon smoked a Marlboro on our way up to the house, which was designed to look like a miniature Southern plantation home with columns and a porch wrapped around the front. From inside The Cure played, that song about cats.

Simon stopped in front of the house. "Maybe this is stupid."

"We don't have to go in."

The cigarette quivered in his fingers. "Yeah."

"Let's go for twenty minutes and if we don't like it, we leave."

He stood silent in his black shirt, untucked over black jeans. I wore his suit pants and a T-shirt. Charlene and Melissa and

Traci-with-an-I held no sway over me because I had Phoebe, and while I liked The Cure there seemed no way to express it at Lewis-Palmer High and that was all right. Two people danced on the wraparound porch like they were casting spells on one another. It made me jealous. Even when I was with Phoebe—kissing her on the uncomfortable rock or holding her hand after a picnic in the park; running to intercept a poorly thrown ball or watching a *Star Wars* movie—I was so aware of my own feelings and aware of my feelings about my feelings I could never dance like that.

Simon suffered from the same disease. He took a long pull on his cigarette, for strength. "Adam."

"Yeah?"

"Let's do this."

It was dark inside the house and everyone was in black. These were not Monument people. Nearly all the men wore eye makeup and the women were cartoon witches with silver rings and huge hair. We were the youngest at the party. The furniture was new and the art on the walls wasn't of people or places: it was random colours mashed together. There were a few bronze statues of body parts. Through one of the doors I could hear people grunting and growling and giggling. A sign on the door said, "Enter at Own Risqué." I thought of Phoebe, what she would make of a place where people made a party out of touching one another down there.

A man in what at first seemed like a dress stood in the hall, telling a story. His hands danced as he spoke. Every finger had a huge silver ring on it. As we got closer I saw his dress was not a dress. It was a black silk robe with a red scarf. He spotted

us and paused. The man was about as tall as me, and thick.
"Welcome, gentlemen, welcome."

Everyone who had been listening to the man's story turned
to us. It did not feel welcoming. We were not really invited.
We did not belong. We were going to be in trouble. Simon
glanced at me with fear in his eyes, a plea. I wanted to take
him by the arm and lead him out so we could change back
into our regular clothes and rent *Lethal Weapon* at my house
so that when we saw *Lethal Weapon 2* we got all the jokes.

"Go get yourselves drinks. You're of age, of course?" The
man in the robe said this to me and then reached out and
touched Simon's shirt. "I reckon you, young man, are the first
Negro to set foot in this house."

Almost everyone on the Front Range was white. In the
movies, racist was about the worst thing a person could be,
but while I guessed no one in Monument was in the Ku Klux
Klan, "Negro" was not exactly the foulest word Simon had
heard. This man did not say it kindly, like a grandfather who
does not know any better. I thought he would introduce
himself, or at least ask our names, but after declaring Simon
a Negro he returned to his friends.

Charlene stumbled out of the kitchen with her purse
swinging and a Bartles & Jaymes wine cooler. "Cuties! Isn't
this amazing? It's like we live in a real city."

"Yeah." Simon looked back at the man in a robe. "Amazing."

"Come with me."

Simon followed her and winked at me. I hoped this meant
he wanted to go off and kiss Charlene. I pointed in the opposite direction. "I'll get a drink."

I didn't want a drink. In the living room, among the torso and pelvis statues, I didn't know how to stand or what to do with my hands. I felt the pitiless heat of a lip pimple coming on.

I sat in a puffy leather chair in an unlit corner. A woman took out a gold cylinder and used it to spill a tiny pile of white powder on the coffee table. I knew what it was. She and two other women snorted it through a short metal straw and they kissed one another messily. She waved me over to join them, and I lifted my hand as though I already had a snoot full of cocaine. My mother would be ruined to know I was at a party like this. The rum and Dr Pepper turned on me after a while as I watched the men and women play. They were thirty, forty, fifty. I wanted to call Phoebe. It comforted me to know she was in her bedroom in pink pyjamas, with teddy bears and Jane Austen books and a piano, a picture of Gandhi, a poster of Nelson Mandela. She was brushing her hair for forty-five minutes. I wanted to tell her I loved the way she smelled, the freckles on her nose, her ankles.

It was too much after a while to watch the kissing and pawing, so I walked into the kitchen and listened to a woman talk about her dissertation. I had trouble following the conversation but I pretended I understood and I nodded when everyone else nodded. Some of the people knew what to say when she complained about the academy. Without warning she turned to me and said, "Whose boyfriend are you?"

"Boyfriend?"

She spoke slowly now, as though I were four—not fourteen. "You're too young and too pretty not to be *someone's*." There was a gap between her front teeth, smeared with black lipstick. She drank something bright red from a tall glass. "Who's your pederast?" A few of her friends repeated the question in wonder and shocked amusement and then they waited for a response, staring at me. I felt betrayed—hadn't I spent several minutes listening to her talk about German philosophy? I didn't know the meaning of the word *pederast*. When I didn't answer she said, "It's okay, kitten. I know you didn't come here to talk," and a few of them laughed. The others looked at their drinks and apart from the music everything in the kitchen was silent.

I did not walk away, not at first, because if they understood I was confused and hurt it would be a gift to this woman. I wanted us all to forget and talk about something else, horses or music or football, even German philosophy. I could tell them about Jason, who was going to be in the NFL. I could tell them I was going to be a starter on the Lewis-Palmer Rangers even though I was only a sophomore. It went hot behind my eyes and I knew if anyone said another word against me I would cry. I covered my lip with my hand, in case a pimple had shown up, and no one else spoke. After a while I said, "Please excuse me," and I walked out the door and into the soft night. The house boomed behind me.

It took me nearly an hour to walk home along the Santa Fe Trail, a gravel path where the train tracks used to run. The pines smelled good. I didn't worry about snakes because there was enough moon to see by. On the edge of town I heard some rustling and thought at first it was an animal, a cougar maybe, but it was a couple kissing in the weeds. The boy had his hand up the girl's jean shorts.

I wanted to be that boy and I wanted Phoebe to be that girl. I wanted Beatrice, and I shoved the wanting away like that nightmare where I drink Winona Ryder's blood on a school bus. The stars made me feel like a gnat.

I walked up our driveway and spotted Beatrice in the backyard of Marv's house, smoking a cigarette and drinking a glass of red wine. She wore a cocktail dress with shiny bits that reflected the streetlights. Beatrice sang in a small and tender voice a song I could not hear.

three

Simon punched the wall next to my bed at 3:14 in the morning. I turned on my lamp. He was on his hands and knees, his breath was stout with rum, and there was something all over his face.

Melted eye makeup.

"What the hell?"

"Damn it, I'm sorry, Adam." He slouched and swayed. Then he punched my wall again and the picture of my mother and Jason and me at Uncle Oscar's log cabin at Redfish Lake, in Idaho, fell and the glass on the frame smashed. Simon ignored it and crawled over me to the other pillow. His knee dug into my chest and I shoved him off. He lay next to me on the bed and maybe it struck us both as weird because we looked at the ceiling for a while. Then I asked what was on his face even though I knew what it was.

"Charlene put it on me so I'd fit in."

"Why would you want to fit in?"

"And I *drove home*. I did it because you weren't there. You blew me off."

I had a headache from the four or five ounces of rum, the gooey sweet Dr Pepper. The punching and glass-breaking had startled Gary and Maggie out of sleep. They hopped, growling, down the stairs and into my basement bedroom, their collars tinkling. Maggie jumped on the bed and went straight to licking the inky mess from Simon's face. Gary, the white mutt, stood next to the bed and whined until I picked him up.

"What happened?"

"A cop pulled me over by the Coffee Cup."

"You should be in jail."

"Thank you."

"I just mean . . . it doesn't take a detective to see you're smashed."

"It was the fat cop, the one who does all the presentations about drugs."

"And?"

"And he made me pray with him."

"About what?"

"My soul. My 'soul of a savage.' He called me a savage."

"Why?"

"Because I'm Black, you idiot. No one calls you a savage because you look like everyone on *Happy Days*."

"He didn't arrest you?"

"No, he told me this story about how he got into trouble a few times, in high school, but then he was saved."

"So he gave you a warning?"

"*Negro*. Did you hear that? The way that faggot called me 'Negro'?"

I had never heard Simon say "fag" or "faggot" or "homo" or any of those words. "Who was that guy?"

"If you hear anything about me, about tonight, it's a lie."

"Like what?"

"It's a lie, Adam."

"The cop—"

"'*Savage*'!"

"Did you do something to him?"

"I prayed with him! Then I had to leave the Beetle and he drove me home. I begged him not to. I offered him money. I said my father would beat me. But he knocked on the door until my parents came. He wouldn't even let me wash my face. He said my face was 'part of the package.'"

"What does that mean?"

Simon cried and tried to stop himself and cried again and he turned over and buried his face in my second pillow. He said "savage" and "Negro" a few more times, and "faggot" and "fucking faggot." I tried never to use my second pillow or even touch it—someday, my mother would stay overnight in Denver and Phoebe would come over and I would light candles and put on Prince and hide my Ninja Turtles and sprinkle flower petals on the sheets and she would be the first ever to lay her head on it. Simon's tears and eye makeup could stain Phoebe's pillow, but there was nothing I could do about that until morning. *It's just a thing*, I told myself—one of my mother's phrases.

"In Kenya, drinking and driving isn't evil like it is here. They would forgive me that in a moment. But this . . ." He pointed to his face.

"Charlene made you."

"Men in Kenya do not wear eye makeup. You think the rednecks and headbangers are bad here? In Kenya you can go to jail for this. It's worse than *murder*. Your neighbours will burn your house down. Your parents will be fired and your brothers and sisters will lose their opportunities."

"Why didn't you tell them it was a dress-up party?"

He took a deep breath. He needed desperately to blow his nose. When he was drunk he sounded more Kenyan. "I showed up, like this, at two o'clock in the morning, *with a policeman*."

I grabbed the box of Kleenex.

"My parents think he will tell everyone, and so it is done."

"What's done?"

"My father told me I am no longer his son."

"He didn't mean that."

I let him cry again, for a while. He said he was out of the house, out of their lives, forever. After football practice and before work I had done some laundry. There was a clean pair of pyjamas in my drawer, *Miami Vice* pyjamas. I got up and tossed them to him. "Go wash your face. I'll tell my mom you're staying over."

"Should I speak to her?"

I nearly laughed. "In the morning."

My mother was sitting up. The dogs came in with me. "Sweetie, what's going on?"

I told my mom what had happened. She didn't care about the picture frame.

"He can stay in Jason's room as long as he likes. In the morning I'll phone Mr. and Mrs. Kinoro. You'll have to write down this Charlene's last name for me. Our poor bunny down there, so confused."

"He's not confused."

"Well. It's hard."

"What's hard?"

She didn't answer. "I'm real proud of you, Adam."

"Because I left the party early?"

The light from the hallway lit her face. For a year she had been taking a drug for her depression and it had turned her cheeks puffy. "What's a goth?"

Advil and water got me through football practice, though the sun was out and we focused on tackling drills. The coaches liked to crush me because I was Jason's brother so they partnered me with the biggest, meanest, dumbest linemen, and by lunchtime when it was finished I was a box of saltines that had been run over by a dump truck.

In the history of the school, only eight sophomores had made the starting lineup. By the end of my freshman year I was faster than Easy Thompson, I read the ball better and I tackled better, and he knew what was happening when the coaches started pulling him from tight games. It was awkward for the coaches and for me because Easy was a senior. They couldn't make me a starter, not officially, not as a freshman, and I understood it even though Jason and my mother figured it was weak on their part. In the real world no one keeps you on the team because you're a good guy. By the time we'd made playoffs in November Easy would pull himself out all the time, with a sore knee or a fake concussion, and I would go in there and slay ass. Still, I was young for the job and the coaches didn't want it to seem like a blood coronation—so they made a spectacle out of walloping me up and down the field during practice.

Simon was up, sitting with my mother and Beatrice under the parasol on the back deck, when I returned with my gear. All three of them were wearing sunglasses and drinking lemonade, as if our grasshopper-infested backyard were a beach. Simon was in a pair of my shorts and a University of Nebraska T-shirt. When colleges were wooing Jason four years earlier, he and my mother had visited the campuses, and they always gave him a bag of shirts and pins and hats. Jason chose Oklahoma State and left all the other swag in the closet.

I tried not to look at Beatrice, though I did say "Hello, ma'am" to her before I did anything else, as my mother had taught me. She was wearing a wide-brimmed red hat and a cream dress. Her shoes were not shoes at all but cork-heeled sandals with straps that snaked up her thin ankles and calves. She sat in front of a sheet of paper with a rectangle on it, my mother and Simon leaning over it with her.

41

Beatrice was speaking and drawing at once: Jefferson Street with a long, boxy building, three storeys high, with balconies, across the street from our house. "If the town sells us both plots, we can build twelve apartments."

"You have that kind of money?" My mother put hei hand on Beatrice's forearm.

"Not currently, Helen. But we can get it."

Simon looked up at me and said nothing.

"We? *You and I* we? How?" My mother laughed. She poured me a glass of lemonade. Her hands were shaking. "And if no one rents the apartments?"

"We'll do our research beforehand, to be sure there's a market for them. But it's fifty miles to Denver and only twenty to The Springs. People drive a lot farther than in the east. This town will only grow. And let me tell you: this is much safer than investing in stocks. My brother and I have done this several times."

"Where?" Simon pulled the pen from Beatrice and drew a question mark on the paper.

Beatrice looked at him.

"Anyway, I'm out." My mother pointed at the question mark. "I don't have any money to invest. I can barely . . . anyway."

"This is what I'm saying, Helen. You don't have to live that way anymore. Rich people aren't any smarter than you."

"But don't they say you need money to make money?"

"They do say that, and they're right. What *I* say is, if our plan is good, we don't need a dollar of our own money. People will give it to us."

"Who? What people?"

"First things first: on Monday we go to town hall to see if those plots are for sale, and for how much."

"Forty, I heard. Don and Geraldine looked into it."

"Forty thousand for both?" Beatrice pulled the pen back from Simon, wrote *40* on the paper, and circled it.

My mother nodded.

Simon got up out of his chair and stood next to me, and we stepped to the side so we could see the paper around Beatrice's hat. She did some calculations: ten shares at ten thousand each. "Let's say thirty-five for the land. If list price is forty, the owner is the government, and if it's been sitting there unsold for a couple of years we might even get it for thirty. Five cash partners. We take the other five shares as management compensation. It's our idea, our project. Hell, let's just say we rent out the apartments at five hundred each."

I did the math in my head. "Six thousand dollars a month."

Beatrice removed her floppy hat and looked back at me. "That's it, Adam. We manage the property and pay our investors a fair return. When this project is finished we start a new one."

"Where does the rest of the money come from, *Beatrice*?" Simon said her name like he suspected it wasn't real.

"You mean for construction? The bank. The land is our collateral."

"And you buy the land with investors' money?"

"Yes, *Simon*." She mimicked him.

"So you risk nothing."

"Time and energy." She pointed at my mother's left temple. "Our formidable intelligence and talents that might be directed elsewhere. Everyone wins. This is dead simple. You're unsatisfied with your work and your prospects? Do something about it, dear Helen, because no one will do it for you."

Simon rolled his eyes at me.

"In the meantime, as we prepare and market the building, we turn it into a garden." Beatrice started sketching a plot. "Nothing too fancy. We're already well into summer. But it'll interrupt things. The neighbours must all be thinking, like I was thinking when I looked out the window this morning: What happens in those empty lots across the street?"

"The one on the right was the Hastings house." I hadn't meant to say the name of the house with such Scooby-Doo portent, but that's how it came out.

Beatrice turned to me and said it the same way. "The '*Hastings* house'?"

"After the Hastings family left, all the kids figured it was haunted," my mother said. "Little Adam had nightmares about the place, along with Big Red—the old brick school down the way." She still hadn't looked up from Beatrice's sheet, from the drawing of the apartment and the numbers and Simon's question mark. "It did look haunted."

"Haunted houses are real." Beatrice nodded slowly. "Haunted places, haunted ground. Some things don't die."

No one said anything. My mother reached over and drew little flowers on the square of garden.

Beatrice clapped her hands. "Maybe we can do a purification ritual. Those two empty plots of land are going to change our lives. We want it to be ready before we begin."

My mother had not smiled like this, in the middle of the day, since before Jason left. Most Saturdays that spring my mother had not changed out of her pyjamas or gone out of the house. She had watched marathons of *Murder, She Wrote*. Two nights ago Beatrice was a stranger, and already it felt like she had lived here for years. It felt like my mother often wore sunglasses on the deck and talked about property development.

I could see Simon was about to laugh out loud, about the prospect of a purification ritual, so I pressed my foot on his and complained about being sore from football practice. I didn't normally complain—I *liked* to be sore after early-morning workouts. For the rest of the day it felt like you'd already done the painful and difficult tasks. Everything else was easy.

The foot-press worked. Simon smirked and lifted his sunglasses, one of the novelty pairs with neon-yellow temples soda companies gave away at track meets.

My mother sighed. "I called Simon's parents."

Simon spoke in his father's deep accent. "I will have to pray very diligently to understand why God has punished us."

"He's going to stay in Jason's room a bit longer."

It was quiet enough to hear a squirrel, and then Simon went into the house. I knew not to follow him. My mother topped up my glass of lemonade. "When is the swanky wedding?"

"Three o'clock. I need a suit."

"Your dad left a bunch of suits."

"I can't wear one of those things, Mom."

"Why not?"

I had showered at school and in the heat I could smell the grassy residue of Irish Spring on myself. "No one wants John Travolta at the wedding."

This seemed to wound my mother. It had been funny when Phoebe said it.

"Phoebe's mom was going to buy me a suit."

"You said no, I hope."

"I said no."

"Good. We can't have it going around that you . . ."

"Everyone knows we're poor, Mom."

She sighed, removed her sunglasses, and cleaned the lenses on her shirt.

Beatrice stared at me with her arms crossed. "You should never say that. You only become wealthy if you think and feel wealthy, if you say wealthy words."

I couldn't tell if she was joking. "Maybe they'll have something at Second Glance."

"Let me drive you. I took Marvin to work today so I could run errands. I'll buy some flowers and shrubbery for the *Hastings* land."

"That's okay, ma'am."

"She can help you pick." My mother rubbed suntan lotion into her arms. "My boy's colour-blind as a schnauzer."

I went downstairs and dumped my football bag. I did thirty push-ups and then went down the hall to Jason's room.

Simon was lying on the bed.

"Hey, want to come with me to the wedding later? Phoebe said you could come for the cocktail part."

He slid a pillow over his eyes. "I have urgent plans to decapitate myself with my fingernails. But thanks anyway. What are you going to wear?"

"I'm headed to Second Glance."

"A second-hand suit?"

I shrugged.

"You will need help."

"I'm cool."

"It is not cool to buy a grey suit that is actually a pink suit."

"Beatrice is taking me."

"Oh."

"She has other errands to run, so . . ."

"Right." He pulled the pillow off his face.

"What?"

He studied me like I had become someone else and he had missed the gruesome transformation.

"Simon, Sye—*what*?"

"What is she *doing here*, in our town, married to old Marv? I admit I don't know much about business, but I really don't think it works the way she says. Helen is hypnotized. Don't you find her odd, the whole thing odd? Those dresses? In this neighbourhood? Marv! And that phony manner of speaking."

"How is it phony?"

"It's inconsistent. Don't you hear when the trailer park kicks in? Why Marv? Why Monument?"

"You came here. Your family."

"My family came here because they found a hotel for sale at the right price."

"And she found Marv."

"This is what I am saying. He's a sweet enough old man, but Marv is not an investment opportunity. His property is a graveyard of junk."

"Can't we just let a mystery be a mystery? It's love."

He covered his face again.

Second Glance was a mould-scented shop in a converted warehouse on Washington Street. In the late nineteenth century, the Denver & Rio Grande Railroad made a stop here. Some people bought land. They named the town after the hunk of straw-yellow limestone that shoots out of the sandy ground halfway up Mount Herman. European and Eastern ranchers and merchants moved here and wiped out the Indians. There were some old-time frontier buildings on Front Street, most of them gone now. In 1895 there was a train wreck and some people died, and when we were younger we would go to the site of it at dusk and tell one another we saw ghosts.

Monument never grew the way people had hoped because the gold rush didn't come to anything. A group from the city tried to convince the state government to preserve our frontier streets, but the stores closed because nearly everyone drove twenty minutes to The Springs or Castle Rock to buy cheap clothes and frozen veal cutlets.

Beatrice and I did not speak in the truck. It was her job to say something about the weather or to ask me about school but instead she only sighed and sneezed once into her hand, high-pitched and gentle as a kitten. It made no sense to drive and I had tried to tell her so. We could have walked in ten minutes. In Marv's truck she sat like a ballet dancer, dressed like we were on our way to a garden party in a black-and-white movie. Her fingers were long and tanned, and her rings belonged in a European crypt. Through the opening in the arm of her sleeveless dress I could see a delicious flash of her white bra. It was hot and I might have opened the window but I did not want any of her to escape into the real world. I did not want to arrive at Second Glance. I did not want time to pass. She parked in front of the old warehouse with its hand-drawn sign out front, white with orange letters. She turned off the engine and slowly drew the key.

Then she looked at me and knew everything I had been thinking. There was no kindness in her eyes. It was too much, so I looked out the window at a poodle pissing on a bag of garbage.

"Your friend doesn't think much of me."

"Ma'am?"

"I think I know why."

"Oh, he's just having a hard day."

"I'd advise him against making an enemy of me."

The poodle trotted across the street without looking for cars. "Simon doesn't want enemies."

"He thinks I'm a liar."

"No, ma'am."

"You can tell him: Saint Petersburg, Florida. Edmonton, Alberta. Ithaca, New York."

I didn't know why she was naming these places. "Ma'am?"

"He asked me, 'Where?' Where my brother and I had built apartments. Well, there's his answer. You tell him."

"Okay."

"Get out now. It's hot in here."

The owner of Second Glance, Marion, was wearing a Lewis-Palmer Rangers T-shirt. Even I did not have one of those. She had her hair up in a messy grey-yellow bun.

"Word is you're a starter this year." She sat behind the cash register with two empty birdcages on the desk in front of her. She sprayed Mr. Clean on them. "You'll be heading off to Oklahoma State yourself in a few years, I reckon. Reckon the scouts are already following you around."

"Oh, I don't know."

Marion squinted at Beatrice, who stood half-smiling in the middle of the store like the Queen at a goat market. "You an aunt? A family friend?"

"Might you have any men's 42 Regular suits?"

"We're not so much on suits here. There's a few on the rack, but I don't know the sizes, I have to say."

None of the 42 Regulars were any better than my father's abandoned suits. Simon and I had rented *Wall Street* one night after work. I wanted to look like those men, like a big-city man of business, like Phoebe's father.

Marion abandoned her birdcages and stood behind us, looking at the sad men's rack. Her breath smelled like a tuna-fish sandwich. "No one in Monument's so much on suits. Apart from Sunday, what's the point I guess."

"Is there anywhere else?" Beatrice was boxed in by Marion and me. When she turned she put her hand on my bare arm for a moment, to move me. It was only a few seconds but I resisted and stretched it out, like taking extra long to eat an Oreo. I could smell the Irish Spring on myself again. My forehead was wet.

"We're the only used shop in town, I'm afraid."

"A man needs at least one suit, Adam." Beatrice led the way out of the store. "A real suit."

"When's the first game of the season?" Marion called out after us. "Who are you boys playing?"

Modern You was in the pretend frontier village on Front Street, in the same complex as the Coffee Cup Café. It carried the smells of cigarette and unwrapped presents. This was the only store in town where someone like Phoebe could go, because it had some brand names—but she didn't. Now that so many of her friends could drive, she went for Ralph Lauren and Abercrombie & Fitch in the cities instead.

The man who owned Modern You wore a name tag. It said *Gord—Haberdasher*. I recognized him from the Tri-Lakes newspaper because he was on the town board of trustees. His cheeks were blotchy and his breath was alcohol. He promenaded into the men's section arm in arm with Beatrice.

The suits were more expensive than I had imagined. A few were on sale, for around $400, but most were between $600 and $1,200. It made no sense to me. They were just wool pants and jackets of the same colour. I did not like Gord the Haberdasher, who pretended nothing was wrong with his prices. I did not like that he put his arm around Beatrice and asked where on God's green earth she had come from and why she had chosen *this dusty town* of all places, a dynamite woman like her who could be a runway model in Italy.

When Gord the Haberdasher complimented her she looked over at me with special amusement, like we shared a secret about the weakness of regular people. It was unfair to dislike Gord. He was sad. I had to look away.

"In another world I'd be a princess."

"Would you?"

"Maybe that's a bit grand. But I am a direct descendant of Red Cloud, on my mother's side. Have you heard of Red Cloud?"

"I have not. Enlighten me, Madam."

There was no time for enlightenment. I looked at the suits myself. There was a grey one and a blue one on sale, in the 42 Long rack, for $449 each.

"He was the chief of all chiefs, of the Oglala Lakota, and the leader of the Cheyenne and the Arapaho between the Mississippi and the mountains."

"Between the Mississippi and the mountains? You're the goddamn empress of Idaho."

I took the two suits into the changing room but I did not close the door.

"What are you doing here, Empress? Shouldn't you be in Cannes or, I don't know, wherever the Cheyenne live?"

"I was called here."

"Pardon me?"

"I said I was called here."

"Who called you?" Gord the Haberdasher pointed at me, though he continued to look at Beatrice. "Let me know if you need anything, Adam." He lowered his voice, as though she were his now, and he closed the change-room door.

Then they whispered for a while. I took off my pants but I kept my T-shirt on. Jason's black dress shoes, half a size too big, had a thin layer of dust I had not seen so I spit on them and shined them with the hem of my pants. Someone entered the store and an electronic cathedral ding-dong sounded. New voices filled Modern You. Both suits were too big.

There was a little knock on the door. "You okay in there?"

"Yes, ma'am."

"The suits fit?"

"They're too big."

"One moment."

I was still wearing the grey one. It was double-breasted and I didn't know how to button it. There was a single pleat in the front of the pants and they bagged out stiffly. The suit would have been ideal for a clown wedding.

"Open the door." Beatrice knocked again.

Beyond her the new women shout-talked about shoulder pads with Gord the Haberdasher, who laughed deeply at everything they said. I opened the door a crack and Beatrice pushed inside with five more suits and a white dress shirt. She put her index finger to her lips, which didn't make any sense. Where would Gord the Haberdasher think she'd gone? None of the suits was on sale.

It was a large changing room. Beatrice hung up four suits and handed me a dark blue one.

I waited a moment. "You have to get out."

Again she put her finger to her lips and she sat on the little wooden stool and crossed her legs, the stiff cotton dress crinkling over them.

The blue suit was $815. Since she didn't want me to speak, I pointed at the price tag and shrugged. She mouthed, *put it on.*

I covered my eyes and pointed at her. She shook her head and leaned back into the wall of the change room. I reached for the latch that locked the door and she blocked it.

"Please, ma'am," I whispered.

"Please what?"

"I can't change with you in here."

"Why not?"

"Close your eyes. You have to."

The darkness came into her eyes again, and any trace of her smile was gone. I could see the bones at the top of her chest, below her neck; even a couple of her veins.

The doorbell dinged again and Gord the Haberdasher greeted someone else. In Monument everyone knows everyone, and everyone knows it is safe in a change room. I did not want Beatrice to be in the change room but I did not want her to leave. She stood up and snatched the $815 blue suit from me, hung it up. For a moment I thought she was going to hit me and I lifted my arms to defend myself. She reached for my shoulder and I knocked her arm away. She waited and watched me. When she reached again I did not try to stop her. She removed the grey double-breasted jacket and draped it over the stool. My T-shirt, a hand-me-down from Jason, had a cartoon Spuds MacKenzie surfing on it. *Chicks dig me 'cause I surf,* said the shirt. She lifted it up and over my head and I stood in front of her, hot and cold at once. I folded my arms and gently she unfolded them, looked at me in my near-nakedness. She slid her fingers down to the waist of the grey clown pants. I could not watch so I took her thin forearms in my fingers and lightly held her as she unclasped the pants. I looked at the ceiling. The ceiling was a bunch of pipes painted white. Her breath was on my neck. She was so close the tip of her breasts brushed against my bare skin.

This was not allowed.

I closed my eyes. The pants fell to the floor with a whisper. "Oh," she said, and looked at me. I could smell her breath now, her calm breath of tobacco smoke and cinnamon. I wanted her to touch it. Phoebe had never touched it. I was wearing white Fruit of the Looms, size Medium that should have been Large.

"Please."

"Please what, Adam?"

I released her arms so she could touch it and I put my hands on the top of my head. Instead she reached back for the blue suit and took the pants off the hanger. She went down on her knees to help my feet into them. Her face was only a couple of inches from my Fruit of the Looms. I closed my eyes and I was no longer in Modern You and Michael Bolton was not singing "How Am I Supposed to Live Without You" and the women were no longer talking about those poor kids in Tiananmen Square. Beatrice pulled the pants up. Then she stood and looked at me and before she clasped them she dug her fingernails into the soft part of me below my waist. I knew not to cry out. Nothing about her face changed.

"You like that?"

I could not figure out how to answer. I had liked some of it. It felt like I was bleeding. Did she mean the suit? She did not mean the suit. Maybe she did. After a moment she took a step back and nodded. I did not understand why she had dug into me with her fingernails but there seemed no way to ask her. She reached for the jacket, eased me into it. In the mirror my cheeks were speckled. I was ashamed for wanting her to touch it, for saying please, for my feelings, for thinking we were anything more than what we were.

Beatrice moved out of the way. The pants were too long but the suit fit. She moved behind me and tugged at the jacket, lifted it so she could see me from behind. Then she whispered into my ear. "Yes."

"I can't buy this."

Without another word she unlocked the door and stepped out and I reached for the wall, to hold myself up. A few minutes later there was another knock on the door so I opened it. Gord the Haberdasher looked at me as though I had slapped him. "Why'd you take your shirt off?"

Beatrice put a white shirt and a blue tie next to the cash register. "He looks good, doesn't he?"

"Is this for game days? You a starter this year? The first game is, what, the end of August? Early September?"

"It's for today." Beatrice pulled a tissue out of her purse and dabbed the sweat from my forehead.

"There's a football game in July?"

"A wedding. His girlfriend's sister is getting married."

"You're dating a Brandt?"

I shrugged.

"Well well well. You know, we should get ol' Jason in here. I bet he could use a few suits."

Beatrice put her hand on Gord the Haberdasher. "Let's talk about a discount."

He ignored this and pulled me out and yanked at the jacket the way Beatrice had done, slipping his plump fingers between the pants and my waist. I was so embarrassed for feeling the way I had felt in the change room a new splash of sweat popped on my forehead. I wanted to be wearing a shirt. Gord brought a stool and I stood on it and I was so woozy with everything I had to put practically all my weight on the top of his head for a moment. He clipped up the hems. Two of the other women watched. One of them winked at me and said, "We are so proud of that brother of yours and now look—look at *you!*" There was a sign up on the wall, offering same-day alterations.

"We'll need it in half an hour, Gord."

He folded his arms and spoke quietly. "I thought we had an understanding."

"And we'll need the shirt ironed." She took her wallet out of her purse and slipped an American Express card out of it. "I'll pay now."

"What? No, ma'am."

Beatrice shot me a stern look and turned back to the haberdasher, holding up the card. The name on it was Marvin T. W. Walker. "Twenty percent off? Either that or we buy a suit on sale."

"Ten," said Gord.

"Fifteen."

———

The farmers' market in front of Big Red, the abandoned
school, was busy at this hour. Folks waved hello. I knew some
of them wanted to say hi but they didn't recognize Beatrice
and there was something about her—dressed the way she
was, thin the way she was, with her chin up. The deaf woman
who used to work at the hair salon sat on a couple of milk
crates, selling chicken-salad sandwiches neatly wrapped in
wax paper. I bought a couple without asking if Beatrice was
hungry first. We had learned how to sign *thank you* at the
poor-kids' summer camp at Palmer Lake a few years ago.
The sandwiches were only two dollars. Beatrice opened the
wax paper on hers and touched mine with it, crust to crust,
like they were drinks. A white-bread-sandwich *cheers*. Trucks
rolled up and down Second Street playing the same radio
song out their open windows, "Eighteen Wheels and a
Dozen Roses." A dust devil lifted a mess of dirt from where
it was too dry for grass to grow, and it knocked over vases
and flowers and ruined a pan of fried onions in the Mexican
tent. "*Dios mío!*" the woman said. I liked that. We protected
our sandwiches.

A man who was once a state policeman played the banjo
on the corner, by the hippie couple from Manitou Springs
who sold frozen pike. Beatrice put a dollar in his case and he
said, "Thanks kindly."

We sat on the grass, behind the tents of the market. She
stared at the little church, the original Catholic church of
Monument, as she chewed. It was a toy store now. I'd always
wondered if that was an insult to the priest, even though
there was a big and new St. Peter a few blocks from our house.

When Beatrice was finished her sandwich she sat back, with her hands behind her, and stared at me. The staring and the silence and the sun made me sweaty so I told her about Phoebe's family and about my Uncle Oscar's cabin at Redfish Lake, nine hundred miles north and west of here, one long day's drive. She listened but said nothing. My skin hurt where she had dug in with her fingernails. I had peeked and it wasn't bleeding. It was almost time to go back for the suit. "You know I'll pay you back, Miss Beatrice." It pleased me to say her name out loud.

"It was a nice sandwich. We're even."

"Is it true what you said, about your ancestor? He's real?"

"The fiercest and most intelligent Indian warrior of the 1800s. He's on a postage stamp."

"Is that where you grew up? On a reservation?"

"No."

"Where did you grow up?" I was thinking about what Phoebe had said, that she sounded like a city person.

"Canada."

"Wow. You're not even American?"

"Well . . ."

Nothing came after *well*. "Your brother builds apartments all the time?"

"Whenever he can. He's had some setbacks, and capital's not so easy to find these days. With everything computerized, you make one little mistake and Big Brother knows."

"You have two brothers?"

She laughed and stood up. We walked to Front Street, to the plaza that looked like it was from the frontier days. Most of it was pretend. Our fingers touched in the sunshine; in that moment Beatrice was fourteen too and this was our date. I said sorry and she laughed at me again. Beatrice leaned against the truck and lit a skinny menthol cigarette while I went back inside Modern You. The wedding was in less than an hour now, so Gord the Haberdasher tied my tie for me. The elderly woman who did the alterations fussed with a rack of windbreakers with golf logos on them, watching us, and when Gord complimented her work she accused him of saying that to all the seamstresses.

"How old is she, Adam?"

"Who?"

Gord the Haberdasher pointed out the window at her.

"I don't know."

"What's she doing here?"

"She married Marv."

"What? Marv Walker?"

There were no other Marvs in Monument and he knew it. Gord the Haberdasher laughed.

"What's so funny?" The seamstress joined us and brushed some lint off my left shoulder. "Marv's a good man. He'd do anything for anyone. And cowboy handsome, those nice blue eyes of his. Not long ago, at least to an old-timer like me, he was an athlete like young Adam here."

"Marv had prospects, sir." I looked up as his knuckles brushed my Adam's apple.

"Maybe twenty, thirty years ago. Maybe. But now?" Gord the Haberdasher snorted. "He's all worn out. Why him?"

"You don't understand women for hell." The seamstress slapped my arm. "Most of you don't."

"I sure don't, ma'am."

"That's all right, Adam. I admire your candour. You'll be okay in the end."

Gord the Haberdasher turned me around so I could look at myself in the mirror. I was not supposed to enjoy wearing a tie, but I did anyway.

"When's your first game?"

The seamstress laughed. "You already asked him that, Gord."

"I'm a little discombobulated. Marv Walker of all people. Ol' Marv and that fine mountain flower."

Phoebe had said I didn't need to buy her sister and the groom a present. He was a wealthy man, the son of important people in Denver. But on the way to the church Beatrice told me it would make my mother and me appear weak and poor if I arrived with nothing. There was just enough time, so we stopped at the bookstore in the Higby Mercantile on Second Street. I had never been inside. There were two women behind the counter, in the middle of the room, and one of them nodded at me in my new suit as though I were a junior senator.

There was a small section on "Marriage and Relationships" by the window. I found a baby-blue hardcover book of proverbs and verses about love with a silky, built-in place marker. I opened it to a poem by W. H. Auden.

Lay your sleeping head, my love,
Human on my faithless arm.

I showed it to Beatrice. Without looking at the page, she recited the whole poem aloud in her scratchy voice. She went on and on, just above a whisper, her eyes on me like an actor before a camera. Classical music played in the bookstore. I glanced away from her, at the posters of good and famous people on the wall—Emily Dickinson and Mark Twain—but then the bookstore fell away completely. I looked down, following along on the page with a pretend smile, but it was only because if I looked at her any longer the floor would open up and I would fall forever. I desperately wanted her to finish. When she was done she inspected the book as though nothing had happened. "Let's buy two copies, one for them and one for us."

For us?

I took the books from her and bustled to the counter. It was a relief to look at someone who was not Beatrice. It was so much easier. There was enough in my wallet to buy both books along with a congratulations card, and when the clerk asked if I wanted them wrapped I said, "Yes, ma'am." Beatrice continued to browse. I didn't know how to sign the card so I wrote something I had heard in a movie.

With many happy returns on your day, I wrote, and then realized it should have been *wedding day* so I made it *day of wedding.* Now it sounded really stupid but the card was $3.99 so it would have to do.

St. Peter Catholic Church was so close that at Christmas I

could hear midnight Mass from our yard. Beatrice stopped the truck in between our houses and the church. She opened her window and turned off the engine. Men and women in suits and dresses, who looked like they belonged in suits and dresses, shook hands and chuckled. Phoebe's family, the Brandt family, was one of the few that had arrived with the railway and never left. Her uncle was in the House of Representatives.

"Big wedding."

"Everyone knows the Brandts."

She rested her left arm on the open window. "Phoebe Brandt. A pretty girl with a pretty name. Maybe I'll go to your wedding someday, in that same church. You and Phoebe ever talk about that, getting married?"

Phoebe had already picked out her dress. Her list of invitees changed every week. Our wedding would be in early June, 1996, a month after we graduated from Stanford. I slid the second book across the seat. "Congratulations on your marriage, Miss Beatrice."

"Can I unwrap it?"

"Marv will flip about the suit."

Beatrice flicked the air.

"The haberdasher asked your age."

"What did you tell him?"

"Twenty-two."

"I did waste many years on nonsense. I like your idea very much, Adam. Let's pretend all that time never happened." A bee flew into the cab of the truck. Beatrice did not look away from me. It bounced against the windshield a couple of times and then flew out.

"How do you know that poem by heart?"

"School."

"At school in Canada you memorize poems?"

"What will you tell your mom?"

"You mean about the wedding?"

"About your suit."

"Nothing."

"She's a good mother. She'll ask."

"What would you like me to say?"

"You found the suit at Second Glance."

"That is what I'll say."

Beatrice reached slowly for my left hand and lifted it to her mouth and kissed it. Then she bit my index finger hard enough that her teeth left a mark. The church bell rang and the street began to empty. Beatrice started the truck and looked away from me when I opened the door. I did not want to misunderstand this.

"Thank you," I started to say, but she accelerated the moment my hard shoes hit the pavement.

Phoebe was a bridesmaid. She wore a gold dress and matching high-heeled shoes. Her red hair was up in a complex arrangement and she carried a bouquet of calla lilies. A string quartet played below the altar as she entered with her sister's friends.

The church was like the really big houses of wealthy Coloradans, with soft carpet and wooden beams and fake stone and a kicking speaker system. By the time I took my seat in the back—on the bride side, far from where my mother and I usually sat on Sunday mornings—there were only a few spots left. It was good that I was sitting, because I felt dizzy enough to stumble. I looked up at the windows stained with blue flowers or flames or something and the naked doll-Jesus crucified on the back wall. I smelled my hand where Beatrice had put her lips and her teeth. During the ceremony I kissed the spot she had kissed and licked my finger and tasted her.

It would take more than an hour to walk to the Monument Hill Country Club from St. Peter, so I fetched my skateboard. I might have been the first person in the history of the Front Range to wear a suit on a skateboard, but it didn't matter because the Empress of Idaho had kissed my hand. As I neared the interstate to cross into Woodmoor, some men in trucks, young and old, rolled down their windows to call me a faggot. One of them recognized me as he passed and apologized. "Hey, sorry, Little Lisinski. Didn't know it was you."

My mother did not approve of the golf course because of all the water it took in what was more or less a desert. Before the depression hit her, she had tried to get a group together at church to make the golfers find their own water, but no one wanted to make any of the rich people angry. The kinds of people who had memberships at the country club could end up doing you or your kids a disservice. Monument was small. And in the end, wasn't God in charge of that sort of thing?

The country club was up on a hill, so by the time I arrived I was so sweaty I had to splash water from the fountain on my forehead. There were two artificial ponds close to the clubhouse. A soft chemical smell rose up from the grass in the sunshine. Phoebe's father had offered me a position at the club, something "more suitable to a young man of ambition" than Eugene's Gas Stop, but I hadn't seen how it could help me.

From up here you could see Pike's Peak. Phoebe and her sister and parents were having photographs taken at the reservoir. I waited on the club's second-floor terrace, talking to a few kids I knew, friends of Phoebe's who were there because their parents knew the Brandts. Two of the girls were currently on Phoebe's list of invitees to our own wedding, though the third had been crossed out for a cruelty at cheerleading practice. When a man in a uniform walked past with a tray full of champagne flutes, I took one, and the disinvited girl, Sarah, did the same. The other two looked at us like we had just stolen a purse.

Phoebe stopped ten feet in front of me when she arrived. "Oh my goodness."

I pretended not to understand her surprise.

"Adam?" She mimed rubbing her eyes. "Is that you?"

The people at the salon had powdered her face and neck and the tops of her breasts. Phoebe took my hand and pulled me to a corner of the terrace. She looked like a movie star.

I touched her neck. "They covered your pretty freckles."

She shoved my hand away. "You'll smear everything. Where did you get this suit?"

"Modern You."

66

"It's like . . ."

"Like what?"

Phoebe backed away again, laughed, and circled me. "I love it. My skateboarder, my football goon. You even stand different. You're just—different." She took my hand again and pulled me across the terrace and into the banquet hall. There was a long table on the stage, where her parents and some other men and women their age stood drinking and laughing. Her parents, Steve and Laverne, were in the middle. We waited on the outside of a circle that surrounded them. Steve had curly red hair on the sides, though he was bald on top. He wore a tuxedo with tails, like orchestra conductors on television, and Laverne wore a shimmering beige dress. She was tall and athletic, like Phoebe. Their elaborate, poofy dresses would have slipped right off Beatrice.

We stayed far enough away that Phoebe could describe the men and women who surrounded Steve and Laverne. She called them *the supplicants*, a word I did not know. "*I want money*," she whispered, as a man told a story that made him seem heroic. As others spoke, she imitated them, too. "*Give me money. I don't know your daughter's name; please give me money.*"

Phoebe's uncle, the congressman, spoke on a giant black cellular phone in the corner and another group of men swarmed around him—waiting. Phoebe was still holding my hand in hers. When I tried to pull her away from all of it she yanked me closer. Then she reached through the crowd of men and women and grabbed her father's sleeve. "Dad?"

Steve Brandt put up his hand to the others. "Yes, sweetie?"

67

"Adam really wanted to say hello."

Steve Brandt was not a handsome man. It didn't matter. He moved with patience and grace through the crowd and extended a hand. "Thank you for coming, Adam."

"It's a real honour to be invited, Mr. Brandt. Mrs. Brandt."

Both of Phoebe's parents were in front of me now. Phoebe stood up straight and I stood up straight. I was acceptable because I was an honour student, a starter, and because my brother was wide receiver for a Division 1 NCAA football team. Jason was a striver, so my blood had striving in it—even if I was poor and fatherless.

"Very dapper." Laverne Brandt winked at me.

"You look more and more like your brother." Steve's hand was still in mine. "You might even end up bigger."

I handed the book of love poetry to Phoebe's father and he looked at it and returned it. "There's a table for this, Adam. If I take it I'll end up opening it, and it's probably a corker. I won't want to give 'er up."

"Oh, that's so thoughtful." Laverne touched her chest.

"Doesn't he look terrific in a suit?"

I felt like a small pony that had come from behind to win the Derby.

Steve agreed I looked super and shook my hand again, told me to have a hell of a night.

The master of ceremonies, a family friend who hosted a talk-radio show in the city, asked the guests to take their seats for dinner. Phoebe would not let go of me.

"What is it about you today?"

"I had a glass of champagne."

"It's not that." She looked around to make sure no one was watching us and kissed me on the lips. "Maybe it's the suit."

"Maybe."

"I like it."

"I like you."

"Like, Adam? You *like* me? I'm your favourite gum, maybe?"

"Love. I love you."

Phoebe took in a deep breath and sighed it out. "You're not real. You're some kind of imposter."

One of the other bridesmaids pulled at her arm, dragged her toward the head table.

"Break it up, you two." Phoebe kissed me once more. Our teeth clanged. Her foundation smelled like Hallowe'en. I stepped down off the stage and walked to table twelve at the back, where I sat with couples who had plenty of questions about Jason, the Oklahoma State Cowboys, the National Football League, and my own prospects for greatness.

Five more times, when no one was looking, I licked Beatrice on my hand.

Television light flashed on the walls and ceilings of Monument. I had come to the end of the paved streets, the end of sidewalks, so I walked among the invisible cicadas in our weedy neighbourhood south of Second Street. It was just after midnight—two hours past my curfew—yet I could still hear the trucks and cars of teenagers and dropouts roaring up and down Old Denver Road.

I could always feel the hard rumble of the train before I heard it. The ground and the air changed. Then every other sound on Jefferson Street faded into the shake and roar. The train turned toward me, lighting the backs of our houses, before it veered south again. When I was a kid I imagined that one day it would turn east toward us and keep going, right through our kitchen. Cracks in our walls and foundation webbed longer every year. The Denver and Rio Grande Railroad was why they'd bothered with Monument in the first place, and now, the richer you were, the farther from the train tracks you were able to live.

We had a front door and it worked perfectly well, but we never used it except as a minor storage room for shoes we lacked the courage to throw away. We'd taped a message on the door: GO TO THE BACK PLEASE. Once I asked my mother why we never went in through the front and she'd started to answer, with the typical confidence of an adult, and then she'd stopped herself and said, "I don't know. It's always been that way."

My mother had left a shopping bag on the hood of her car, with food in it. Whenever I asked my mother how she was doing she always said she was tired or exhausted or overwhelmed, though she went to bed early enough. There was always a day off or a two-week holiday she could mark on the calendar, months into the future—not that we went anywhere. There were posters on our guidance counsellor's door about planning ahead and living in the moment. Once I had suggested to my mother that she live in the moment and she asked what I meant by that in a way that suggested it was best not to answer.

Between our houses there was a vague smell of skunk. I moved closer to Marv's, where it was stronger: marijuana. Through the open window it sounded at first like Marv was in trouble. But that wasn't it.

I ducked into the darkness by the fence, in case either of them moved the curtain aside and looked out. Back in December, at the party after our last playoff game, we gathered at the house of a graduating senior named Heath. Heath's parents were away, so there was beer. Downstairs, a bunch of boys and girls watched a porn video. I had seen love bits in movies—most horribly, with my mother in the room with me—but nothing like that. Standing on Heath's yellow carpet watching the video, I'd felt like I was in that dream where I'm naked somewhere with no hope of clothes.

Crouched on the gravel between our houses I listened past Marv's grunts for her breaths. I had seen Marv shirtless many times—cutting the lawn or working in the garage, watching one of Jason's games with me in his living room. I knew his great chest and back with its long brown and white hairs, the deli-meat smell of him.

Beatrice would be tiny before Marv on the bed, a chickadee. I was aroused and nauseated. I sneaked back over to my mother's car and pulled the paper bag off the hood, moist on the bottom with condensation.

The climactic scene of *Dr. No* was playing for Simon, though he had fallen asleep on the couch. I put the apples away and watched from the kitchen until my breath and my heart slowed. It had all come down to James Bond and the filthy doctor fist-fighting over whether or not something atomic would happen. Jason had sent me a boxed set of the Sean Connery 007 movies for my birthday. In the movies all the gentlemen kissed all the ladies' hands. It was nothing to them.

When the movie ended I turned off the television and ejected the videocassette. I helped Simon up off the couch.

"Shit." He wiped his eyes. "Brother, you didn't find *that* at Second Glance. What's the matter?"

"Nothing."

"Come on."

"I'm tired, is all."

During the wedding dinner and the speeches, Phoebe had watched me from her table. We'd slow danced so close that I could smell the tang of her underarms. She'd whispered in my ear about the suit and my posture. She talked about us together in Ethiopia, helping starving babies in our gap year, studying and romancing at Stanford, and then on our way to work together in our suits. I would go left and she would go right but first we would say goodbye with a kiss on some messy street in Manhattan. During one of the really miserable country songs we walked onto the ninth hole and pawed at one another against an elm tree. She let me squeeze her ass through the silky gold dress. I kissed off half a pound of her foundation.

Simon and I stumbled around in the basement bathroom, brushing our teeth.

"You said Second Glance."

I shrugged. My mouth was full of Crest.

"You're supposed to be saving up for a car. I can't drive you around forever."

My eyes were red. I did not want to go to football practice in the morning, I did not want to go to church, and I did not want to work in the afternoon. My window was open to let in some breeze. I did not want to listen beyond the bugs to hear what was happening next door, but I lacked the strength to close it. Even in the basement, our little house was too hot, but in bed I abused myself and then I read a Valentine's-themed Archie *Double Digest* to cool down, to bury how deeply I hated myself for my deeds and for my feelings, and then I abused myself again in the still air of July.

four

arv had fought in the Korean War and he kept a
Winchester Model 70 from his time there. It was the
first weapon in his collection. Every few months he would
clear the concrete slab behind his house and line up his rifles
and pistols and his two machine guns to clean and oil them.
On my way to football practice he was putting them into
some kind of order, preparing for the ritual. When I was
younger I helped him. I'd imagine holding a gun with bullets
in it, pointing it at someone bad, and I'd vow to gather a
collection of my own like his. I would oil guns before church.
Then that feeling passed, like wanting to play with Matchbox
cars, like wanting to watch *Sesame Street*.

"I guess it's good they have you all practicing so early on

a Sunday, but Beatrice and me were going to make us—make the group of us—a nice breakfast."

"Mom and Simon will be up soon."

"It ain't a party without you." Marv winked, scrambled up from his porch, reached for his ruined spine, and stretched up out of the shadow into the morning sun. "Nothing fancy, mind you. Scrambled eggs, hotcakes, sausage. Tater tots. I know you hate breakfast sausage but I got some venison ones in the freezer. When you back?"

I remembered my suit, on his credit card, and schemed up a way to tell him about it. There was enough in my account to pay him back. I did not want Marv to go to my mother. I did not want to hurt his feelings, spoil his understanding of me. "Ten-fifteen, probably."

"You'll have to hustle to make it to church on time."

"I might not go today."

Marv walked closer to the fence and looked down at my dad's bicycle. "Yeah, I don't think Beatrice is much of a churchgoer, if she has her own way."

"She doesn't have her own way?"

"Oh, you're damn right she does. You think I can control a woman like that?" He took a long breath in and sighed it out. "I says to her this morning, I says, 'You and me finding each other as you pass through this giant old mess of a country. Isn't that proof of God?' And she says . . ."

I waited.

For a while Marv was off in a reverie and then he remembered I was there. "Anyway. We ought to get you a better bike."

"Yeah."

"Everything all right, son?"

"You bet, Mr. Walker. I didn't sleep well, is all."

"That's a sign of intelligence, they say." He reached out for me but he wasn't close enough to mess my hair. "I don't know."

"Have a nice breakfast, Mr. Walker."

That seemed to release him. He put his hat back on and he looked over at his guns like a proud father watching his children compete in the Olympics.

Monument always smelled like bacon on Sunday mornings before church. Thousands of pounds of it fried and floated in a greasy, invisible cloud over our windless town. This morning it was a delicious curse, because I had been too agitated to eat anything more than an unripe banana. I rode my father's clickety ten-speed up Second Street, past a few elderly folks in suits and dresses but almost no cars and trucks. That changed when I crossed the interstate, biking over the people from Denver and The Springs who drove below Monument without a thought about us.

I knew how many there were of just about everything in our town—but I could not keep track of the churches. Any empty store or warehouse could transform from a bank or a machine shop into a new kind of church, and all it took was a hundred chairs. From kids at school I knew that some churches even had guitar music now, though the singers only sang about Jesus. That is what love meant, in those songs: not romance, but delivering yourself to the Lord. You didn't even have to get dressed up. There were churches on the north edge of The Springs, indoor stadiums surrounded by perfect parking lots. A few boys on the team went to those churches and said it was more like going on a field trip to the opera house in Denver than sitting in St. Peter with its incense and ancient songs.

More and more of the boys were too Christian to train on Sunday mornings, so all we did was run for an hour and then hit the weight room. The coaches chose our partners so we would "mix it up"—big with little, senior with sophomore, lineman with cornerback, offence with defence, smart with stupid. My partner that morning was Squeak, a three-hundred-pound boy who already looked and sounded and limped like a forty-year-old man. He was an offensive lineman who drove in from a farm every morning, a senior. This was his last year of classrooms and football, his last year of running. No college had scouted him.

He was on the bench press, ready to drop two hundred and fifty pounds on himself, when he said it. "Simon Kinoro's your boy, right?"

"Yeah."

"Is he Wendy?"

"No." I stood over him, to spot. "Who'd you hear that from?"

Squeak and some of the other giants of Lewis-Palmer High, farm boys with low IQs and shaved heads, walked through the hallways like a gang. Squeak wiped the sweat from his head with a *Don't Tread on Me* towel. "My older sister was at some vampire party a couple nights ago."

"Oh yeah?"

"She said there was a Black boy there. And some quiet one who just hung out in the corner and watched everything."

"We were there. Ready?"

It was a lot of weight, even for Squeak, and while he struggled with it I struggled with what I might say. The veins on his forehead were pregnant worms. He finished and sat up, wiped his head again. "She said Kinoro was a total Wendy, fake eyelashes and makeup."

"He didn't wear fake eyelashes. And it was a dress-up party. Charlene and Melissa put makeup on him."

"Kinoro went into some room. Weird shit goes down in there, weird Wendy shit."

"There was no room like that."

"You calling my sister a liar?"

"Simon isn't Wendy."

Squeak stood up and looked at me. We were about the same height, but he was three of me deep. "It's none of my business, Lisinski. Just fucked-up, is all."

"It was a dress-up party. Simon likes that. It's a Kenyan thing." I wanted to pull him into the bathroom and ask him, beg him, to speak to his sister and tell her to stop. "He isn't Wendy."

"You could end up captain next year. You could end up in the show."

"You figure?"

"Like Jason. But Jason didn't fuck around."

"What do you mean?"

"Wendy shit. This Wendy shit. Kenyans, for fuck sakes."

"Sometimes you end up in a place you don't expect. And when you get there you think: Hey, why not?"

"Why not what?"

"Act like a goth. Like everyone else."

"My sister didn't say *goth*. She said vampire, faggoty stuff. She said Wendy."

We knew Black kids from television: *The Cosby Show*, mostly, and crime shows. Simon was not like that. His parents arrived with money and bought the hotel in Woodmoor. It went around they thought they were better than everyone else because they spoke with proper grammar and Simon's father was cousins with the vice-president of Kenya.

I lifted and Squeak encouraged me to do one more and shouted at me, "Push, you little bitch!" The coaches didn't care.

It was noisy in the weight room, with shouting and cussing and N.W.A. on the stereo. I knew what Squeak and some of the other boys with shaved heads said about Black kids, when we played teams from Denver where real Black kids lived. Yet they chose the weight room music: rappers from Los Angeles pretending to shoot cops.

Lifting the weights had emboldened me. "Squeak, can I ask you a favour?"

"You can ask."

"Believe me that Simon isn't Wendy."

Squeak crossed his arms. They were huge and scarred from farming. One afternoon he'd told me the story of each scar, horror stories of animals and machinery. "You ain't in his African head. How do you know?"

"If you tell people he's Wendy it'll be wrong and a lie. You know what'll happen."

"Maybe it ought to happen."

Marv's guns lay gleaming on his concrete pad. He was not with them. The smell of oil and polish sat heavily in the heat behind our houses. Though I had showered after practice, I was sweaty again from riding the ten-speed with gear on my back. I climbed onto the back deck and nearly walked into Beatrice lying on one of our loungers in a red bikini with slices of cucumber on her eyes.

"Is that Adam?"

"Yes."

She pulled off the left slice. "Everyone else is off to worship our Lord and Saviour."

I had taken my time, riding home. On Second Street they'd been filling an empty field with storage units. No one was working now because it was Sunday so I'd studied the site, the decisions they'd been making, the number of units they could put in a strip before they had to add a road through the complex. There was a chain-link fence but I'd jumped it and prowled around—the longer I studied the storage farm, the more likely I'd be to arrive home too late for church. Each unit was the size of my bedroom. I wondered how much they would charge, each month, and how they would keep varmints and thieves out.

"I guess I missed them."

For a while Beatrice squinted at me with her left eye. Then

she replaced the cucumber. "You're too pale. Put on some shorts and join me."

Now that both eyes were covered I didn't worry about her watching me watch her. The red bikini top was untied. It covered her breasts, but the straps dangled freely. A gust of wind could blow it away. Pubic hair escaped from her bottoms.

"What did Phoebe say about the suit?"

"She liked the suit. Thank you."

"That's all?"

"I looked different to her, she said."

"What kind of different?"

I did not want to talk about Phoebe. I did not want to go inside and put my bag away. I wanted to look at Beatrice. There was a tiny silver ring in her belly button. She had a long scar above her waist. Her skin was the colour of a nut and I might have told her so if I'd remembered the name of the nut. "A better boy than I really am, maybe. Not so poor?"

"You and your mother won't be poor for long." She said this as though it were as simple as switching to decaf.

"What do you mean?"

"You'll see."

I stared at her for too long, and then longer. I imagined she could snap her fingers or wiggle her nose and everything would change: the hot summer air would cool and the grass would turn to ice; the cats would chase the dogs; the houses of Jefferson Street would levitate, spin, and return to their foundations.

"I started poor, too, my brother and me. But it isn't about the money you have. It's about how you think and feel."

This made no sense to me. If you have nothing, how can you feel you have something?

"Do I sound stupid to you?"

"No, ma'am."

"Like all the dumb rednecks?"

"No, ma'am."

"I didn't even finish high school. My parents were losers. They abandoned my brother and me so they could drink themselves to death. Yet look at all I've achieved."

"You have a ten-thousand-dollar coat."

"Yes I do. Yes I do."

"You've lived all over."

"I have. And I could tell horror stories about what people have done to me. Bad men. Do I tell?"

"Um . . ."

"Don't say *um*. Don't ever say it, or *like*, superfluously. Don't end statements as questions because it's fashionable, because you heard someone do it in the movies. It's like painting a sign on yourself that says 'Yokel.' When you're in New York they'll see it and smell it anyway. Don't let them hear it."

I carried my football bag downstairs and stood in the cool of the basement. I took off my shirt and my pants and I put on a pair of swimming trunks. There was some bread in the refrigerator so I smeared peanut butter on a slice and I cut cucumber and put it on a little plate. We had two loungers on the deck. I prepared one and pulled it away from Beatrice and ate my bread and my cucumbers standing up. It was a hundred degrees, had to be. I lay next to her.

"Why are you here, ma'am?"

"You mean here in town? I was passing through the West and—"

"I mean our house."

Beatrice had long fingers. Her nails were long and pink and sharp. I had four scabs where she had clawed at me in the Modern You change room. There was nothing special about this, I reminded myself, nothing special about me. She made everyone feel this way.

"I love Marv, but he doesn't have decent chairs and his smelly guns are out."

The sun was above us and it was unusually humid, like a storm might open up over town at any moment, but there were no clouds and no wind to blow them up and over the mountains. The heat was crushing and after practice I did not want to be outside in it. There was a thin, delicious layer of sweat in a tiny pool at the base of Beatrice's neck.

"Are you looking at me?"

I looked away and willed myself to get up and go downstairs, where I belonged. But I stayed.

She ate the hot cucumber slices from her eyes, said "Yuck," held her top on and turned over. There were two faint lines on her back where the bikini straps blocked the sun. She reached for the bottle of Hawaiian Tropic and wiggled it.

"Do you mind?"

"Mind what, ma'am?"

"I don't want to burn."

"But . . ."

"You don't want to? That's okay."

I opened the plastic bottle and poured some in my hand. It screamed coconut. The heat had turned it into something between cream and oil. When Jason or my mother asked me to put lotion on them I did it as quickly as possible because touching their bare skin was like dipping my hand in a pail of last night's dinner. Phoebe had never asked me. "Where do you want it?"

She reached up and slid her hair off her neck. There were flecks of grey in the black. "Everywhere." I started in the groove of her lower back, above her waist, so I would not lose any lotion.

"That's good, Adam."

Her skin was hot. It sucked up the coconut lotion and shone. Beatrice slid over so I could join her on the lounger and I leaned over her with both hands, reached from her back up her spine, over her muscles and ribs to her neck and shoulders. I rubbed it into her arms even though she had already done her arms.

"Oh that's good."

I could not speak. When I finished I stood up and turned away from her, as I did not want her to see my swimming trunks.

"And my legs?"

I kneeled on the wood of the deck and started in the middle of her left leg, worked my way down to her veiny foot. She was more muscular than she looked from afar. I started again in the middle and worked my way up, stopped a few inches from her bottom. The bikini was cut so high I could barely look at it. I moved to the other side of the lounger and did the same on her right leg.

"Can you go higher, on both legs? The easiest place to get a burn is right along your bikini lines."

My hands trembled so much I dropped the bottle and some of it spilled on the deck. I closed my eyes, to calm myself, to pretend for a moment that I was elsewhere. It was winter. I was in the parking lot of the high school and a mean wind was blowing off the mountains and I was not wearing a jacket and no one had room in their car to drive me home.

I put lotion in my hands and rubbed them together. I started where I had left off, from where it was already moist.

"You can slip your hand under the fabric if you like."

I had never touched a girl here. It was the softest part of her. I finished the right side and moved to the left and I took my time. Her breaths had changed too. Her back rose and fell quickly now and when she spoke her voice was different, more insistent.

"Now slap me."

"What?"

"Slap me."

"I don't . . ."

"You see my ass?"

"Yes."

"Slap it."

"Why?"

"Slap my ass!"

I did, with my right hand.

"Harder."

I slapped it harder. Then I did it again and again.

"Is it red now? Can you see it's red?"

"Yes."

"The left side now. Take your time. Surprise me."

I did it. She moaned a little. Then it was quiet.

"Now softly. Between my legs."

"What?"

"Put the lotion all the way up." She spoke as though she had just finished running. "It's bad to get a sunburn there."

I slid my right hand up the inside of her thigh and she spread her legs a bit and I was sick and hungry and I wanted to laugh and I wanted to run away. I did the other side.

"Are you okay, Adam?"

I walked into the house with the bottle of Hawaiian Tropic and I threw open the curtains so I could see her. A tea towel hung on the oven handle. She looked up and watched me, tilted her head. Both dogs sniffed at my legs. I opened the fridge door, to block her view of my body. She sat up, holding her bikini top in place, and then she looked around and lowered it so I could see her breasts. Actually see them. Once in a park by the railroad tracks a girl named Carla had lifted her sister's shirt and I had seen her breasts, her enormous nipples, for an instant. Carla had said, "Tits!" Her sister scream-cried and ran home. I squeezed lotion into my hand and threw the bottle on the counter and I pulled my trunks down. I soiled the tea towel.

The cool of the fridge pleased the dogs. They huddled in front of the fruit and vegetable drawers. Beatrice paused a moment and replaced her bikini top, lay back down on her front. I thought she might laugh at me, at my shame. She did not, and she did not look away. Instead she watched me close the curtains to keep the dread afternoon sun out of the kitchen. I stood for a moment in front of the back door, to show her I was not afraid, and then I carried the balled-up tea towel downstairs and threw it into the washing machine so no one would touch it. I crawled into bed and stared at the ceiling.

I was afraid.

five

The Hastings family were the chronic inbreeders across the street, generation after generation of brothers and sisters marrying and having children who then married one another and had children who married and had children. It created fat ghoulish mumblers who wore nothing but dirty sweatsuits and stole cats and dogs from the neighbourhood and drank their blood in family rituals. If you stepped onto their property, even by accident, they would see it as a legal invasion and kidnap your ass and hustle you into the basement for a rusty murder. Or so all our older brothers told us.

After Jason moved out and I was alone in the basement at night, I knew the spirit of that place and its deranged people was liable to visit me in the witching hours. The Hastings house was larger and grander than the other houses on Jefferson

Street, including ours. It had one and a half storeys, with peeling blue paint and windows covered with bedsheets instead of curtains. The yard was a garden of weeds in summer and in winter they never shovelled the snow from the front. Libby Hastings, the youngest, was ten years older than me. She wandered around town and used the bathroom at the Gas Stop because Gene did not let us say no. One day Libby and her family were gone and the town—which had owned the house—dispatched tractors and earthmovers to knock it down and clear it.

For what?

A few hours after I had rubbed lotion on her body, Beatrice stood on a pile of deep black Hastings earth across the street. She held Marv's hand and my mother was next to them, off the pile. Beatrice waved at the crowd in front of them, people from St. Peter who had changed from suits and dresses into cut-offs and T-shirts. They all held shovels or rakes.

"I still don't understand."

Simon was explaining to me about capital, about how it worked. We stood in front of the picture window with our shirts off, watching and drinking root beer. We were not expected to go out there and help. It was adult time.

I had always thought capital was money and apparently it *was* money—but it was also more than money. Simon did not see how Beatrice and Marv and my mother could develop the Hastings Land into apartment buildings without capital.

There was an orderly row of little trees in burlap sitting along the street where the sidewalk ought to be, and flowers and shrubbery in plastic pots. The shrubs were Russian sage, which my mother called Monument Lavender. If you thought it was real sage or real lavender and tried to eat it, you died.

"It doesn't matter. Anyway, this scheme won't work."

"Why not?"

Simon sighed. I was good in school but Simon had a way of making me feel like I belonged in special ed. Once when I mixed up *seen* and *saw* he threatened to disown me as a friend. I only half-listened to his second explanation of capital because I was thinking about putting lotion on Beatrice, slapping her ass red, moving my fingers under the fabric of her bikini bottoms. I wanted to know her horror stories.

"Adam?"

"Yeah."

"You get it now?"

"One thing: if everyone gives them money, won't they have capital?"

"It's capital, I suppose, but it's not *their* capital."

"Isn't that the whole point?"

"The point of what?" Simon stepped into his Gas Stop coveralls.

"Of buying real estate with someone else's money."

"But then it's theirs, Adam. Not yours. We shredding?"

We grabbed our skateboards and started walking. The mess of Jefferson Street was too rough for our skateboards, so we had to carry them to Second Street. When we passed my mother and Beatrice and the neighbours they had begun to dig holes for the little cedar trees. The plan was to make the Hastings land into a garden, to make it an attractive and beautiful oasis in the crummy part of town. Kenny Rogers was playing from a silver ghetto blaster. Its extension cord was plugged in at Marv's house.

"What, you think you can trust a bank?" Marv was speaking to a man I recognized from church, whose daughters, Kellie and Sadie, were legends at Lewis-Palmer High for having gone all the way one night in a game of strip poker. There was something different about Marv, the way he stood. His posture was better. His voice was louder. From across the street he looked younger.

We stopped to listen.

Beatrice stood behind him, on a mound of dirt in her bare feet. She wore a red dress and a wide straw hat. "They're failing all over the country." She removed her hat and waved it around. "Savings and loans from Texas to Washington State. And why? Why?"

Kellie and Sadie's dad shrugged. "How come?"

"Well. It's all hocus-pocus."

"Computers!" Marv was holding a cedar. "Computers moving money around. Is that where you want your nest egg? There's only one sure investment in the world."

Marv dropped his cedar in a hole.

"No one in New York City can take this away from you." Beatrice kneeled down and picked up a handful of dirt. "Once it's yours."

Simon pulled me along. On the bottom of his skateboard there was a picture of Rudy from *Fat Albert* playing a guitar. My mother held a shovel. On a normal Sunday afternoon she watched television and ate caramel popcorn yet here she was, digging for Beatrice. With her free hand she blew me a kiss.

———

At eight o'clock the sun went orange and lit up the dust and though it had been there all along it seemed only now we could taste it in the backs of our throats. On Sunday nights even the people who had nothing better to do than cruise Old Denver Road stayed home for beer and barbecue. Gene had stopped by the Gas Stop at seven and had ordered us to shut down an hour early—at nine. He could save twelve dollars on payroll.

All afternoon and evening I'd listened to Simon talk about *Dead Poets Society*, which was playing at Chapel Hill. He had seen it Thursday, the night Beatrice arrived in Monument. It was a cry to his heart, to either seize the day or shrivel into misery. *Carpe diem!* I did not believe *carpe diem* was at all helpful, not where we lived. In Denver, sure: go ahead and seize the day, wear eye makeup. Not here. I hadn't told him about my conversation with Squeak in the weight room.

Beatrice arrived with the truck at a quarter to eight. Simon was inside mopping while I sprayed the pumps with Windex. I hoped she would go inside to buy gum or a Dr Pepper. Instead she walked slowly to me, in high heels. She wore a white tank top and a white skirt with pictures of bees on it. I pretended everything was all right but nothing was all right.

"Congratulations are in order, Sir Adam."

I hadn't spoken to her since abusing myself behind the refrigerator door. I was more or less certain I had become a sexual deviant. I had to go to the library to look this up, to see if the new crack in me meant I belonged in a mental institution. When I first started masturbating I had worried it would give me AIDS. The library had helped. "For what?"

"Marvin and your mother and I went for a drink at O'Grady's this afternoon after we finished with the garden. In Palmer Lake. We sat outside, on the patio. Glorious."

I was having trouble concentrating. Her breath was a warm cloud of beer but the rest of her was coconut.

"The town manager was there, a man named Ray who played baseball with Marvin in high school. They're old pals. On a whim Marvin invited him for a beer. He joined us. There we were, the four of us."

I tried to imagine my mother on the patio of O'Grady's, with the manager of the town.

"We pitched him."

"What does that mean?"

"We made him an offer. Unofficial, of course. On the land."

"Oh."

"And guess what he did?"

"He said yes."

Beatrice hugged me. I had Windex in one hand and a crumpled ball of filthy paper towel in the other. "He accepted, Adam. And not forty thousand, either."

Coconut. The skin of her arms was soft around my neck but she was all muscle and sinew and bone. "No?"

She released me and backed away. "Twenty-nine. Can you believe it?"

It was twenty-nine times more than what I had in the bank. Now that she had told me her news, she smiled for a while.

"I don't need gas. But I guess I should buy something, to be neighbourly. What do you recommend?"

"We got the usual gas station stuff."

"Like?"

"Soda. Gum. Candy bars. Air fresheners. Oil filters and that."

"Ginger ale?"

"We got ginger ale."

Simon was mopping inside, which meant he did not want me or anyone else to come in and mess up his clean floors.

"Oh, I adore that smell." Beatrice leaned in over the threshold. "It reminds me of being a girl, at the swimming pool in my hometown."

Simon ignored her. I pulled a can of ginger ale out of the cooler and I counted out the change for her fifty-dollar bill.

"What's with him?"

I didn't want her to know what Simon thought of her ideas about capital. "He went to a movie the other night and it's messing with his head."

"It should mess with your head too." He pointed the drippy mop at me.

"What movie?"

"It's a movie set way back, when everyone in America was rich and white and wore uniforms to school. That's how it still is in Kenya, if you have the money. Not the white part but everything else."

"Oh, we have plenty of that here too." Beatrice looked at me to agree with her.

Simon spent thirty seconds explaining what he had been telling me all night, about poetry and truth and theatre and the dangers of small-town life. "There's a special sinister aspect of the movie. I figure all the dads who hate creative sons also hate Black people. You can imagine them at a lynching."

"A lynching! You're so well-spoken, Simon." I knew Beatrice was complimenting him to tease him, or something. "I'm compelled."

"Go see it. Go tonight. You won't be the same tomorrow."

"Sold." She pressed the cold can against her forehead. "Young Adam doesn't want to see it?"

I shrugged.

"Adam needs to see it more than anyone." Simon pulled a five-dollar bill from his float and handed it to me. "You should take him. I'm insisting."

There was only one reason for a boy and a girl to go to a movie together. Robin Williams was not my favourite, and in the previews it all looked old and boring.

"Don't you want to see a movie with me?" Her hair was pulled up with a bunch of clips. "I thought we were chums."

Simon pointed the mop at me again. "I'm paying, so there's no reason to say no. Our friendship depends on it. It's about your white superiors. I'll even drive you to Chapel Hill."

Beatrice walked backwards to the truck, pointing at me. "Brilliant. Meet you there."

At eight-thirty we finished with our shutdown chores and sat outside with rum in our Dr Pepper. There had not been a legitimate customer for twenty minutes. I was so nervous about going to a movie with Beatrice that I drank too fast. A bright blue IROC Z28 convertible pulled in and Simon said, "Unit," which I found hilarious—we called cars "Units"— until it wasn't hilarious at all. The driver was a girl, Lindsay

Brandt, Phoebe's cousin from the city, and Phoebe herself was in the passenger seat.

"*Stupid good-lookings.*" Phoebe imitated Madame Yes from *The Flintstones,* which we grew up watching in rerun every day after school.

"'Lookings?'" Simon glanced about. "Are there two of me?"

The girls stayed in the car. Lindsay tried not to make eye contact with Simon because she fancied him. Phoebe had told me, using the word "fancy" as a verb, and I had vowed never to tell. "There's a pool party at the Novaks'. We're all invited."

"I could show off my pectoral muscles." Simon flexed. "Who will be there?"

Phoebe listed some kids, mostly rich ones from the ranches and some of the smarter juniors and seniors from the football team.

"Damn." I looked at Simon and back at Phoebe. "We can't tonight. If only we'd known."

"You guys have plans? It's Sunday."

"Yeah. Geez."

"What are you doing?"

"Heading into Denver, to this party at an art gallery."

Simon stared at me. Swearing was not his bag but he murmured, "The fuck?"

"Actually, it's above an art gallery."

Phoebe opened the door of the IROC, stepped out, took my hand, and pulled me around the corner of the shack. "You're going to a party in the city? Whose party?"

"Simon's friends."

"Why didn't you invite me?"

"It could end up pretty late."

"I don't care about that." She took my face in her hands so I couldn't look away. Her eyeliner was a bit crooked. "What's going on?"

"Nothing."

Phoebe released me and took a couple of steps back. She was already wearing a bikini under her tank top. I recognized the straps. Five fat men in leather and denim roared up Old Denver Road on their Harley-Davidsons, heading toward Palmer Lake. Phoebe hated men on Harleys more than she hated men in monster trucks. This was our first awful moment since we had started dating, and neither of us knew what to do. It wasn't too late. I could call Marv's. I could tell Beatrice we'd have to see *Dead Poets Society* another night, tomorrow night, so Phoebe wouldn't think I had transformed into another boy. I could see her—touch her—in a bikini. We could kiss in the water. I had never been in a swimming pool at night.

I nearly said what she wanted me to say, that we would not go to Denver. The words were there. "Actually" was how they began. *Actually, we'll head home after work, put on our bathing suits, and meet you at the Novaks'. We don't have to go to Denver.* That would have pleased Phoebe more than if I had just said *yes, yes, anything* when she had first invited us, because it would show how she'd changed me. It would have pleased me, too, because it would have wiped out all my fears and these new lies. I was so comforted by the thought of a simple, chlorine-smelling night with kids.

"Sorry."

"No, it's cool." Phoebe's upper lip twitched, like she had bitten into a bad peanut, and she turned away. She would not beg and she would not shout, blame me, question me further. The rum and Dr Pepper were not helpful, as I was numb to any path out of awkwardness. I wanted her to leave so I could think about how to fix everything later.

And she did. With a haughty wave, Phoebe stepped back into the IROC and Cousin Lindsay drove off.

Simon stared at me. When I was ready I looked back at him.

"As I believe I stated earlier: What the fuck?"

"I already said yes to Miss Beatrice."

"Yes, but that was before we were invited to a pool party. It's just a movie with Helen's wacko liar friend."

"You said it would change my life."

"It could change your life tomorrow. What's wrong with you?"

"She isn't a wacko liar."

Simon raised his eyebrows. "This business idea of hers, it'll get Helen into trouble. I can imagine what my father would say about such a scheme."

"Yeah—your father's not a wacko."

"He's a different sort of wacko. This one: I don't believe a thing she says. All her business experience. It doesn't make sense."

"Because she's a woman?"

"Because she is a liar."

"Anyway, I said I'd go. Wouldn't it be rude to cancel?"

"It would be *normal human behaviour.* I shouldn't have organized this. You shouldn't go anywhere with her."

"Come on, Sye."

"Just cancel and we'll to go Brad Chadston's house."

"No."

"Now you have lied, and I have to lie for you to secure
the lie. What if someone sees you at Chapel Hill? This is not
so clever."

I imitated him instead of trying to argue: "Clevah."

"You're acting mental." He took a long drink of his rum
and Dr Pepper. "This sucks. I love swimming pools, the
scantily clad. Now what? I spend the night watching *Cagney
& Lacey* with your mom."

It came to me. "I have a couple of pimples on my chest."

"What? Let's see."

"No. Gross. I get it from my shoulder pads, when it's hot
like this."

"This is why you said no?"

I looked away and nodded.

Simon laughed and then he stood up and hugged me.

The lobby of the Chapel Hill Cinema reeked of popcorn and
carpet glue. There were no kids from Monument but after I
bought popcorn I did not linger. *Dead Poets Society* was up
against *Batman, Lethal Weapon 2,* and *Indiana Jones and the Last
Crusade.* At 9:15, five minutes before curtain, I was alone in
the cinema with two elderly women. One of them had a silver
four-legged walker. They sat in the front so I sat in the back.

Just as the lights went down, Beatrice entered. I waved and she waved back, as though she were surprised to see me.

"Marv didn't come?"

"He rather overindulged at O'Grady's, I'm afraid."

"What did he say?"

"About what, Adam?"

"You coming to the movie with me."

"He's asleep."

The first trailer was for *When Harry Met Sally.* We whispered.

"Miss Beatrice, what if Marv—"

"We're friends, aren't we? Nothing wrong with that." She put her hot hand on my arm. "You can't help it, can you? You were born with the worrying DNA, like Helen. She nearly passed out today when we made the offer to Ray. Afterward, she chanted, 'Thirty thousand dollars, oh God, thirty thousand dollars, oh God, thirty thousand dollars,' like a nun." She lifted her hand away. "What will you tell your mom?"

"Thirty thousand isn't so much."

"About tonight? Seeing a movie with me?"

"Simon will tell her."

Beatrice took a small handful of the popcorn. On the screen, Meg Ryan was faking an orgasm in a deli. "I think he loves you."

"Who?"

"You know who."

"He's my best friend."

"*Loves* you." Beatrice considered the popcorn in her hand. "No butter?"

"They just have the fake stuff here."

She took the bag from me and stood up. "You mind?"

The second preview was for *Uncle Buck* with John Candy. When Beatrice walked back into the theatre her high heels clicked on the concrete. She sat back down just as the screen grew by a few inches in every direction and the feature reel rolled. I pulled a few pieces of popcorn from the side and they were drenched in oil.

Dead Poets Society opened in a stone hall of the sort we did not have in our town or anywhere near it, a group of boys in uniforms with their serious parents. An old man asked them to recite the four pillars and they stood up and said, in unison, "Tradition. Discipline. Honour. Excellence."

Beatrice tapped me. "Is that what you do every morning at school?"

"Yes."

My answer pleased her. She gripped my arm again, dug deeply with her nails, and snuggled next to me. The air conditioning at Chapel Hill was famously bad. On that Sunday night it was too cold, and even though I had been sweating all day I did not welcome it. Neither did Beatrice. She shivered in her white tank top.

I liked *Dead Poets Society* right away but I could not concentrate. She rubbed her arms.

"Miss Beatrice, we don't have to watch this."

She spoke right into my ear and I shivered. "You just have to keep me warm."

I did not have a sweater or a jacket. "How?"

"How do you think?"

101

Minutes passed. The boys retired to their dormitory rooms, sneaked cigarettes. Their conversations were naughty. Beatrice asked if I wanted any more popcorn and I said no. She moved the bag to the seat on the other side of her. She shivered. I didn't know how to keep her warm so I did what she was doing. I reached around her and rubbed her upper arms. She laughed and removed my hands. I watched the movie some more and felt stupid. Then she lifted her skirt and placed my hand above her knee. Now that my hand was there I did not know what to do with it. We were not in the sun and there was no coconut lotion.

I rubbed up and down, like I could start a fire on there.

"Slower." The movie light shone on her face. Her lips were thin, smeared with popcorn oil. She had a strong chin and a small but pointed nose. It was a face you might fail to notice at a party, but for her big eyes. She was a girl from Japanese cartoons.

Beatrice shifted on her seat, opened her legs, and moved my hand to the inside of her right thigh. She put her tongue in my ear and said, "Don't hurt me."

I pretended to watch the movie for a moment, to be sure the women near the front were not moving from their seats. Over the dialogue and the music of the film I could hear her breathing and the sound of it was enough to warm me. I do not know how long I was moving my left hand on her thigh before she reached down and slid it all the way up.

She was not wearing panties. It was hot where her hair began. I pulled my hand away.

"No?" She turned to me.

I wanted to tell her yes yes yes yes. Instead I whispered a stutter. It had surprised me. I didn't know. Panties: I had expected them.

At school we only admitted our inexperience to our closest friends. In the fantasy world of freshmen and sophomores we were all gigolos. Only Simon knew the truth about me, which was the truth about nearly every teenager in our town. I was eleven when Jason left so I couldn't ask him for advice. No one in real life asked for advice.

Beatrice took my left hand in both of hers and put my fingers into her mouth, slid her tongue around them, licked them wet. Then she adjusted again on her seat. She joined my fingers with hers and touched herself. It was softer than coconut lotion and hotter. I followed along, watching Robin Williams recite poetry to some boys gathered around him in a classroom.

Into my ear she said if I told anyone, ever, it would be the end of me, the end of everything. She moved her fingers away and let me do it alone. On the screen, the boys romped in their uniforms.

None of the elderly women could hear her. The popcorn bag fell on the floor and it spilled in a dry splash. She scratched my arm and hand and kicked the seat in front of her. We were no longer in the cinema. She reached around for my neck and squeezed, dug into my skin again and looked at me with hungry and furious eyes. "We should go."

The monument of Monument is a yellow slab of limestone that squeaked out of the earth millions of years ago. You can see it from just about anywhere in town, from the interstate, even at night. When the moon is out it glows in the dark pine.

"Can you visit it?"

From Chapel Hill to Monument it was only about fifteen minutes. "You just drive up Mount Herman Road."

"Shall we?"

Nothing moved in the town. Folks with front porches sat on them, with beer. Monument was small enough that people turned their heads when a truck went by on a Sunday night, but Second Street was deserted. We crossed the railroad tracks on our way toward the mountains and I directed her left. There was a sign for Dirty Woman Park.

"What is that?"

"A long time ago a woman lived there and her crap was everywhere. There were pigs and chickens in her actual house with her. I don't know. She just wasn't tidy."

"What an awful name. I bet they'll change it."

My arm and hand were bleeding a bit where she had scratched me. My neck too, a little. She had not said sorry or a thing about it.

Up Mount Herman Road I showed her where to park, under the canopy of a ponderosa pine. There were no other cars or trucks at the trailhead. Right away she opened the creaky door and stepped out.

"It smells amazing!"

I led her to the path. "Now, ma'am: you have to look down, for snakes. They won't bother you unless you step on them."

"How reassuring."

The trail was wide enough for a horse and rider to pass.

Where the scrub oak was thick and unruly it was hard to see the ground in the watery moonlight. Sticks could be snakes. Beatrice shrieked a couple of times and laughed at herself, and then she took my bloodied hand. I understood it was my job to take care of her. When the trail opened we surprised two mule deer. They spotted us and leapt away.

Beatrice pulled me close. "Are there bears here?"

"Not really. But cougars."

"Do they attack people?"

I had never heard of anyone getting mauled. I had never heard of anyone stepping on a rattlesnake, either. I could not really protect her or anyone. I wanted to be here, alone, with Beatrice, but I also wanted to stop and turn around and go home.

Every now and then, in places I could not predict, I missed my father. I never really knew him, the way a boy is supposed to. We never went fishing together or hunting or to a game, like I had done with Marv, and I do not remember him reading to me or teaching me numbers or letters or even scolding me for poor behaviour. He was a different sort of ghost than the ones who haunted me from the Hastings house. But whenever I could not figure out what to do in matters a mother might not understand, whether to say yes or no, I thought of him. I sought him out.

An invasive species popped out of the wild grasses. Each plant narrowed into a sort of cob at the end, growing straight up. Toward the end of the school year, in biology class, we'd walked through this valley, yanking them up. Yet here they were. I told Beatrice about the big weeds and it seemed to bore her.

Monument Rock was hidden by pines. We turned left and there it was. Beatrice stopped. I had been here a hundred times but I saw it through her eyes. It was a mysterious and sacred thing. Before the rock, on the right, there was a pond. Dogs swam in it during the day. In the moonlight you could not tell how filthy it was in that water. Insects skimmed along the perfect surface.

"If you touch it—"

"Touch the rock?"

"Yes. If you touch it, you have good luck, they say."

"Who says? Who are *they*?"

"I don't know, Miss Beatrice. When you come here on a warm day it's what everyone does."

She studied the sandy ground as she made her way around the pond.

At the rock she did not touch it, not yet. She lit a cigarette. Bats flew overhead and we both looked up and watched them. I struggled not to say anything. A real man pretends it is entirely normal, even tedious, to see a cloud of bats on a hot night, though my instinct was to point in wonder. She smoked and stared. No one could catch me and punish us so I looked at Beatrice as deeply and as sincerely as I could. I tried not to look away. I tried not to laugh. Again she reached into her bag and this time she pulled out an old silver flask. She unscrewed the flask and took a drink and handed it to me. It was warm vodka. I had tasted vodka once before, at a teammate's house when his parents were in the city for a Broncos game, but only with Hawaiian Punch. This was a swallow of skinny metal. I took another drink.

"Easy, soldier."

"I don't quite understand what's happening, Miss Beatrice."

"Adam—"

"Marv is my friend."

"We can go home. I'll just touch the rock and we can go home. Unless you want to stay with me."

"Yeah, okay."

"Why, Adam?"

"Why what, Miss Beatrice?"

"Why do you want to stay with me?"

I did not know how to answer.

"Goddamn it, Adam. Am I beautiful?"

"Yes."

"Tell me so."

"You're beautiful."

"How?"

"Really super beautiful."

"More beautiful than Phoebe?"

"Different."

"So not as beautiful?"

"She's my girlfriend."

"And what am I?"

"My neighbour."

"What part of me is beautiful?"

"It's hard to put into words."

"Not my body? It isn't beautiful?" She dropped her cigarette in the sand and squished it with the hard toe of her shoe. Then she spun around and took a step closer to me. "I don't have a body like Phoebe."

"Maybe it's the way you look at me."

"Tell me how."

I opened my mouth to answer and made no sound.

Already I was drunk and she had moved so close our noses were nearly touching. Coconut and her cigarette. She said it so quietly I wondered if she had actually said it. "What would you like to tell me, Adam? I want you to tell it to me."

Was there a way to say it without saying it? "I think about you."

"When?"

"All day. And when I'm falling asleep."

"And what do you think?"

"I just do."

"I was hoping you were going to say you wanted to fuck me."

"Fuck" was by far the most popular word in school. Kids said it about everything. Hearing it this way, after good slugs of vodka, was not at all the same.

"Will you say it, Adam?"

"Say what?"

"You know."

"Out loud?"

"Yes."

I looked up. Were there bats? I was not sure how far we had gone, if this was a trick, if she really wanted me to say it. Before I said it I practiced it with my lips, with no sound. Then: "I want to fuck you."

"Again."

"I want to fuck you."

"Say it with my name."

"Miss Beatrice, I want to fuck you."

"The other way. No miss."

"I want to fuck you, Beatrice."

"You're seducing me."

I was not sure what this meant.

"You're seducing and corrupting me. A married woman. A married woman who arrived in your town with noble intentions. Yes?" She wanted me to say yes. It was all I could say. I was bursting to say it. "Yes, Adam?"

"Yes."

"I'm helpless before you."

"Yes."

"Tell me what I am."

"You're pretty, Beatrice. You smell so good. You're noble and helpless."

"Go on your knees."

"Why?"

"On your knees."

I fell to my knees in the sand and when she beckoned me closer I crawled. She leaned against the rock, reached behind to touch it. Then she lifted her skirt over me. I reached up for her, her ass and the inside of her skirt, to balance myself, and with her free hand she pulled my hair. I was sure she was going to pull out the clump she had. It hurt worse than her fingernails in me. She pulled my hair and my eyes burst with tears and she put my mouth where she wanted it and told me what to do with my tongue and with my lips and I did it.

six

my mother and Simon were nearly at the end of *Gold-finger.* I didn't know what a person looked like after doing what I had done so I stopped in the dark kitchen and washed Beatrice off my face. I ran water over the back of my hand and my wrist. The house smelled of cigarette smoke and fish. An empty box of crispy-breaded Atlantic cod sticks sat next to a greasy cookie sheet on the stovetop. Two beige crescent moons of cod remained.

In the truck Beatrice had set out some rules. No one could know. It would hurt them and hurt us and if I told anyone I would make an enemy of her and that was the last thing I would ever want in my life. We could not leave hints or clues. We were special. Regular people would not understand. I asked her what I ought to say about the scratches and we practiced it.

"The fish is for you, sweetheart. Zap it in the microwave."

I was not hungry. Or maybe I was. I drew a glass of water, lay the fish on a plate, and put it in the microwave for thirty seconds. Simon asked my mother to pause the movie. He was wearing dress pants and a brown sweater, like a professor.

"Do you understand now?"

"Yes." I sat down.

"*O Captain! My Captain!* Right?"

My mother lit her bedtime cigarette. "I'll have to see this movie."

"It's about poetry. And *poetry*." Simon pointed at my mother's cigarette. "Can I have a drag, Mrs. Lisinski?"

"God no."

The first bite of fish stick burned my tongue. "Is there tartar sauce?"

"We ran out, sweetheart, sorry. What did Beatrice think of it?"

"Oh, she liked it a lot."

"Even a sociopath can't help but be enormously inspired." Simon went into the kitchen, opened the fridge door. "Would you like mayonnaise?"

"Sociopath?" My mother stopped rocking her chair. "What?"

"No thanks."

My mother turned from Simon—*sociopath?*—to me. She sat up. "What happened to your neck?"

"I'm fine."

She put her cigarette in the ashtray and the dogs hopped off her and she inspected me. Since she was looking I showed her my hand and wrist too.

"A cat scratched me."

"What cat? These don't look like cat scratches."

"After the movie we heard this meowing, like a cat was in distress."

"In *distress*?"

I knew I should have used a different word than "distress." Beatrice's word. "We followed the sound and there it was, in a box in a garbage can. I picked it up, to free it, and . . ."

My mother narrowed her eyes a little. She went to the bathroom and came back with rubbing alcohol and the bag of cotton balls.

"No, Mom!"

"You can get terrible infections from cat scratches. Even blood diseases. And these are deep."

It burned like hell all over again, only this time I screamed because Beatrice could not hear me. My mother called me her baby and a big-hearted cat hero and a dummy and returned to her chair and her cigarette. The dogs jumped back on her. It was too hot for flannel pyjamas but she wore them anyway, red ones, and they were covered in dog hair.

"Is everything okay with Phoebe?" my mom asked.

Simon put the jar of mayonnaise and a spoon on the end table. "Yeah, Adam. How are things with Phoebe?"

"Fine."

My mother crossed her arms and looked at me.

"It's a life-changer." Simon broke the awkwardness. "If you'd like to go I'll see it again, Mrs. Lisinski. I'll buy your ticket too."

"You bought his ticket?"

"He didn't want to go. I forced him. I am a shameless promoter of *Dead Poets Society* even though there aren't any Black people in it. They should be paying me a small but meaningful fee."

"You use such big words. I don't know what you're talking about half the time."

"I'm Kenyan." He turned up his accent. "It is in our nature to be very deep."

I liked that my mother had stopped staring at me. She put out her cigarette and the dogs jumped off her. "I don't know if I'll sleep. Forty thousand dollars."

"Twenty-nine."

Simon raised his finger. "And none of it yours!"

"That makes it worse, to be honest. If I lose one cent of these folks' money . . ."

"You won't, Mom."

I could feel a sarcastic comment ready to burst from Simon, so I squinted him into silence.

"Goodnight, boys. I drank too much."

"You don't want to see the end?"

"Maybe you don't know this, Simon, but Adam's been watching these movies on a loop ever since they came in the mail. I know what happens." She got up and kissed me on the forehead, messed my hair. It ached, my hair. "My good boy, my darling." She looked down at me so intently and so sincerely I had to look away. "You're still my baby."

113

Simon mock-gagged himself.

"And you always will be. What did you learn today? How did you challenge yourself?"

"The cat thing, I guess."

We finished watching *Goldfinger*. On our way down the stairs, we sang the theme song with Shirley Bassey vibrato. We prepared for bed and sat in the basement living room where the castaway furniture aged.

Simon checked his white Swatch. "Maybe it isn't too late to go to Brad Chadston's soirée."

"I have practice in the morning."

"You really did like the poetry and everything."

I nodded.

"Sorry you had to see it with Alexis Carrington Colby."

I didn't want him to know it upset me when he spoke poorly of Beatrice. "I *like* that outfit."

"If we can just survive high school we'll be okay. Away from here, nothing can stop us." He went into Jason's room and came out with three paperback books. Two of them had Black people on the front: *Selected Poems of Langston Hughes* and *Black Love* by Gwendolyn Brooks. The other one had an old photograph of a wild, bearded white man on the front. His shirt was dirty. Walt Whitman, *Leaves of Grass*. Simon slapped the books against his leg. "It's all in these pages."

"What is?"

"America."

"I don't get it."

"You saw the movie."

"Yes, but—"

"It's why we live here. Why my parents *really* moved to Colorado, though they don't know it. Why we needn't worry about anything. It's all in these books. We don't have to worry about teenage nonsense. There's no time for it."

"Is that why you're dressing like a poet now?"

Simon opened *Black Love* to a marked page and cleared his throat and changed his stance so he looked like a lounge singer ready to belt one out. He recited:

Black love, define and escort our romantic young, by means and redemption,
          discipline.

I clapped but I didn't like what he had read. It made me feel the way hip hop made me feel, that Simon and I weren't the same at all. These words pushed him farther from me.

"You see? Almost everything they sell us at the mall and teach us at the school: it's meaningless."

"But I'm not Black. I don't fit in that."

"You don't fit?" He laughed. "You fit everywhere!"

"No, I don't."

"I'm the only Black kid in every room in this town, and at wrestling meets and baseball tournaments in Denver even the Black kids don't accept me." He picked up the books in a pile again. "This is where it *matters* that we fit."

Simon was an enthusiast: about music, about clothes, about wrestling and baseball. Now, thanks to a movie, he had books of poetic mania. "Our romantic young"! I wanted to tell him about Beatrice but I had promised.

"Phoebe called."

Everything turned a different colour. The ticket-taker at Chapel Hill had snuck into the theatre and had seen us. She was a friend of Phoebe's sister and now Phoebe knew and soon everyone would know where my fingers and my lips and my tongue had been tonight. I had to call her. I needed some lies. "From the Novaks'? What did she say?"

"I didn't talk to her. Your mom did."

"What?"

"Don't worry. I waved my hands around and she covered the receiver and I told her to say we were out in the city."

"She didn't believe me?"

"Maybe someone saw you at the theatre."

My mother worked in a strip mall on Old Denver Road where Monument becomes Palmer Lake. The football field was in the opposite direction, on the other side of the interstate. So there was no reason for her to drive me to practice, but she insisted.

I lay awake for hours, thinking about who might have seen me at Chapel Hill. It would take less than an hour for all the kids in Monument to know. Two hours for the parents.

It was Monday. There were probably fewer than ten people in the whole Tri-Lakes area who had to dress up for work. A couple of them walked up Second Street. The shirtless, sunburned men in baseball caps were back working on the only construction project in town: the storage farm. A mother and some children trotted about on horses in the field

opposite, overlooking the floor of the valley where the interstate ran like an ugly river. Phoebe had been to New York
but I had not. I had not been anywhere, so this was how I
imagined adult futures: driving to work, driving home, listening to call-in shows about George Bush and the recession
and the Broncos.

The morning cloud had already burned off. It was hot and
stagnant at nine o'clock. Practice was starting earlier and
earlier in the mornings, to avoid the midday sun that sucked
the team's motivation away.

Our car was a red 1985 Dodge Charger with a white stripe
on the side that said "Shelby" for some reason. It did not have
air conditioning. My mother smoked in it because the people
who had owned it before us had smoked in it. A belt needed
changing and it squealed when my mother put her foot on
the gas. Gene kept offering to change it for us, with "labour
on the house," but whenever I asked if he could do it he said
he was too busy. He was too busy fishing.

We stopped at the lights on the west side of the interstate.
My mother took a couple of Tylenol without water. Lewis–
Palmer High was alone on a plateau opposite, before the
land rose again into the dry foothills that eventually gave
way to the plains.

"All right. Tell me."

"Mom, there's nothing to tell. Did you have too much beer
yesterday?"

"It's just hormones, is it?"

"What's just hormones?"

Instead of specifying she dished a sarcastic laugh.

The more I said, the more clues I felt I might reveal. "I'm good, Mom. Great, even."

We passed the hospital and a field of wild grasses.

"Everyone warns you about the teen years. 'They're gonna distance themselves from you. They're gonna distrust you. They're gonna go secretive and weird on you.' But you never believe it. You think, 'Not my Jason.' 'Not my Adam.'"

"I'm sorry, Mom."

She turned toward the school. "For what, sweetheart?"

"I don't know. The way I'm making you feel. But I'm fine."

"You and Simon made me *lie* last night, to poor Phoebe. Why?"

We pulled into the massive, mostly empty parking lot. A couple of guys, older ones with cars and trucks, slung bags on their backs. They watched us as we parked along the sidewalk. My mother turned off the Charger, tossing her lit cigarette out the window.

Beatrice had said not to leave any hints and here I was, leaving them everywhere. My mother took my wounded hand in hers and touched the scabs. "There's nothing wrong?"

"Nope."

"No drugs? No trouble?"

"I promise, no."

"There's nothing crazy going on with Phoebe?"

"I'm happy. Mom, you're gonna be late for work."

"All these people talking about Jason all the time, *Jason this, Jason that*. It's not too much?"

"It's hard to be his brother sometimes, because he's done so good. Sorry: he's done so well. But I'm proud of him."

"You're just as special."

"I'm special in the *after-school special* way, I guess. But people are right. I'm not like Jason."

"Adam."

"And I'm fine with it! Mom, there's nothing wrong."

"You are special. When you discover how, whether it's through football—maybe it is, you're an absolute star—or a subject in school, or inventing, or art, business, whatever it is, *whatever, anything,* you tell me. You tell me and together we'll make it happen. We'll give our all, just like we did with Jason. If it takes money I'll ask Uncle Oscar for money, no problem, I have no shame. Not with you. If anyone tries to stop you or hurt you . . ." She lifted my hand up and kissed the scabs. "And sweetheart, you'll leave this place on a rocket ship. Not a real one. I mean maybe a real one, if you want to be an astronaut. Do you want to be an astronaut?"

"I get car sick."

"Anything!" There were tears in her eyes. "Do you understand what I'm saying?"

"Yes, Mom. And thank you."

"Why did you make me lie for you last night?"

The story about the chest pimples, and my bashfulness in swimming pools, had worked so well on Simon I tried it with her. She laughed and cried some more and called me her sweet baby forever. "I make myself crazy sometimes."

"At what?"

"Being a mom and dad at once, *watching the signs,* making sure you know you're loved and supported. Protected. Protected is the thing. If you're protected, you can achieve greatness. We have no money and I'm sorry about that. I'm so sorry. But I'm working on it. And Beatrice is making me nuts. I'm hardly myself around her. Can you believe it? I'm going into the real estate business."

Beatrice.

"She's a marvel, isn't she? Maybe in Denver women like her are everywhere."

"Maybe."

"We're buying *land* together. She has architectural drawings from other projects she and her brother did in Canada and Ithaca and we're gonna put them on a sign, to get investors. But four people have already asked to invest. We're incorporating a company today. Can you believe it?"

"Sure."

"I woke up this morning and I couldn't stop shaking. Then there's you."

"It'll all work out."

"Stupider people than us got stinking rich from real estate. That's what Beatrice says. Oh man, I need a drink of water."

Beatrice and Adam, Adam and Beatrice.

"You know, I wish I'd met her years ago. Someone who figures: It's there, why not take it? All my life, even when I was your age, I figured I wasn't good enough. That's why I've tried to make sure you and Jason think different. For me when I was your age—golly, last week—everyone was smarter, luckier, richer." She shook her head. "Not that I knew anything about richer folks. Phoebe and Simon, I never knew kids like them when I was in school. It's a credit to you, that you chose them as friends, but it must be a lot of pressure."

"Not at all." It was so painful to sit here, listening. All the guys were walking past and gawking at us.

"We. Will. Get you there. Right? Wherever it is you're going, we'll get you there."

"Thank you."

She wiped her eyes. "Well. We're good then. Sorry for freaking out. I didn't sleep worth a hell last night. I drank a bunch of beer."

"You're a good mom."

With this she looked at me for a while, like I had either punched her or kissed her, and she put her head on the steering wheel and full-on cried, snot and everything, in her charcoal scrubs with blood stains. I tried to close my window, to stop the eight guys I could count on the sidewalk from hearing her. But they had already heard and seen enough.

Practice was set to begin in five minutes so I muttered, "I better flee, Bruce Lee," and variations on it, until my mother released me. She was wearing makeup again today and it had gone Uncle Fester on her. She kept an emergency kit of fancy wet wipes and eyeliner in the glove box. I opened it for her on my way out.

"I embarrassed you just now, didn't I, with the other boys?"

"Not at all, Mom. I love you."

When I walked into the change room everyone on the team launched into a symphony of fake weeping. I stood up tall and told them all to go fuck themselves. When a junior backup quarterback named Kyle wouldn't shut up about my mom I slammed him against the lockers and offered to hospitalize him.

———

I'd planned to phone Phoebe before we hit the field but I chickened out. After my shower, as I dialled her number, I was sure she had photographs of me, wet-faced, crawling out from under Beatrice's skirt at Monument Rock. But there was nothing sinister in her mother Laverne's voice when she told me Phoebe was out at tennis lessons. She had called, last night, to invite me to dinner.

"Really?"

"Yes, Adam. Really. Just smart casual, all right?"

Her father was a lawyer. Maybe he was organizing an ambush, though it seemed unlikely.

Three of the boys offered to give me a ride home, because I was Jason's brother. Hallsy, a linebacker, lived closest, so going with him made the most sense. Most of the other players lived on ranches or in the new subdivisions behind Monument Lake and along Raspberry Hill. Poor kids were almost never athletes.

There was no point asking Hallsy what "smart casual" meant. He wore jeans and a T-shirt most days, and Converse sweats rolled up to his knees. Older guys like Hallsy wanted to get me alone because they were close to graduation and they figured I could help them in some way. I could tell Jason about them and Jason would tell the scouts and the scouts would pluck them from Monument to the Big 12.

"Kyle's mental. He always takes it too far."

The more I thought about it the more I hated what I'd done to Kyle in front of everyone. Kyle could have ripped my throat out but I'd known he wouldn't. No one would have allowed it. No matter why I'd done it, to protect my mother's honour—there was no courage in it. "Yeah."

"If anyone ever bothers you, just tell me. They're fucking dead, bro."

I thanked him, and hated myself for it. I was a coward no matter what I did. I asked him to drop me at Norm's Convenience on Old Denver Road.

In the summer when I was a kid and Jason was busy with football, my life was a bike ride or a skate between Monument Lake and Norm's. It's where I spent my allowance on peanut butter cups and Big League Chew, where I learned to write *Adam* in Korean. Norman Park was a small but ripped man with hair that always looked like a windstorm had just died down. He was from a big city called Daegu with a lot of apples and an important statue of Buddha wearing a hat.

"No one ever bought one of these before." Norm lifted his glasses to inspect the issue of *GQ* I had chosen. Sean Connery was on the cover. "It's not for women?"

"The 'G' stands for 'Gentlemen's.'"

"*Penthouse* is not about penthouses." He flipped through it with his reading glasses on. I had taken Tae Kwon Do classes from his wife, June. "Why do you want this?"

"For clothes ideas."

He looked at me. "But you're *jock*. You and Jason both."

"I don't know, Norm."

"Just wait."

He went into the back and emerged with a box full of magazines with the covers ripped off. A bunch of them were old issues of GQ. I did not need ten of them, and my football bag was heavy enough, but I thanked him and sat on a hunk of cement outside with a Mountain Dew Slurpee. Nothing in four of the coverless issues had anything about "smart casual" in the fashion section. The men mostly wore suits. If smart casual was *suits* I was in trouble, because I only had one and I had already worn it to the wedding.

I didn't want to throw any of the GQs into Norm's dumpster because then he would think me ungrateful and tell June. I piled all but the latest issue in my bag, slung it on my back, and flipped through the magazine as I walked down Second Street past the storage farm. It was too hot for the woman and her children to be on horseback. The horses were alone now, just standing there and staring and thinking whatever horses think.

The pages smelled of Drakkar Noir, which is how most of the boys on the Lewis-Palmer Rangers football team smelled. It was fifty dollars for a proper cologne like Drakkar Noir and we did not have money like that.

Marv's truck was not in his driveway. I watched for signs of Beatrice from the deck. At noon every third Monday the town tested its air raid sirens. My limited knowledge of nuclear war suggested that hiding under a sturdy table was not meaningful, so whenever the sirens went off I thought of the worst: dying a virgin. Up on the deck I flipped through GQ and watched Marv and Beatrice's house. There was an article about politics in Washington and one about wine, and another about the man who had just sold Domino's Pizza.

Marv's back door was propped open with a new terracotta flowerpot full of pansies.

"What are you doing?" Simon wore another pair of old-man slacks and a button-up shirt with a buttoned-down collar. He was eating a bowl of Cap'n Crunch.

"Thinking." I looked away from Marv and Beatrice's house, up at a jet leaving a zipper in the perfect blue of the sky.

"And sweating. It's a hundred and five out here." He chewed. "What are you reading? Did you talk to Phoebe?"

I showed Simon the magazine and told him about "smart casual." We studied outfits in the magazine, circled a few, and went through my closet eating Cap'n Crunch. Simon put together a combination of Levi's, my new dress shirt, the jacket from my suit, and a red pair of Chuck Taylors Jason had left behind.

He walked around me like I was a disappointing swimsuit model as I ate cereal. "This is super-white and fancy-but-not-too-fancy. Just boring enough. You look like almost everyone on *Cheers*."

"Jesus."

"Everyone in *Cheers* is white and they just came from work to get drunk with their white friends. You look exactly like them. Especially Frasier."

"Jesus, man." I stopped chewing my Cap'n Crunch to think. "*Cheers* has no Black people?"

"They're 'always glad you came' . . . *unless you're Black*. It's like Monument. Of course you don't notice but—"

"Monument has Black people."

"Yeah. Me. And you know what it feels like to be the only Black guy in the bar, with everyone staring?"

"Like Eddie Murphy in *Coming to America*, I bet. I bet it feels amazing."

"As you yourself just said: *Jesus, man.*"

Simon's parents were still at work at the hotel, so he planned to go home and pack his bags, then come back here and transfer his socks and underwear to Jason's drawers. "I can buy a couple hundred dollars' worth of cereal and spaghetti sauce to pay my way, so I won't be mooching. It'll be fun."

The lie I dreamed up in the moment was not a good one. "First let me check with Beatrice. I promised I'd help her and Mr. Walker with some things."

"You don't know how to do *things*."

"I can check oil."

"Mr. Walker *is* actually handy though, isn't he? A blue-collar man? He helps *you* guys, doesn't he?"

"He's at work, though."

"No one wants to do home renovations in heat like this."

"Let me just check." I thought of what Beatrice had said about Simon in the theatre. That he *loved me*. I watched him watch me as I changed back into my shorts and T-shirt.

"What?" Simon tipped the bowl to drink the milk.

I hopped the short wooden fence into Marv's yard. Now that I had talked myself into seeing Beatrice I had no idea what I might say. This was surely breaking her rules but I had no choice.

I knocked on the open door. Even just looking through the window, I could see the kitchen was transformed. All the dishes were away. There was a bouquet of yellow flowers on

the table and all the crummy calendars and newspaper cut-
outs were gone from the wall. A poster with a photograph of
Paris had replaced the clutter. It smelled like pie, maybe
cherry, with a cough of cigarette in behind.

On my third and final series of knocks Marv walked into
the kitchen with his cane. How could Marv be home? I nearly
ran off. There was a look of pain on his face and when he
spotted me he laughed it away.

"Hot dog, Adam. I was just thinking about you."

"How come?"

"I saw Henry Jarvis at the Coffee Cup earlier this morning.
Asked about you. He said not to say anything, doesn't want
you acting superior, but he says you're gonna have a hell of a
season."

"Oh yeah?"

"Says you're probably better than your"—Marv leaned forward on his cane and told the next part like a dirty secret—
"than your goddamn *brother* at this age. More tools. More
talent."

"Nah."

"I'm just so proud of you. It's strange to say it and strange
to hear it, I bet, but I've known you since you were a baby and
it's a hell of a thing, a *hell* of a thing, to see you turn out this
way. Good at school. Good at ball." He beamed at me with
his free arm out, like he wanted me in there for a hug. But I
didn't know if I was supposed to head in. Then it seemed to
occur to him that we were in the kitchen. He opened his fridge
and pulled out a Miller. "You want a banana or something?
Glass of milk?"

"No thanks, Mr. Walker."

"Well. Want to just hang? *The Price Is Right* ain't gonna watch itself." He walked into the living room. There were flowers on every table and new paintings on the walls, all by the same artist, it looked like—Native Americans on horseback in the mountains, with tipis and arrows and headdresses. Marv sat on his couch, which was covered with a big, bright Navajo blanket. On the TV, Bob Barker was just about to ask the contestants how much a fancy camera cost.

"Beatrice told me about the cat scratching you up last night."

"Yeah."

"Ouch. What kind of person puts a little creature like that in the garbage?"

"I like your new haircut."

Marv touched his head. "Young bride makes you feel young!"

"You aren't old, Mr. Walker."

"The hell I ain't. But you know what she is? An absolute miracle."

"Yeah."

He had not stopped smiling. "Shit."

"Yeah."

"Sit down, son." He took a long drink of his Miller. "Did you . . . did you come by because you need something?"

"I was just wondering if you know what 'smart casual' means."

"What?"

It felt good to explain about the dinner invitation, about

Laverne Brandt, to pretend I had come for suggestions. It sounded real and I could see, as I explained, that it pleased him. He celebrated with a good gulp of beer.

"You figured, of all people, you'd ask me?"

"Sure! You and Miss Beatrice."

"Shit." He chewed on his index finger and squinted for a while. "I guess a nice pair of pants and the kind of shirt you tuck in? With buttons all the way up and a collar? Yes, I'd say that'd be about smart casual."

"Thanks, Mr. Walker."

I understood why Beatrice liked him. He was still smiling at me. "You and Phoebe are getting pretty serious over there."

"I don't know."

"Her dad's richer than Croesus."

"Who's that?"

"I don't know. It's a thing to say."

"Yeah."

He pointed his bottle of beer at the TV. A woman was doing Cliffhangers, which is the best game on *The Price Is Right*.

We watched her play. She made poor choices and really blew it. "I better go, Mr. Walker."

"Bea's with your mom." He pulled something out of his pocket and handed it over.

Darling Marv,
Got errands to run. Then off to Denver with Helen this
afternoon to incorporate statewide and to put our marketing
together. Can you taxi to work just this once? I'll get myself a
car for the future. Be home for dinner. Love B

"I woke up and the truck was gone. But it doesn't matter. I got sick days." He rubbed his belly. "Something was off at the Coffee Cup this morning. I felt awful right away."

"Really?"

Marv looked at me, still smiling. What made him seem so much younger since Beatrice arrived wasn't his haircut. It was his eyes. There was something entirely new in them: more white, more colour. I thanked him and walked out of his house feeling like a genuine reptile.

I showered just after five. When I got out, the door to my mother's bedroom was closed. I knocked on it. "Mom?"

"Hi, sweetheart." Her voice was recognizably shaky.

"Are you all right? Can I come in?"

"I suppose."

There were thick blinds in my mother's room, to keep the heat and the sun out. She sat on the side of her bed in the dim light that sneaked in, wiping her eyes.

"Look at your brave mother. Bawling again."

I pulled a few Kleenexes from the box and handed them over. The fan was on overhead. The smell of her perfume hung in the room. I sat next to her and put my arm around her. Her jewellery box was a pink mystery to me. It sat ripped and ancient on her chest of drawers. There was a ballerina on top. Her own mother, who died young of throat cancer, had bought it for her when she was twelve. I was wearing just a towel and I was still pretty wet. When she had her troubles with depression I learned not to ask why she was sad. Sometimes people are just sad and nothing you say can make it stop.

Once we went to see her psychologist, to figure out how I could help her when things were dire—in months like November and December, when the light changed and things turned desperate between Thanksgiving and Christmas. I learned to check on her, at least with a knock, every time I wondered what she was doing in her bedroom. If I didn't, and things were miserable, and she'd lost herself in the misery, she could make a real mistake. The psychologist said I should listen to my heart in times like those.

"Look." She reached back for a neat pile of glossy papers and placed them on her lap. On each paper there was a drawing of a white apartment building with balconies. It was plain and boxy, but new. At the top it said JEFFERSON GARDENS, and our phone number and my mother's name were at the bottom next to *For investment inquiries.*

"What is this?" I asked the question even though I knew the answer.

"Adam, I quit my job. And I'm so scared."

On my way to the Brandt estate I stopped at the garden across the street. Beatrice had just been here, watering, because all around it smelled of wet soil warming in the late-afternoon sun. The ghosts of the Hastings land were gone. There was a big version of my mother's glossy papers in the shape of a realtor's sign, again with her name and our phone number on it.

JEFFERSON GARDENS

Most of the people in Monument worked in the cities—
and that's where they bought their clothes and their gifts,
their beer after work, their books, their cars, even their food.
It left our town with a sort of emptiness, but I never felt it.
This was all I knew. My mother and people older than her
spoke of a time when a small version of everything was still
here: dry goods, a general store, plenty of places to eat and
drink, actual banks. But most of the families in Monument,
the kids in school, had arrived here in the last ten years or so.
New kids showed up every September. People talked about
building new schools in new neighbourhoods. None of them
seemed to care about that other, older sort of railroad town
where you could walk to everything. No one in Monument
walked anywhere—except me.

On Second Street the flag over town hall was at half-mast,
to commemorate the death of a great old man whose name I
didn't recognize when I saw it in the newspaper. There was
a wisp of unmoving cloud in the sky. The sun eased toward
the soft peaks of the low mountains.

Some of the places in the strip mall, like the Coffee Cup
Café, were actually old. Everything else was new, most of it
really new, because the stores never lasted long. Blockbuster
and Modern You were surrounded by *For Lease* signs, empty
storefronts that had once held an antique shop, a toy store, an
aerobics studio, and one hundred kinds of muffins. Why Not
Flowers was the newest of the new shops.

The Why Not Flowers woman was beginning to take in
buckets of roses that had been sitting outside with price tags

on them. I was no expert but I could tell a lot of them were tired and wilted. Rather than pretend to know anything about flowers I told the woman I had twenty dollars. This was a disappointment to her, though she tried not to show it.

"You're a Lisinski, aren't you?"

"Yes, ma'am. Adam."

As she selected the flowers she frowned at them. She was a big woman and the heat out here in the front of the store had just about soaked her hairline. I wanted to tell her to stand inside her flower fridge, in the back, but I did not want to be rude.

"Your mom, Helen. She's friends with the new woman."

"That's right."

"I saw her here, the new woman."

"Oh."

"Not in the store. Over at Modern You with Gord." She looked at me and then she looked away. "A few times now."

"She likes clothes."

"Not sure she walked out with any clothes, but it's none of my business, is it? Now, where are you off to tonight, young Mr. Lisinski?"

"Laverne and Steve Brandt's."

She tilted her head to one side. "You know what? Most of these flowers are gonna be garbage in a couple days anyway."

"That's why my mom doesn't like flowers."

The woman frowned at me.

"I mean, she likes them. But it's hard on her, to watch them die. Like goldfish."

"It's the beauty of the thing, Adam."

"Yes, ma'am."

"Some things, we do them even if they don't make the greatest sense. Everything dies. That's like saying, 'Why bother living?' Isn't it? Since we're all just gonna be dead eventually."

"Yes, ma'am."

The little bouquet she had been building turned into a much bigger one. She went into the fridge and came back with more: leaves and tiny white snowflake flowers, lilies and roses and maybe a purple sunflower. I imagined Beatrice in Modern You with Gord the Haberdasher. When she was finished she showed the bouquet to me. "How is that?"

"It's really nice."

She frowned at me again.

"I mean, wow. It's the prettiest bouquet I ever saw."

Now she winked at me and wrapped it all up. "You be sure to tell Laverne Brandt where you got these. I'm taping a business card on it. You'll tell her?"

"I sure will."

It was painful for her to take the twenty-dollar bill but it really was all I had. Payday was not until the end of the week.

It was forty minutes to the Brandt estate, between Monument and Palmer Lake, and it was still plenty hot outside. But I knew if I walked on the road someone would recognize me and offer me a ride, a football fan or some parent, so I took the Santa Fe Trail.

I needed time to think about what the florist had said. Gord the Haberdasher could lock the door of the store and flip up a *Be back soon* sign. He could do anything in there, with anyone.

The Santa Fe Trail runs between the backyards of Northern Monument, close enough to smell the meat cooking through open windows. Kids screamed the rules of their game at one another. It was safe here. The last person murdered in Monument was back in frontier times, and no kids had ever been kidnapped or molested by some passing stranger. People from the cities came here to get away from all that. At school my English teacher said there were more churches, per population, in Monument than anywhere else in America.

I knew from Phoebe that it was correct to arrive a few minutes late. Never early. A dinner party was not like a job. Now that I knew the truth about Gord the Haberdasher, about Beatrice, I challenged myself to never again think of slapping Beatrice, my fingers on her, my mouth down there.

My only route to Stanford, with Phoebe, was through football. I tried to think of football. We did visualization exercises with Coach Jarvis. The pictures of the Stanford campus were of dry hills and buildings the same colour as those hills, and palm trees. No real winter! I thought of Jason and his adventures in Oklahoma; my brother at a party where girls chanted his name. I admired the branches of a big cottonwood tree near the creek as though I were already in Stanford or in New York or farther, the lonely cottonwood an emblem of my faraway childhood home. There I was, telling people about the cottonwoods and scrub oak and ponderosa pine trees of my town, in a tuxedo on some European coast in 2020. In this visualization exercise I wore a heavy gold watch.

The driveway into the Brandt estate ended in a circle. In the middle of the circle, surrounded by geysers, a stone mermaid reached for the sky. One afternoon in the snowmelt of springtime, while I'd waited for Phoebe, Laverne Brandt had explained the meaning of the statue. The lonely mermaid and I had certain things in common. She was half a fish and I was poor and neither of us was happy about it.

There was a car I didn't recognize in the driveway, a long, silver BMW. It was 7:13 when I rang the bell. Gabriela opened it. "Welcome, Mr. Adam."

Gabriela, her husband Lorenzo, and their three children—two grown up and one, Verónica, who had just graduated from high school—lived in a "cottage" on the Brandt estate that was twice the size of our house. They worked for the Brandt family in various ways, in and out of the mansion. Gabriela was the cook and Verónica cleaned up. When we'd pass Verónica in the halls at school, she and Phoebe would say hello to one another like sisters.

I had not seen any of them at the wedding.

From the foyer I could hear piano music. The Brandt mansion was so big you didn't have to take your shoes off. There were already flowers everywhere. Gabriela reached for my bouquet and I hesitated—I was supposed to give it to Phoebe's mother and say admiring things about the shop. I had wanted Laverne to look at them and smell them and tell me they were a magnificent choice and to thank me. Gabriela understood. "I will prepare them and put them in a . . . *florero*."

"A vase."

"Yes. A vase."

"*Muchas gracias, señora.*"

"*De nada.*"

I continued to practice my freshman Spanish by asking who played the piano. And where. Gabriela commended me, though I knew my grammar was a mess.

"*En la biblioteca, Señor Adam.*"

The carved wooden door to the library was from a village in India where they specialize in such things. Steve and Laverne Brandt had been on holiday there, before they had children, and they'd bought the door and had it shipped home. Three times they'd told me the story of how they'd had to build a whole house *around the door*—ha ha ha.

Phoebe was playing the piano. I knew nothing about classical music but I did know Bach was her favourite. Whatever she was playing, it sounded old. Laverne walked over in her apricot dress, putting an arm around me and leading me to the piano, where Steve and another couple stood with highball glasses.

I did not think I could make it through the night without telling her: "I brought you flowers."

"Oh?"

"Do you know Why Not Flowers, Mrs. Brandt?"

"I don't understand the question."

"Why Not Flowers?"

"Oh, the store."

"Yes, ma'am."

Laverne squeezed my arm and looked away. "That's just terrific, Adam. Thank you."

The man in the couple mouthed "Hello," turned to the piano, and then back to me. We knew one another. I thought it must have been from the Gas Stop. Or maybe he was a football father.

Then I understood the discomfort in his eyes and remembered: this was the man who owned the goth ranch. Tonight he wore no eye makeup, no silver rings, no black silk robe or red scarf.

Like me, the man wore a blazer with jeans, and so did Steve Brandt. Simon knew his smart casual. The goth man's wife was short and plump and blonde, with the icy eyes of a husky. She wore white silk pants and a matching top with stiff shoulder pads.

Phoebe finished and lifted her hands off the keys, held them for a moment. No one said anything. Then she looked up and smiled and the adults put their drinks down and we all clapped.

"Adam." Laverne pointed at me. "What composer was that?"

Everyone looked at me.

"Was it Bach?"

"Very good, Adam. *Very* good." Laverne clapped again, turned to her husband and friends. This was not her first drink of the evening. "Baroque composers, yet. You've come a long way in, what, half a year?"

I decided to look out the library window instead of answering. The sun was just about to dip behind the mountains. Massive rocks dotted the property, which was surrounded by a white wooden fence. There were a few horses in the field. One of them, a pinto, was trotting in a circle for no reason I could figure. Phoebe's parents made her feel guilty for not riding the horses. One of them had been her tenth birthday present. It was named Soleil, after the actress who played *Punky Brewster,* which was Phoebe's number one show when she was ten.

Steve lifted his glass. "To young love."

"Dad!" Phoebe pushed him and he nearly spilled his drink. "Oh my God."

"Sorry—make that, 'To, like, totally, like, *liking?*'"

The adults laughed and touched glasses. This was enough to blow some of the foulness from the room. Phoebe took my hand for a moment and squeezed, whispered, "Sorry." I was relieved. She had heard nothing of the movie or my adventures at Monument Rock.

"How is Jason doing?" Steve did not wait for an answer. He turned to the goth. "Adam's brother Jason, Jason Lisinski, you probably heard the name, plays football for Oklahoma State. They say he'll be a first-round draft pick."

"Wow. You must be proud."

"Yes, sir."

"I'm Emory Wagner. This is Karen."

"Adam Lisinski. It's an honour to meet you both."

Steve explained about the Wagners owning a technology company in Denver. They were all "investors." I did not really know what that meant, as a job. Steve and Emory's parents had known one another; their grandparents too, but they were new friends. The Wagners' weekend getaway ranch was just outside town, Steve said. I pretended to be surprised about their ranch. Emory Wagner lifted his highball glass from the piano, apologized, and wiped away the condensation it had left behind with the sleeve of his blazer.

"We don't get out here often enough, is the tragedy of it." Karen enunciated so carefully I thought at first she was making fun of someone's accent. "When we bought the ranch we thought: Every weekend. Well! If only."

"They have horses too," said Phoebe.

"Neglected creatures." Karen looked up at Phoebe. "Maybe you two could ride them for us, when we can't get out here. They're looked after, of course, but not *adored*. That's the thing."

"We could do that." Phoebe poked me. "A pretend fox hunt of an afternoon."

"Yes, ma'am."

"Splendid. We've been feeling enormously guilty about it. Right, Emory?"

"Enormously."

Steve and Emory led a conversation about intellectual property rules. The universities wanted to retain far too much of a researcher's idea as it became a product or a company. "Snakes!" Laverne said. Steve topped up everyone's glasses with whiskey from a slender decanter. Phoebe asked about my neck and hand. I told everyone about finding the cat. How could anyone be so cruel? Good for me, rescuing the poor animal at what Karen called "such personal peril."

Finally Phoebe led me away from them to the window. She was wearing a baby-blue dress.

"How was your art gallery party?"

"We were the youngest guys."

"You missed an amazing night at the Novaks'. I was walking around in my bikini the whole time."

"Damn it."

"A lot of guys were there, older guys. I was getting a lot of attention."

I imagined myself pretending to shake Brad Chadston's hand and head-butting him instead.

"You could have been there."

"It was for Simon. He really wanted to go to the party."

"I see. So between Simon and me, you pick . . ."

"You."

"Except last night."

"Phoebe, come on."

"All I'm saying is . . ."

She trailed off and I knew why. All she was saying is that she wanted to make me jealous and mad.

"There's a thing going around about Simon."

"What thing?"

"He's not Wendy, is he?"

"No."

"I mean, when I heard it, I thought: 'Oh. Right. Yeah.' He's not a normal Black kid and—"

"He's just Kenyan. Anyway, how do you know about Black kids? Charlene and Melissa put makeup on him."

She raised her eyebrows at me. "Did those bitches put it on you too?"

"No."

"Good." She picked something out of my hair and dropped it on the slippery wood floor.

"He's living with us right now, in Jason's room."

"What? Why?"

"He had a fight with his parents."

"That's not such a rad idea, having him live with you right now."

"Why not?"

Eyebrows.

"He's my best friend, Pheeb."

"Exactly."

"And his parents don't understand him."

"Do any parents understand any kid? Honestly, my mom would buy me a Power Wheels Barbie Corvette at the mall if I didn't physically stop her."

"Simon had no choice. They kicked him out."

Phoebe looked out at the mountains and the horse. It was still running around. Maybe it was insane. The sun was about to set. "It doesn't mean you have to go to Wendy parties."

"It wasn't."

"At an art gallery?"

"I'm his only real—"

"You're right. I'm sorry." She took my hand. "I love that you're loyal to him, Wendy or not." Phoebe pulled me across the library to a black leather chair with a reading lamp over it. She picked up the book on the table next to it, *Supreme Power.* "When I'm done this I want you to read it."

"What's it about?"

"The seven principles of success. Or disciplines. The seven *somethings* of success. I know it sounds corny but you read it and think: *I get it.*"

"Get what?"

"How confident people are confident."

"What's the supreme power?"

She touched her temple, then my temple.

"It's about Jedi mind tricks?"

"Kind of."

"I should get my mom a copy."

Gabriela knocked on the big Indian door and opened it. Verónica came in behind her. She was taller than her mother but not as tall as Phoebe. When Phoebe and her sister's clothes were too small Verónica inherited them. "If you would like to make your way to the dining room."

"Thank you, Verónica." Laverne led the way, and turned back to her new friends. "Doesn't she look fabulous? You should have *seen* this girl when she arrived here all those years ago."

I looked at Verónica and she looked away from me, at her own arm and the door. It made me feel like I was doing something to her, something nasty, just by being here.

Phoebe took my hand again. "Be good. But be careful, too."

"Are we still talking about your power book?"

"About Simon."

"He isn't Wendy. And even if he was—"

"It doesn't matter if he is or not. What I'm saying is it's too late. People are saying he's Wendy so it's already happened. Do you want them to say you're Wendy?"

"I don't care." This was, of course, not at all true.

Phoebe mumbled something I didn't hear.

We passed Verónica. I tried to look at her again, to say a proper hello or to mouth a silent apology, but she was not having it.

There was a toilet on the way to the dining room. I ducked in to wash my hands and calm down and when I came out Emory was there. His arms were crossed over his chest. I was taller than him, stronger too, but I knew from my own fights that it was a sport of its own. A smaller and lighter boy

143

who knew what he was doing could nearly always whip a big one. Besides, we were at Phoebe's house and he was old. On the other side of him I could hear Laverne telling a story about her hairdresser's car. He pointed at me. "You keep your mouth shut."

"About what, sir?"

Before I could answer he stepped in close and grabbed my wrist where Beatrice had scratched me. "You don't say *anything*. That's the deal with *him*, and the deal with you."

He was strong, but not as strong as I'd thought. My eye twitched. I wanted to ask him what I would even say, what he was afraid of, but I could not bring myself to speak.

"You think this is funny?" He squeezed harder.

Verónica's mother Gabriela walked into the hallway and stopped. Her hard shoes slid an inch on the floor. "Mr. Emory?"

I wanted to manufacture a sudden illness and go home, but Gabriela coaxed me back into the washroom and encouraged me to stay. I was too upset to pretend I spoke or understood Spanish. Mr. Emory, she said, was a scoundrel, but not a dangerous one. She drew cold water and put it on a facecloth and pressed it to my forehead, hummed a little song like I was six.

Afterward she led me across the hallway to the sliding dining room door. Before she opened it she told me to take a little breath. I did.

"I'm sorry, Gabriela."

"For what, Adam?"

"All this."

She put her soft hand on my cheek.

At the long table Steve asked if my mother would be offended or horrified if I had a glass of wine with dinner. I assured him she would not. Dinner began with a simple tomato soup. Gabriela walked around the table with a bottle of red and a bottle of white. All the adults but Emory chose white. Phoebe chose white. I chose red, to be with the scoundrel.

I had wine at home, at Thanksgiving and Christmas and special birthdays, but it was never like this. Emory sniffed it and swirled it in his glass and told about the region in California where it came from: the Napa Valley. He and Karen had visited it a couple of weeks earlier. Something was really happening in California. They had decided to invest in a winery, he announced, and Steve and Laverne applauded.

It was quiet for a moment while we sipped our wine and our soup.

Phoebe knew how to sit, how to eat soup, how much to drink with every go at her glass of wine. She tilted her head as she spoke. "I'm curious, Mr. Wagner. What was it that drew you to the computer industry?"

"My father was an investor in Hewlett-Packard."

"Wow."

"It was my choice, Phoebe, but it was also not a choice."

At his ranch house, Emory Wagner had moved and spoken like a sexy graveyard Pee-wee Herman. At the Brandts', he was just a regular businessman.

Steve lifted his drink and pointed it at Emory Wagner but addressed me. "In families like ours, Adam, we grow up with

145

a responsibility to remain on a certain trajectory. The word we use for it is *succession*. And it can be tricky. What if I were like your brother, for example? A brilliant athlete? It would have put my father in a genuine predicament. Luckily, I was a woefully ordinary boy."

"Oh, you were not." Laverne pretended to slap him. "He was a *god* at Stanford. I had to fight through an army of girls to get him." Then she laughed by herself for a while.

"It's not like succession forces you into a life of misery." Emory looked about him, to bring everyone but me into the conversation. "We do have other interests, beyond tech. Wine is an example. Horses, as we said."

I had tried to copy Phoebe: the way she sat, the way she ate. I did not want her parents to say, after I left, that I was a quiet and nervous boy. The wine had turned something in me. "Goth rock?"

Karen looked at me and turned to her husband. The beginnings of a smirk formed on her face and she sat back in her chair.

"Not so much, no." Emory inhaled into his chest. "But that's the idea. As long as the business is taken care of, we can indulge other interests."

"Business and family first." Steve pointed at Phoebe. "Right, princess?"

She squeezed my thigh under the table. "*Princess*, oh my God," she whispered.

"Of my two girls, she's the one with the head for business. Or so I predict."

Emory shook his head at me, slow and menacing. His wife

glared at him and did not speak for the rest of the dinner. With each spoonful of soup, as the wine faded out of my brain, I regretted saying what I had said.

After dinner we went to the library again. The adults drank cognac out of tiny fishbowl glasses. Laverne asked Phoebe to play the piano again. This time she started playing "Careless Whisper," the Wham! song. When it was time to sing she sang, and looked at me to sing along. But I could not. I had not read *Supreme Power*. It made me nervous to hear her sing at first, the boldness of it, but then I was proud to be her boyfriend. Steve was right about his daughter.

After the song, as everyone applauded, Karen walked to the fireplace and looked up at the painting of a prince on horseback surveying his land. Everyone in Colorado wanted to be on a horse, but we all drove. We watched horses on television and looked at them in pictures—even though they were right there outside, crazy with lonesomeness, running in circles, waiting for us. Phoebe started another classical song to shut everyone up, so I walked over and stood next to Karen. It was a wintry and sad song. A heartbroken person had written it.

I turned back, though not all the way. Emory watched us with his arms crossed again. The cognac smelled good.

"You've been to one of the parties?"

I said nothing and looked at the painted prince. He was calm and assured.

"How old are you, Adam?"

"Fourteen."

"Sweet Christ. You won't say anything?" There was no more artificial fanciness in her voice.

"Of course not, ma'am."

"Thanks."

"I wouldn't know what to say."

"Join the club." She sipped her cognac.

After the cognac it was time to leave. Emory led the way by looking at his watch. They were planning to wake up early in the morning for a ride before heading into the city, he said. Back to work, to regular life, after a long weekend in the country. In quiet, in beauty, in paradise. He thanked his new friends for their warm welcome and announced it was their turn next time, soon. Perhaps their secretaries could arrange it. This ritual of saying thank you and goodbye went on for a long time, and then there were handshakes and—hell, why not!—hugs and French-style cheek-kisses. There was no polite way for me to stay any longer than the others, to sneak off with Phoebe, so I did my best to be thankful and to shake hands with everyone. I waved to Gabriela and Verónica, who stood at the base of the stairs. I could not apologize to Verónica, for making a servant of her. I could not thank Gabriela for restoring me. The Brandt family stood in the doorway, the golden chandelier light behind them.

"Can we offer you a ride home, Adam?" Karen remained in the light.

Emory was already at the car. "Wow, what a great idea!"

"Isn't it?" Karen slapped the roof of the car a couple of times. "We could talk about goth rock."

Her husband rubbed his hands together and laughed.

"Thank you for the offer, Mr. and Mrs. Wagner. But I think I'll walk."

Emory slammed his door closed. With a final wave back toward the light of the house, Karen opened her door. I saluted the mermaid and walked down the driveway. The German car passed slowly. Its windows were closed and neither of them looked at me. Once they were a couple of hundred yards away from the house the car accelerated and growled toward Old Denver Road.

I wished I had said more to Karen, to comfort her. While it might have made for an awkward moment or two, Steve and Laverne were drunk and had been more interested in talking than listening.

The Brandt door was still open. Phoebe stood between her parents, each of them with an arm around her. From afar it looked like they were joking with one another. I bought lottery tickets for my mother every week because I wanted to live in that clean, orderly, beautiful house. Someday I would have children and they would not live like me. They would live like Phoebe. They would *be* Phoebe. I would be a parent like her parents, the prince, confident without trying too hard. I would not have to remind myself of anything. I would drink cognac. I would ride my horses.

Phoebe was so polite around adults and so courteous and so careful and clever that no matter what I did or said I ended up feeling like a muddy Rottweiler. Last year we'd both been in the academic top five of all freshmen. She ended up number two and I was number four, but to get there I'd had to study like a maniac. To her it was nothing. Number one was a smelly, wild-haired boy named Geert who stuttered and threw tantrums in the hall if there were loud noises. Phoebe volunteered on the yearbook club, in the drama club, and for plenty of her mother's charitable causes. She played on the senior girls' basketball and volleyball teams. She was a regional tennis champ. She spoke Spanish and French and, at Christmastime, she had performed in *The Nutcracker* with the state's best ballet company.

I waved as I passed to the other side of the gate, and they waved back and closed their door. The crickets and cicadas sang in the fields and in the distance, along the pond, the frogs called out. I walked into the ditch where the ground was softer. At the junction, where the Brandt driveway met Old Denver Road, a truck was parked in the shadows of the trees. I stopped when I realized it was Marv's.

Beatrice had drunk too much champagne and she had told him about me, about us.

The moon was bright enough that if he was looking he could already see me. There was no way to hide. The field was flat. Unless I sprinted and dove into the pond he would run me down if he wanted to run me down. I walked deeper into the field, crouching like a Viet Cong, and then I sprinted to the line of tall aspens that hid the Brandt estate from the rest of El Paso County. I ran in the ditch, back toward Monument. I could hear the old truck revving and then retreating.

Headlights bounced and flickered over the road and into the ditch. The truck's deep horn blew twice. Its old shocks squeaked and clanged as it thumped over the windrows. My long shadow ran in front. I could not outrun it so I stopped and put up my hands for some reason.

The truck slowed and crossed into the shallow ditch, clonked into park. Dust rose like phantoms into the headlights until Marv turned them off. After the racket of the chase, my own crazed thoughts, the silence was eerie over the road.

"Why are you running from me?" Her voice was soft in the quiet.

I laughed and stood up. I had whacked my shin on something and I could feel it starting to bleed a little. "Are you alone, Miss Beatrice?"

"Yes."

"Jesus, I thought you'd told Marv. I thought he was after me."

"Marvin? Even if I did tell him—you think he'd . . . ?" Now she laughed.

It burned to breathe, maybe from the dust. From my worries. I laughed some more.

"Would you like to get in?"

I did and she started the truck. She wore a tan dress. Was it last night or the night before or *never* that she had lifted her skirt over my face?

"Did you have a nice time with Phoebe?"

I did not want to tell her about Emory Wagner. "It was nice."

"You got some time alone with her, did you? Afterward?"

"No."

"It was just dinner and goodnight?"

"Yes."

"And what do her parents think of you?"

"They think I'm like Jason, so they approve."

"What does that mean? 'Like Jason'?"

"Different like him. Not just some poor useless kid without a dad from a shit house on Jefferson Street."

"*Are* you different like him?"

Every day, at some point, I asked myself this question. When I did not charm myself with fantasies, the answer was obvious. There were millions and millions of boys just like me in America. The tires had picked up clumps of dirt from the ditch and we jiggled in the cab as they fell off on the pavement. "No." Then for a while neither of us spoke.

An owl flew in front of the truck, into and out of the headlights. The massive span of its wings made it feel otherworldly, the bird and our seeing it. Beatrice stopped the truck and the engine growled and shivered.

I had never seen one flying. So much time passed that I lost track of it, and of how long we were sitting there in the dark, as though I'd had much more than one glass of wine at the Brandt estate. It made me feel small, a wisp of a thing, the way the stars and the history of the earth and the NFL and Stanford all made me feel. Once the spell of the owl had passed I said what I had been thinking. "Why are you doing this?"

"Doing what?"

I could not say it. What was I supposed to do, alone with her in the truck? Kiss her? Is that what Gord the Haberdasher did?

We went under the Rio Grande bridge. The lights of the town shone faintly on her face. A small truck roared by with a bunch of girls in cowboy hats in the back singing "Boot Scootin' Boogie."

She drove down Old Denver Road past the Gas Stop, closed now, and the grocery store, the post office. The city was a few yellow lights shining on empty pavement. She pulled over at Second Street, in front of Norm's parking lot. *Adam* in Korean.

"You want me to take you home?"

The way she said *take you home* made me think of Christmas when Jason and I were both small. Mandarin oranges, cookies, my mother in her terry-cloth bathrobe, Bing Crosby and David Bowie without eye makeup singing "Little Drummer Boy," the smell of the big coloured bulbs melting the plastic needles of our tree, Charlie Brown and the Grinch. I could go home. Some of the kids at school spoke of despising their parents. They wore it like a medal. I prayed for my mother before I went to sleep at night. I wanted her to be happy and proud of me more than I wanted most things.

Home was a right turn.

The bench seat of Marv's truck was a blend of leather and fabric woven together, with Xs of duct tape over the holes and tears. It had no seatbelts. I slid an inch closer to her and I tried not to look away from her big eyes. She reached up and touched my neck, where she had scratched me. I was scared but I pretended.

"Don't take me home."

I went once to Garden of the Gods for a school trip, in the third grade, and again years later, with Marv and my mother for a picnic. This was just after Jason left for Oklahoma. One of Marv's nieces, living in Virginia, had had a baby. He didn't know her well enough to fly to Norfolk but it gave him a certain feeling and he wanted to celebrate. It was my mother's idea to pick up a six-pack at Norm's and have a picnic somewhere. This was after work one day in May or June, and after two cans of beer each I thought the two of them were going to kiss in the sunset. I was ten or so and the idea did not bother me at all.

Garden of the Gods is a city park in The Springs. Unlike the plain yellow monument of Monument, the rocks are red. In third grade we learned how it was a sustaining and holy place for the Ute people. In their legends this is where they were born, thousands of years ago. I remember my teacher at the time, Mrs. Hamill, receiving a reprimand of some sort from a parents' group because our lesson contradicted the Bible.

I knew it was slow geological mayhem that had made Garden of the Gods possible, shoving the rocks up through the sand of the foothills. I forgot why it was red, though. We passed a sign that said the park was closed after eight and I knew Beatrice saw it but she didn't seem to care. She stopped on the edge of the main lot and turned off the truck.

"Jesus fucking Christ." Beatrice leaned on the steering wheel. From our parking spot we could see down over some spiky rocks and a meadow. There were no clouds, and with three-quarters of a moon it was eerie down there. The bald top of Pike's Peak was icy in the moonlight. "I can't believe this place. And you live twenty minutes away."

"You do, too."

"Yes." She was distracted by the look of the place.

I told her what I knew about the Ute people, and how other Native Americans had come here to camp and hunt. I wanted to tell her more about it, and the names of the other tribes, but I realized I had forgotten most of what I'd known about it in grade three.

"Are there ceremonies?" I asked her.

"Pardon me?"

"The chief of all chiefs, of the whatever."

"Red Cloud."

"You mentioned him in Modern You on Saturday, when you were buying my suit. Who was he again? Your ancestor?"

"Chief of the Oglala Lakota and wartime leader of the Cheyenne and Arapaho."

"You have special ceremonies, things you do?"

She pulled down the visor and looked into its little mirror. "They took all that away from us."

"Who did?"

Beatrice opened the door. "You did."

I followed her out and she handed me a blanket, from behind the seats. "I don't understand."

"Not *you* you. But *white people* you." She turned around in a circle. It had not fully occurred to me that she was not a white person, despite what she had said in Modern You. Beatrice lit a cigarette. "Marvellous. They were . . . what was your question, Adam?"

"Do you have ceremonies?"

"No."

"I don't either. Christmas, I guess. My dad wasn't a Christian but he ran off. We go to church and all . . ."

Beatrice was not really listening. She looked at me but through me at the same time, at the rocks and the scrub oak and the distant meadow, at the stars above Pike's Peak.

I followed her down the path. We went around a big rock and turned right, where everything opened up. "Some places, Adam, they build expectations. Mount Rushmore, right? You think it's going to be massive and you get there and . . . *bloop*. Little faces. Most of the big waterfalls: yeah, they're big, I suppose, but it's really just a bunch of water. This, though. I get the name."

We were alone in the midst of it all, and her enthusiasm helped me see it in a new way and I tried to tell her so but she started walking again. I didn't want her to learn where the name came from: some rich German had wanted it to be a beer garden.

"Where are we going?"

She didn't answer.

"Why are we here, Miss Beatrice?"

The path descends to the centre of the garden, where some people get married and others climb the rocks. In grade three, our tour guide had ended her presentation here. There is a low wooden fence to keep the deer away and to stop people from trampling the special grasses. Beatrice hopped it and led me into the meadow. It was too late to be in here, and against the rules to walk in this part. She no longer seemed worried about rattlesnakes, even though it was more danger-ous in the wispy grass and wildflowers than on the clear horse paths of Monument.

In the light of the moon the red rocks were a witch's fingers. Pike's Peak was in front of us and the meadow itself was a sea. The ground was sandy here too, and under the juniper and scrub oak it was a beach. To the south there were lights from a new subdivision digging into the foothills. It comforted me to know that if I ran, there would be somewhere to go. I started to speak and she quieted me, listening. There were little sounds, of animals hopping and fleeing our footsteps, our voices, our smell: squirrels, maybe lizards, snakes, bobcats.

Beatrice reached for the blanket and laid it before us. Then: "Kiss me."

The first time I kissed Phoebe, after a bike ride to Palmer Lake, she'd asked me to do it. My mother and her friends, my grandparents before they died, they commanded hugs and kisses when I was a kid. *Give grandma a kiss.*

The way Beatrice looked at me, the way she demanded, was different. I swallowed and stepped closer, and even though I had touched her down there with my fingers and with my tongue I felt bashful about putting my hands on her body. She grasped me and squeezed. Her fingernails were long and dug again into my arms. I wanted to ask her not to make me bleed but I did not want to spoil the moment. She kept her eyes open. When she pushed me away there was blood in my mouth, heavy and salty. I wondered if she would always pull my hair and bite my lip, scratch my arms and my neck and growl questions at me that were not for answering.

"You like that?"

I nodded. I wanted to reach up and touch the blood on my lip, even though I knew it was there and touching it would not make a damn difference.

Then she lay on the blanket, on her side, and patted it next to her. I walked in a circle and looked up at the moon.

"Don't be nervous."

"All right, Miss Beatrice."

She waved me over. "Lie with me, Adam."

It was another hot night but I was shivering, feverish. I told my body to stop. I thought about running. The decision I had made in the truck was a mistake. I had to draw the courage to tell her so, tell her to take me home. I wanted a park ranger to interrupt us, give us a fine. She did not have to drive me home. It would take all night but I could walk.

She stood up off the blanket and turned around, her back to me. There were buttons down the middle of her dress. They began at a soft burst of black hairs at the top of her spine.

"Undo the buttons."

"I don't know if I want this."

"Undo the buttons."

I undid one with my trembling hand and another, another. She slid one of the straps of the dress off her dark shoulder and I moved the other strap away with the gentlest slide of my fingertips. Her panties were white and new. She turned to me. She did not wear a bra.

"Touch them."

It took some work to get my blazer and shirt off, and then she kissed me from my neck down to my waist and addressed herself to my jeans. When they were off she stood up again and we kissed some more. She put my hand where she wanted it and I did what she had taught me and she pressed her small breasts against me. She did not scratch my hand. Without her pushing me down or telling me to do it I went on my knees and pulled down her panties, found her spot. I could see her this time, in the moonlight. She did not pull my hair. After a while she stopped me and kissed the taste of herself off my lips. "You're bleeding," she said, and lay me on the blanket. She put her fingers inside the waistband of my Fruit of the Looms and slid them along. It was so different than touching myself I laughed.

"You sound like a boy," she said.

I nearly said it: *I am a boy.*

She pulled off my underwear and there I was, naked in the trees, with a new wind easing down off the mountains and over the grass. She moved her hair over me, to tickle me, and I covered my eyes. I wanted to cry out into the empty night. I had never been happier.

"Has anyone ever?"

"No, ma'am."

She took it in her hand and then she put it in her mouth. I grabbed a handful of wild grasses and weeds on both sides of the blanket. I tried to stay quiet. She slid back up me and kissed me and reached back.

"You ready?"

"Do I need a—"

"Certainly not."

I had always wondered about missing but she lifted herself up off me, in that yellow moonlight, and guided me inside.

159

It was too warm, too wet. Up and down she moved, and moaned, and looked up, and looked at me and laughed, said words no one said, and I put my hands on her breasts and I wanted it to last forever, to stay in there forever, but then it sneaked up on me and I could not stop.

"Well!" she said, and slid up off me and lay next to me. "I told myself I wouldn't do this anymore."

"Do what?"

"You have a lot to learn."

She reached for her purse and slid it over, pulled out her Virginia Slims and a small pack of Kleenex. She wiped herself with a couple of Kleenexes. I wanted to apologize. There was, among the skinny cigarettes, a thin and sickly joint. Every month or so a police officer or a doctor would come to the school and give us a presentation about drugs. Most of us knew marijuana and mushrooms didn't count.

Beatrice lit the joint and inhaled, held it in for a moment, and then exhaled. She handed it to me. "Suck it right deep into yourself, as deep as it will go. And hold it there."

I did, and I seemed immediately good at it, until I launched into an episode of coughing. We took turns, and I coughed so hard I had to spit. Her face changed. It went softer and I understood things about her I had not understood before. Together we laughed and she was a kid too.

"Someone taught you?"

"I was about your age. No. Younger. It hurt at first. It always hurts at first but then . . ."

For a while I imagined her younger. Then old, ancient, old as dirt. I wanted her to be a kid again, like me. I wanted it to be a thousand years ago, both of us Ute kids in the place where we actually came from, no one caring we were here: not Phoebe, not Marv, not my mother. I touched the scar below her waist. "Did you have an accident?"

"I had a C-section."

"That's from a—"

"Stop talking now."

She stood up and looked at Pike's Peak. Beatrice was a naked giant to me, my imagination could not contain her, but she was really a small person, thin and fragile, with lungs and a heart and a brain where things could go wrong. It seemed an hour had passed before she returned to me on the blanket.

I told her about Emory Wagner, about the goth party and meeting him and his wife in normal clothes. I ran my hand down her leg. It was a miracle I was allowed to touch a woman.

"You don't think I'm like that, do you?"

"Like what?"

"A vampire."

"No."

She pulled me on top of her, by my hair. "We are lovers."

PART TWO

seven

We did it in our dusty garage, on a bench press no one ever used. We did it in the spacious back seat of the white Cadillac DeVille Marv had bought for her. After work on a Thursday she met me on my walk home and we did it standing up, in the brick alcove behind the post office on Old Denver Road, the skirt of her beige cotton dress crumpled in my hands. Marv worked shifts so I skipped football practice to do it on the couch, on the floor, and on a peeling-vinyl dining-room chair because it did not feel right to do it in Marv's bedroom. We did it while eating toast and jam. Once I woke out of a dream in my own bed with her wine breath on my face. I was already inside her and she was telling me *shhh* and squeezing my nipples. It was three-fifty in the morning. I had bruises and cuts everywhere and hid them from my mother and from Simon. There were bloodstains on my clothes. I told my teammates it was from skateboarding and I told everyone else it was from football.

Then for five days in a row: nothing. I would wait for her in the garage at midnight. I would see her in the mornings, when she and my mother would go off together in the Cadillac, in their perfume, and she'd speak to me like I was nothing more than the neighbour boy. *Have a terrific day, Adam!*

The Brandts were on a month-long cruise through the British Isles and Scandinavia, so I had no other social obligations. Once every Sunday morning at nine, which was late Sunday afternoon in her time zone, Phoebe called me and told me about Europe and we whispered love at one another. It was easier than ever to say "I love you." I wondered if she would feel the change in me. I did not want to break up with her. I had only improved since last she'd seen me, kissed me.

A day before Phoebe's bleary return to Mountain Standard Time, a week before the first day of school, Coach Jarvis asked to see me after practice. Henry Jarvis was a tall and bony man from Seattle with a pot-belly that made him look half pregnant. He sat under an umbrella, at a table with enormous coolers full of Gatorade. There was nowhere for me to sit, so I stood.

"What happened to your face?"

"I wiped out on my skateboard."

"Lord." He picked at his teeth so vigorously I worried he was looking for something in there to show me. "How you figure you're doing, young Adam?"

"Good, sir. I think good."

"Everyone's allowed to miss three practices before the first game. Three. How many you missed?"

"Five."

"In just a few weeks."

Coach Jarvis waited for me to respond. I knew the rules. There was no point making excuses because I was not sick and I had not been sick. "Sorry, Coach."

"And?"

I knew what he wanted. I decided to give him a shrug instead.

Coach Jarvis rubbed his hair. He kept it shaved to stubble. "It's a smart move to keep you on the team. You're a fine athlete and you got your head on. It's not easy for us to make a sophomore a starter and you know it, you know what all this means. You could, *you really could*, end up where your brother's at. Now. I'll be honest with you, buddy. I don't know if you got what he has."

Again I shrugged.

"I certainly ain't talking about talent. You know you got all that. There's things you can do—"

"Coach."

"I hate saying this, I hate it, but in some ways you're better. Now. What Jason has on you is drive. Just raw, vicious drive. I can't have a quarter effort, a quarter commitment. If you up'n *decide* you won't be as good as Jason, you sure as hell won't be. Yes, yes sir, that boy makes it look easy. He likes us all to think it's voodoo, right? But he worked his ass off and he still does. He ate it and slept it and dreamed it and shit it and you know damn well he did. Tell me how many practices he missed in four years. *In four years.*"

I looked at the Gatorade.

He made a zero with his thumb and index finger. "That's the difference."

I was in love.

"Can I get a commitment from you today, right now: no more missed practices and no more mooning around when you do show up, just pure and intense effort?"

"I'll try, sir."

He made a fist with his right hand and sighed. "What do you mean, *try*?"

Marv was working eight-to-four shifts. School was starting and soon it would be hard to see her. In five days Beatrice had not met me in the garage and she and my mother were almost always in Denver together, or in their skinny office here in town. I walked by Modern You after hours, to see if she might be in there with the haberdasher. When I could not see Beatrice I could not think of the Rangers. "It's been hard."

"What's been hard?"

"Well, Coach—"

"No one is making you play football. It ain't a burden for most boys. If you're having troubles, or something else is more important to you, hey, I get it. Drugs, pussy, guitars, Nintendo, organized crime, none of that's my problem. It's your problem." Coach Jarvis had tiny, smart eyes. His team hat was on the table in front of him. He squeezed it and slapped it on the table. "What are you making me do here, buddy? Jason wasn't only a player to me. He's my boy. I don't want to do this."

"So don't."

"If you can't show up for practice and I keep you on the team, if I *start you*, a sophomore, what does that say to the others?"

"I don't know."

He threw his hat at me and pounded the table so hard the stack of plastic glasses fell over and rolled onto the turf. "Give me your goddamn jersey."

Simon met me in front of the house, where the weeds met the gravel. He had been waiting there, under the shade of our filthy cedar tree. The dust of every passing car clung to it. "You quit the team?"

"They kicked me off. How do you know?"

"Jason phoned."

"How did he find out?"

"One of the coaches, Coach Something, called him right away. The coach said everyone's worried about you, that you've been skipping practices, 'acting like a queer,' and falling off your skateboard and generally fucking up your life and wrecking the team."

I could tell Simon wanted to talk like we always talked, like this was town nonsense and we were above it. But he couldn't. His eyes carried a film of tears. I imagined the conversation with Jason. "He shouted at you?"

"Yes, he shouted at me! He was furious that I answered the phone when no one else was home. He didn't know I'd moved in. He said, 'Don't even fucking *tell me* you're in my room, fucknuts. 'Fucknuts,' he calls me! And I said, 'All right,

169

I won't,' and he said he'd slap me upside my nasty Kenyan head next time he saw me, right after he slapped you upside your nasty head."

"He's a prick sometimes."

"I don't understand. You go to practice every day."

"No, I don't."

"Then where *do* you go?"

He followed me up the drive and onto the back porch. Marv's truck was gone and so was the Cadillac. Beatrice and my mother were at the little office they leased from Don and Geraldine on Second Street. They had finished raising their money from our neighbours and three other investors from the other side of the interstate. They had their contractor. Now all they had to do was negotiate their permits with the town, settle things with the bank, and start building. I led Simon downstairs and made him promise to tell no one, not ever.

"Of course."

"What will you do to yourself if you tell?"

"Hang myself naked from a goalpost."

The dogs had followed us downstairs. Gary was licking something on the carpet, who knows what. The windows in Jason's room were covered with tinfoil because Simon could not sleep with any light. He had been writing poetry of his own, about the Black experience on the modern Front Range, by candlelight. Sunshine ruined poetry. I told him not to say anything until I was done. Since I had not told anyone else I did not realize, until I was telling it, that the truth was a mistake. Beatrice had made me promise not to tell anyone until at least Marv and her and my mother were dead.

At the end Simon wanted to go back and get the dates right. "She started in on you right away."

"What do you mean, 'started in'?"

He pulled a little metal cord, flicked an orange lamp on and off.

"You don't like her."

"Everyone likes her. That's how she gets what she wants. A new car, this crazy business, fourteen-year-old boys."

"It's not like she went looking for a fourteen-year-old boy. We fell in love."

"What about Marv? What about Phoebe?"

"I love Phoebe too. I love them both. And I'm not going to hurt Marv."

"That's not . . . it doesn't work that way."

"It's like someone took all the blood out of me and put it back in, but different."

Simon shook his head. He spoke softly. "I think it's against the law, what she's doing to you."

I didn't tell him about the scratches and bruises, where they came from. "In the Amazon and in Indian tribes—"

"Adam. Does this look like an Indian tribe?"

"Anyway, who cares what the law says? Because no one knows. Except you now, and I wish I hadn't told you."

"Just wait, brother, until she's bored with you. People like this . . ." His Kenyan accent, in the past weeks, had become so proper it would hurt his cause in school. "You have to march back to the field and tell the coach you regret it. And this thing with Beatrice: no more."

I mimicked him, his arm movements and the feminine way he said *You have to march back to the field.*

"It makes you feel better to hurt my feelings, Adam?"

"Feelings? They'll hurt your *body* if you talk like that at school."

"I don't care. You know, you're not the only one. I saw her with another man on Friday."

"What man?"

"The one from Modern You."

I thought about it, about Gord the Haberdasher removing his tie, licking his lips. "I'll kick his ass."

"What?"

I kicked the wall.

"And let's think about it. If she's married to Marv and she's sleeping with the man from Modern You and she's doing who-knows-what with a fourteen-year-old boy . . ."

"Stop saying that."

"Then it's fairly certain there are more. Maybe the mayor. The bank manager, to do this ridiculous deal? Her *investors*?"

I reached out to shove him and he side-stepped me, let me crash awkwardly into the basement wall.

His eyes welled up. Our Gas Stop coveralls hung behind the bar my father had built in the basement. In Monument in the seventies, everybody built crappy basement bars, with leftover carpet all over everything and even disco balls, but eventually they degenerated into terrific places to hang clothes and store abandoned exercise equipment. Simon pulled his coveralls off the hanger and stuffed them in a bag. "When I needed help, you helped."

"Go to hell."

He leapt up the stairs three at a time.

I used Nivea for self-abuse. It carried the smell of the absence of her. When I was finished I put my coveralls in a backpack and skateboarded to the little office on Second Street, between the tanning salon and the used bookstore. My mother was on a chair and Beatrice leaned over the desk. There was a big stainless steel bowl of red grapes between them. They were both on the phone, sharing one receiver. Beatrice popped a grape into her mouth, even as she spoke.

"Golly, it's up to you, Mr. Mercer, how much we can borrow against our principal. Isn't it? Don't you have that authority?" Beatrice winked at my mother and then me. "The value of our asset is considerable. At Wells Fargo they said it was worth seventy thousand."

My mother poked Beatrice and made a face. Beatrice mimed, "What?"

The call ended and they both laughed.

"I can't believe you said that. Seventy!"

"What does he know? He's in Denver. A double lot in Denver is worth double that at least."

"You're going to get us in trouble."

Beatrice turned to me. "Adam, I'm teaching your mother the fine art of negotiation."

"Don't listen, son. This is the fine art of mistruth."

"Mis*direction* perhaps. Fifty, seventy, what's the difference, really?"

"Twenty thousand dollars." My mother pointed at me. "Close your ears!"

They laughed and bantered and high-fived and ate some grapes and poured coffee. The office, a hallway with an opening in the back that was once the storage area for Don and Geraldine's tanning salon, was not air-conditioned. The only time I had ever seen my mother this happy, this confident, her cheeks this pink, was when the colleges were courting Jason. I still failed to understand how all this had happened. Without a dollar of her own money, my mother owned two plots with Beatrice. They were borrowing hundreds of thousands of dollars against the land to build an apartment building. The new sign at Jefferson Gardens would be for rental inquiries, not investment.

Now that I saw Beatrice and heard her voice, I knew she could not have defiled herself with Gord the Haberdasher. With the coffee in my mother and Beatrice their giddiness rose to a crescendo and then they exhaled like they had reached the natural end of a tickle fight. My mother put up her hands and screamed, like a Muppet, and ran across the room and hugged me, kissing me on the cheek.

"How are you?"

"I'm fine."

"Talk to me."

"Fine!"

"Grapes?"

"No."

"Coffee?"

"Gross. No."

"What did you learn today?"

"Nothing so far. Simon's an ass."

"Simon is the least ass-y boy in America. I'm going to ask you the question again, at the end of the day." She looked into my eyes. "You're sure everything is okay?"

"You bet, Mom."

"Not sad? You look a little sad."

"Nope."

"What do all the stickers on your skateboard mean?" Beatrice sat back in her chair, crossed her arms.

After my conversation with Simon, I saw her question as proof of something. There was no way to answer it without seeming like a kid. The stickers meant nothing. They meant I wanted girls to see them on my skateboard—*Thrasher*, NOFX, Bad Religion—and think I was cool.

I had come to tell my mother about Coach Jarvis, to warn her. I had come to see Beatrice. I wanted proof. I wanted her to think of me as much as I thought of her. I wanted her to say *fuck* in my ear and hit me and guide me into her.

My mother looked at her watch and cussed, apologized for cussing, like I was seven, and pulled Beatrice past me toward the door, grabbing both of their purses first. They held hands longer than seemed right. Then my mother shouted, still smiling—she smiled so much now—"Out, Adam. We have to go."

"Where?"

"A reporter from *The Bee* is doing a story on Jefferson Gardens." Beatrice pointed at my mother. "He's taking a photograph of Helen, the property mogul, in front of the land."

"We'll be in the photo together."

"No no no. I'm in no photos. This is your project."

"Bea." *Bea!* "Don't be insane. If you hadn't moved in next door I'd be euthanizing a schnauzer with tuberculosis right now."

"I can't be in the picture."

"Why not?"

"No pictures. Is that okay?"

I listened to their conversation but all I wanted was for Beatrice to wink, to touch me as I passed, to say a word just for me. But they didn't want to be late for their appointment with the reporter, so without saying much more they jumped into the Cadillac.

It was quiet on Second Street when they were gone. A man in a sombrero, dressed in white, walked slowly past and I said hello to him though it took all of my effort. A few clouds floated over Mount Herman, breaking the perfect blue. I skateboarded down Front Street. For a few minutes I stood in front of Modern You, fashioning a plan. Inside the store it was chilly. Gord the Haberdasher was on a stool, hanging a suit. "Livin' on a Prayer" by Bon Jovi was playing.

"Ah, you again." He climbed down. "In the market for another suit?"

"No, sir."

"Well then." He looked down at my skateboard like it was a dead dog. "How can I help you?"

"What are you . . ." I checked to see if the white-haired woman who had altered my pants was around the corner. I did not want her to see me. Now that I was here, mid-way through saying what I had planned to say, I was on the verge of losing the courage. My mouth quivered and I hoped Gord the Haberdasher couldn't see.

"What am I . . . what?"

"Doing with Miss Beatrice Walker?"

Gord the Haberdasher opened his mouth and put his hand on his heart. Then he smiled. "Oh my. Oh me oh my what a question. Why?"

"So it's true?"

"Don't tell me Marv sent you. What a putz."

I turned and walked out. There was no one around but I wanted to be sure so I ran with my skateboard to the dumpster and hid there for a while because there were tears in my eyes. I hated Gord the Haberdasher and I hated Bon Jovi, and I was tempted to ride to town hall to see if the mayor would say *oh me oh my* too.

The youth group at St. Peter was setting up for an anti-abortion ice cream social in the park next to Big Red. Two of the organizers lived up Jefferson Street, sisters whose mother had committed suicide. One was a year older and one was a year younger than me. We said hey to one another at school. One was named Katie but I couldn't remember which one because they both looked like Katies: clean and blonde and happy as hounds. Boys at school eyed the Katies like exotic fruits. Both of them wore straw hats and shorts and matching pro-life T-shirts with pictures of fetuses and a fancy version of the word *Love*.

"I hope you come by, Adam." Katie took off her hat and fanned herself with it. Her sister was working with Father Tim from the church, setting up a pole for a white market tent. It was complicated and she laughed when Father Tim became frustrated and mimed cracking one of the poles over his knee.

"I'm working tonight, sadly."

"Maybe another time."

Katie, the second one, busy with the tent, smiled with so much sincerity it had to be fake. "Another time *totally*, Adam."

Father Tim waved a pole. "Go Rangers!"

It was still fifteen minutes early to show up at the Gas Stop and I couldn't bear the thought of listening to Gene, who'd be coming off the morning shift—not yet. Simon would not arrive until 1:20.

I sat on a curb in the alley behind the station and smelled what remained of the Nivea on my fingers.

Gene's daughter Hailey, who had Down syndrome, came around the corner, trundling after a ball. She spotted me. We hugged and she took my hand and pulled me to the shack. Rather than go inside and talk to Gene, who was busy with a calculator, I bounced the ball with Hailey. She was almost ten years older than me but she was like an affectionate little sister. At 1:25 I pulled on my coveralls. Knowing Beatrice was finished with me, that she had found someone else, made me want to sleep. Then throw up. I went into the bathroom and stood over the toilet until the feeling passed.

"Where's your bud?" Gene knocked and shouted through the door.

Simon was always punctual and polite. When something went wrong at work, with a nutty customer or a faulty pump, Simon was calm. Everyone sneaked soda from time to time because we knew Gene didn't keep track of his inventory. Everyone but Simon. Yet Gene pretended he was doing me the grandest favour by employing Simon, and he lorded it over me.

One minute remained. When I opened the bathroom door Gene was looking at his watch like he was timing a race. Hailey pulled me back outside to bounce the ball.

"There it is. He's late. I knew it!"

"Something's gone wrong." I went inside. "That's the only reason he'd be late. There's a problem with his car."

"Adam!" Hailey called me back. "The ball."

"If he picked another day to do this I wouldn't be so PO'd." Gene was a Mormon and did not cuss. "But I got a tee time. These people!"

I could not say, "What people?" because I did not want to hear Gene's answer. There were racists all over town, I could see it in the way they looked at Simon, but I did not want to hear about it or think about it. "Simon'll be here any minute. Leave Hailey with me. She can help out if it gets busy."

"What?"

"And when Simon comes I'll call Rayleen to come pick her up."

"Oh, like Rayleen won't complain her head off."

"Have a heart, Gene."

He tilted his head at me, like a dog when you sing a song at it. "Don't you say *have a heart* to me."

"Simon will be here."

It was a slow afternoon. Summer holidays were nearly over, so a lot of people were out of town trying to snatch up the last of it, hunting and fishing and driving to Disneyland.

Hailey and I bounced the ball.

In four hours I had pumped less than two hundred dollars worth of gas. I was so anxious about Beatrice abandoning me for Gord the Haberdasher and who knows who else, and now about Simon too, that I imagined my sweat must be coming out sour. Hailey was bored with the ball and all she wanted to do was sit *right next to me* on the barstools in front of the shack and play the name game. Just after six o'clock the Cadillac pulled up, though not to the pumps. My mother stepped out, looking as though she had just survived an earthquake.

"Who's that?" Hailey hopped up off her stool.

"My mom and Beatrice."

"*Beatrice Beatrice fo fee-atrice.*"

I was so heartbroken about her I nearly sprinted across the pavement and kissed her, begged her. But she stayed in the car.

My mother's eyes were swollen from crying. She rolled her lips, one into the other. "Simon's at Memorial Hospital." My mother looked at Beatrice in the Cadillac and back at me. "He'll be okay, but he needs surgery."

"What happened? What kind of surgery?"

"*Banana fanna mo mee-atrice.*"

"I don't know exactly what kind of surgery. Mrs. Kinoro told me but I didn't write it down. The kind of surgery you get when your cheekbone is broken."

"How did he break his cheekbone?"

"It wasn't just his cheekbone, sweetheart."

"Someone hurt him? Who?"

My mother looked up at the sky. "Mrs. Kinoro said she doesn't know. The chief needs your help."

"*Mee mie moe mee-atrice. Beatrice.*"

My mother and Beatrice drove off to find Gene at the golf course. I phoned the police and asked for the chief. He wasn't in. I told the officer I could not talk, not until I was off work, but he kept me on the line, asking muffled questions. A hot gust of wind blew gravel into the side of the shack. There was only one rule and I had broken it. I had told Simon about Beatrice and I had damned him, damned us. A short-box Chevy and an El Camino had come at the same time, a couple of burnouts from the medical equipment factory, and they must have said something to Hailey. She ran into the shack crying, so I hung up on the officer.

I wasn't allowed to say anything to the rednecks. Gene forbade it. If men were cruel to Hailey all we could do was pity them. God kept a special list of men who hurt the fragile, Gene said. I started one pump and then the other. It was against the law and dangerous to smoke cigarettes so close to the pumps but people did it anyway. These men did it. Both of them had gone fat and misshapen from beer and chicken.

"Can I kindly ask you fellas to take a few steps back to smoke? Gasoline spills from time to time."

One of them, the bigger of the two, his face so chubby it made his faded Broncos cap look tiny, winked at me. "You can kindly go fuck yourself, Lisinski Junior. Go ahead and fuck your retard too."

My brother was not universally adored among his peers. Hailey cried like a five-year-old with a bloodied knee, and from the shack it echoed. It was men like this who had hurt Simon, I was sure of it. The bigger one had just shaved. His razor lines were uneven and his cotton-candy cologne overpowered the smell of gasoline. Both of them were dressed like the offspring of a cowboy and a football mascot, ready for a night at O'Grady's. As I checked their oil I enjoyed a fantasy about removing the nozzle from the Chevy and spraying them both.

The other man, whose eyes were already shiny and sleepy from an afternoon of beer, pulled out his wallet. The pump on his El Camino had popped off. "Where's your nigger tonight?"

Simon was so good he spent his spare money on books of poetry. And I had damned him.

On the El Camino pump it said $18.82. It was a seventies car with a recent paint job, lovingly washed and waxed and shined. My job was to bring it to no higher than nineteen dollars, maybe only to $18.90 for serious car nuts. I pressed down hard on the nozzle, overriding the automatic shut-off, and filled it so high a thin stream leaked out. Then I pressed it again, and held it, and gasoline splashed down the side. "Oops."

The man stomped over with his cigarette in his mouth and shoved me out of the way. He cussed and shouted incoherently. His friend laughed so hard I thought he was going to faint. The smoker was stuck between coming after me and removing the spout. If you leave gasoline on fresh paint it will discolour it. He yanked the spout from the El Camino and replaced it on the pump, pulled the squeegee from the bucket and washed where the gasoline had already evaporated. "You're giving me the gas for free."

"Can't do that."

"Like hell you can't."

I took out my pen and my pad of paper and wrote down his licence plate number. "If you want to steal gasoline you'll have to discuss it with the chief."

"Have it your way." The man with the El Camino pulled a twenty out of his wallet, turned around, and reached inside his pants with it.

"No way!" His friend screamed with laughter. "Don't do it!"

A look of confused pleasure came over the man's face as he wiped his ass with the twenty. Then he pulled it out and threw it at me.

"Oh God. You are the fucking *boss*." His friend applauded. "You're a living legend. Kids'll study you."

I put a rock on the twenty to keep it from flying away, and went into the shack for the tweezers Gene kept for mysterious reasons. Behind the cash register, Hailey cowered and cried.

The rednecks stood over the shitty bill like it was a newborn kitten. The second pump said $21.50. Tiny Bronco cap paid me with exact change and made a big deal out of keeping the money away from his friend, who said he wanted to wipe it on his nuts for me. I bent over to pick up the twenty with the tweezers. I wanted to wipe it on him. I wanted Jason and his Black friends from Oklahoma to be here so they could make him eat it.

They stopped laughing like an old engine shutting off and looked at me in my coveralls with shitty money on a pair of rusted tweezers. The man who had wiped it on his ass faked a punch and I flinched. Both of them questioned my commitment to heterosexuality and they returned to their vehicles. I watched them drive out and then I went to hug Hailey for a while.

The phone rang again. "Is this Adam?"

"Yes, sir."

"You aren't allowed to hang up on me again."

I told the police officer what I knew. I knew nothing. The officer was trying to create Simon the Fighter, one of those assholes who go around asking if boys have a problem. *You got a fucken problem?* I agreed he was big and he was on the wrestling and baseball teams but told him that Simon suffered when he stepped on an ant.

My mother and Beatrice were turning in to the Gas Stop. Gene followed in his big diesel truck.

"Do you have any suspects, sir?"

The officer snorted and then recovered. "Boy, we don't even know what happened here. Good chance we never will."

"Why?"

With that, the officer found his revenge. He hung up on me.

Gene marched into the shack. "You two owe me for this."

My mother followed him inside. Beatrice stayed in the car with a cigarette. I was dizzy with worry for Simon, and it was getting harder and harder to see my mother and Beatrice together.

"For what, Gene?" I said. "What did we do?"

"Y'all get yourselves hurt with your boyish nonsense, drinking and smoking marijuana and picking fights."

"Who? Me and Simon?"

Hailey hugged her father. "What happened to her?"

I told him about the rednecks. Hailey ran back and hugged me as I wriggled out of my coveralls. She tried to pull me outside. "Let's bounce the ball!"

Gene wanted me to wash the twenty before I left. My mother, who had remained quiet when he accused Simon and me of criminal acts, shuffled her feet and cleared her throat. It was contrary to her parenting philosophy to come between a teacher and me, or a coach, a boss, a girl.

"With respect, Mr. Eugene, I'm not sure you're being entirely fair."

Gene glanced at my mother and back to me, as though I were responsible for her. He said nothing. He just looked at me and I knew him well enough to know what he was thinking. Either I washed the shit off the money or I was fired. Lots of boys wanted to work at Gas Stop. They dropped off their applications all the time.

"He's a part-time student, making a part-time student's wage, and you're punishing him with something unhygienic and frankly disgusting, just *disgusting*, because . . . he stuck up for your daughter?"

Gene would not look away from me.

"I'll take care of it, sir."

"No you won't." My mother clapped her hands. Then she looked down at them, like they had not behaved. She never sought confrontations. When someone had humiliated or mistreated her at work the best she could do was complain about it to me at the end of the day, over a strong and spicy

Bloody Mary. She never spoke up, and she punished herself for it. Yet she seemed to grow taller in the shack, and her voice lost its quiver with each new word. She was different. "You *won't* have him wash that money, Gene. He did the right thing."

I was about to say, again, that I would clean the twenty. It was like I had to write all my exams for college in an hour and I had not studied. I might have wobbled. There was Gord the Haberdasher with his pants down, Beatrice in front of him, in the change room of Modern You. My mother took my hand and squeezed and whispered, "Shh, baby." I was her baby when I needed to be. The shack was so hot that sweat oozed down Gene's face, but he would not reach up and wipe it away. Hailey sat behind the counter, ignoring our conversation. She ripped open one of the Little Tree air fresheners, a Vanillaroma one, and a sugar bomb went off. My mother reached for her nose. Gene's eyes had rings under them, which always happened when he golfed. He was allergic to one of the chemicals they used to keep everything green. The shitty bill sat on a square of paper towel.

"I'm sorry, Gene."

"What?"

"Like my mom said, I can't clean that money."

"Pick up your final cheque next week." He walked into the bathroom and turned on the water. Before he splashed his face he slammed the door shut and Hailey jumped.

———

The radio in the Cadillac was tuned to the country station. Randy Travis and Keith Whitley and Clint Black may have been different men, but they all sounded the same. If I moved to the middle of the back seat I could see Beatrice's face in the rear-view mirror as she steered. Her big eyes were blank. She would not look at me. She mouthed the words to the stupid song. Colorado had turned purple in the dusk.

We turned off the interstate. A bunch of kids jumped through a sprinkler in front of a housing complex and screamed even though it was too late for them to be awake. My mother pointed at the kids. "How do we keep them safe?"

Beatrice did not respond.

"Just like that. Just like that." My mother chopped one hand into the other. "Just like that a savage, a gang of unfeeling *savages*, can destroy everything that's beautiful. He's a child! If I could find them . . ."

"Find who, Helen?"

"The bastards who did this. Because here's the thing: you never get it back. They take it away from you, that feeling *it's all yours, this is your town, your state, this is your country, your life to build*. And it's gone. For the rest of Simon's life you know what he'll be thinking? You know what's lurking around every corner?"

"Punishing them won't help."

"Oh, yes it will."

"It feels like it helps, for a little while, but it doesn't."

"What will help?" My mother wiped her eyes with the back of her chopping hand.

"Forgetting." Beatrice went back to silently singing along to Clint-Whitley-Travis.

Neither of them spoke as we approached the hospital. My mother opened her window when we stopped at a light. Def Leppard played from a group of trucks gathered in a strip mall parking lot. She lifted herself so her head was out the window and my mother did something I had never seen her do: she spit.

Simon was on the sixth floor. His mother was in the room with him, holding his hand and speaking Kikuyu. The moment she saw me she stood up and backed away so I could see him.

"Hey, fella." His voice was small. The left side of his face had sunk. His lip was cut and his nose was swollen.

"You look amazing."

"Don't make me laugh. It hurts."

Mrs. Kinoro had retreated to the corner. It was a vast private room with flowers and a silver television. "He is not allowed to speak above a whisper." I loved the way Mrs. Kinoro spoke. *Weespah.*

I pulled the chair close to him. "What happened?"

He winked. "I slipped and fell."

"This is utter nonsense. He tells no one the truth. He slipped and fell and fractured his cheekbone, broke two ribs? Look at this lip. Some peculiar fall."

"When is the surgery, Mrs. Kinoro?"

"First thing in the morning. All of the X-rays and scans

are completed. The only hope is that, tonight, as the surgeon takes his beauty sleep, the eye is not permanently damaged."

Simon whispered, "A cheekbone comes in handy, holding your eye in place."

I leaned into him. He smelled of antiseptic. "Was it Squeak and those guys?"

"A dreadful, unlucky fall. One in a million."

"The police want to help."

Simon looked at his mother, who turned away and looked out the window. "Maybe the police can move that pesky curb I fell on."

"Come on."

"No, Adam."

"Did they tell you not to tell?"

He looked at me with his cunning eyes. There were clouds of blood in the whites of them. Even if they had not ordered him to stay quiet, Simon knew what it meant to speak to the police. If there were witnesses, the witnesses would be my teammates. Not one of them would say a word against another, not to the police. By now they would have prepared their story.

"This is why we came to America." Mrs. Kinoro spoke to the window, to her own reflection. "So we would not have these sorts of fears."

"If I could roll my eyes I would."

Mrs. Kinoro turned back to him. "Pardon me?"

"Nothing, Mother."

I did not want to see them fight. "Mrs. Kinoro, can I get you something? A drink? Something to eat?"

"No thank you, Adam." She did not look away from him.

"If you'd like to go for a walk or something, I could stay with him."

"All these 'somethings.' What is, 'Or something'? Does it have a meaning I do not understand?"

"I don't think so."

"Is it too much to ask for precision? I do not need *anything*. I do not need *something*. I am quite comfortable here with my son who was nearly murdered today by . . . *someone*."

"*Maitu. Maitu.*"

Mrs. Kinoro bent close to him and he spoke to her in Kikuyu. Then she stood back up, righted herself in her queenly way, and turned to me. "You are a good boy, Adam."

Simon pulled his hand out from under his covers and grimaced. Every move hurt. He reached for my hand and I gave it to him. I had never held a boy's hand. Both of us had dry skin, from the gasoline and from washing it off so often. Neither of us said anything for a while and I resisted the urge to take my hand back and look away. In my silent fashion I loved him and thanked him and told him I was sick with what my teammates had done to him. His mother looked away. I wanted to whisper in his ear that I was sorry for confessing, for damning him to hell, that he had been right, that I would win Beatrice back and avenge him too. The light from his monitors turned his collapsed cheek the colour of a dark lime.

"It's a routine surgery, I hear. Super safe." This was a lie and Simon knew it. Where could I have learned anything about surgeries?

"I was supposed to be asleep by now. Thank you for the visit, old man. Come back tomorrow night after they put my bones back together?"

From the distant street, the Kinoro house had an old-fashioned glow, pale yellow against deep brown wood. Though he had never said anything, I knew what Simon's father thought of me. He was not moved by American football.

I knocked on the door with my backpack on. Mr. Kinoro opened the door and stepped out onto the veranda. At ten o'clock on a Monday night he wore a tan suit with bedroom slippers. He pulled a toothpick out of his mouth.

"Adam Lisinski?"

"Yes, sir."

"My wife said you were coming."

"I'll just grab a few things for Simon. Books and clothes."

"Join me in the salon." Mr. Kinoro had never said much more than hello to me. I could not imagine what we would discuss in the salon. Whenever I heard "salon," I thought of haircuts.

In our town, people with money built giant houses in the country wrapped with beige vinyl siding and filled with creamy carpeting and crystal chandeliers and marble staircases and vast windows with a view of the mountains. When Simon's parents arrived from Kenya they bought the last old wooden mansion in town, on the eastern shore of Monument Lake. They paid a firm from Denver to renovate it. The mansion was over one hundred years old, with dark wood and stained glass and built-in bookshelves. To keep out the heat in the summer and the cold in winter, thick mustard-coloured curtains covered the windows. Lamps lit up the antique furniture and bookshelves, the dining table, the silver candelabra, fresh flowers. There was a photograph of the salon in the salon: a black-and-white image of the original family, a doctor and his wife and three daughters, prosperous white people, all of them looking like they had decided to resist arrest. Apart from our feet on the creaky wood the only sound inside was the *tick-tock* of a grandfather clock taller than Mr. Kinoro.

I was ashamed of our stuffy little house by the railroad tracks. The cigarette smoke, the dogs, the stained walls, the way it shook when the train passed.

"Sit, please." Mr. Kinoro watched me with his hands behind his back and half a smile, the courtly gesture of a hotelier. I knew from Simon there were two versions of Mr. Kinoro: the patient and kind man who owned one of the town's most important institutions and joined the Elks and Masons and Rotary, and then *his father*, who had learned from his own father and his father's father to be the hard king of his home.

I sat in the red wing chair by the fireplace. He sat in a taller version of it, more of a throne, with flashes of gold in the pattern.

"'Lisinski.' What sort of name is that?"

"My granddad was Croatian and Polish."

"I see. He arrived here when?"

"He was born in Denver. His parents, my great-grandparents, came over."

"As refugees?"

I was unsure of the definition of the word, but I knew my great-grandparents had been running away from European danger of some sort. My paternal grandparents died before I could meet them, in a car accident in the mountains. "Yes."

"It stays with you, doesn't it? That quality?"

"Yes, sir." I was already lost. By the way he looked at me I could tell that was a poor way to answer the question. "Sorry. What do you mean?"

"I mean if we are refugees our children will be refugees, even our children's children. They may not know it."

"You don't think folks can leave it behind, become someone new?"

"This is a romantic distraction from the truth."

"You didn't come to America as refugees."

He laughed like Santa. There was no way Mr. Kinoro could whisper. Like Phoebe he had freckles, but a different sort. "No, Adam. We arrived with capital. Do you know the difference?"

"Simon taught me about that. A refugee can't buy the Overland Hotel."

"Precisely."

I thought of my mother. "But his son or daughter could."

"This is possible, Adam. But if my theory is correct, he will not hold it. He will revert to his true nature, the nature of his blood. There is a calling, Adam, from deep within us. I do not think we consciously hear it. But we feel it, we dream of it at night, and in our days it determines our choices."

I did not like what Mr. Kinoro was saying but it would have been impolite to say so. It would have proven something. "I see."

"Do you?" Mr. Kinoro leaned forward now, his elbows on his knees. He was an unusually fit man for his age, with no pot-belly. "Tell me, Adam. Where is your father?"

"I don't know."

"*I don't know.*" He tried to imitate me. "This is what Simon had told me. I did not think it was possible, genuinely not knowing."

"My guess is Los Angeles."

"Your *guess*. Why that?"

As we spoke I tried to think of the word for what he was doing to me, with the tone of his voice and in his questions and declarations. It was a word I had used in an essay about *To Kill a Mockingbird*. I had found it in a thesaurus and I had looked it up in the dictionary, to be sure it meant what I had hoped and it did. "I don't know, sir."

"That phrase is banned in our house."

"What phrase?"

"If someone asks a question, a serious question, it is inappropriate to simply say, 'I don't know.' Not when we do. You *know* why—you at least have a guess about your father, his whereabouts."

"The sunsets."

"Pardon me?"

"The sun sets in the west. My father liked sunsets but they aren't worth much here, they don't last long enough."

"Because of the mountains."

"Yes, sir. I think he was looking for something he could not find here. Not just sunsets, but that was a part of it."

"You see. Now that is an admirable answer."

I did not want to go upstairs, in the dark, to Simon's room for his pyjamas. I did not understand why Mr. Kinoro couldn't forgive Simon for the eye makeup and take his things to the hospital himself like any regular father. Mr. Kinoro studied me for a while longer, in the *tick-tock* silence of the house.

"Well, Adam." He stood up. "I do not want you here any longer than you want to be here. Open your bag. I took the liberty."

Mr. Kinoro had put together a pile of Simon's things—his pyjamas, his toothbrush and toothpaste, some acne cream, and a few T-shirts. There was a little red Bible on top. He placed them in my backpack.

He stood up and clasped his hands behind him again and smiled. "Perhaps it will help you understand why I will now ask you to leave. To leave, Adam, and to never come back to this house. You're not welcome here. Goodness knows Simon will make his own choices. He will rebel—we all do!—against his true nature, his inheritance. Simon living with you in your squalor, following his worst instincts, is much like your mother starting a property development concern. You see? It's contrary. It fouls up a room. When Simon spends time with you, he tempts himself away from God and beauty, from his best self. Just as your mother pretends to be a businessman, Simon smokes vile cigarettes and dresses up like a *mashoga*."

"Thank you, sir."

He laughed at me on the veranda. On the long path from the house to the road, as sprinklers soaked the garden of peonies and Monument lavender, I thought of something I might turn around and say to Mr. Kinoro. Nothing was good enough, so I walked to the road with my backpack and then I ran.

eight

in the photograph on the front page of the *Tri-Lakes Bee*, my mother is in the foreground and Beatrice stands at some distance, among the raspberries of the Hastings land. The reporter made it sound like Beatrice and my mother were the Astors of the West, two enterprising women transforming our town and—who knows?—maybe the whole state of Colorado, deal by deal. Helen Lisinski was a single mother who had slowly plotted and saved, preparing for fifteen years to launch her career in property development. All she needed was the right partner. Jason was proof of the Lisinski family's long record of excellence. They referred to me as "a star in his own right, on and off the field." What did that mean? We had a shitty car and a tiny house plastered with dog hair and nicotine stains. We microwaved fish. Someone had faxed a copy of the original article to my Uncle Oscar in Tacoma, who was one of the many people to phone that morning.

While my mother spoke to him Beatrice ran up the stairs and onto the deck with a copy of *The Bee*. I stood up to meet her. I thought she was happy. She wore nothing but a hastily buttoned dress shirt and panties, the blue ones. I wanted to cover her up with something but there was nothing.

One of her hands was in her hair, like she was hunting for an insect. "I told him. I *told him* no pictures with me. What the fuck am I supposed to do now?"

"You look really nice in the picture."

"That isn't the goddamn point, Adam."

"You're way in the back."

"It's clearly me. Clearly!"

"Yeah, well."

"*Yeah well. Yeah well.*" When she waved the paper around one of her boobs showed. I looked away. She pushed me, like we were going to have a fight on the field. "*Yeah, well*, right? It's nothing to you?"

"I don't get it. You look nice."

"I won't look *nice* after five sons of bitches roll up on their hogs in the middle of the night." Her voice was different. All of the fancy, all of the poise, all of the care was gone. In her fury a few drops of white spit had escaped her mouth and stuck just to the left of it. "You know what happened to Simon? That's how these gents say hello."

"What gents?"

She rushed into our house. Through the screen door I watched her take the cordless phone from my mother's ear and smash it on the kitchen floor. My mother's smile imploded.

I could not hear their words, but after a few minutes Beatrice screamed and stormed out of the house and past me without saying a word. Marv was now on his measly back porch, watching with his mouth open, so I did not touch her or call her back. I wanted to ask her to meet me in the garage at midnight. I needed it so bad I felt my bones would crack and melt. She could do anything she wanted to me. I was better than any haberdasher.

After a while my mother came out and sat next to me.

"What's wrong, Mom?"

"Nothing."

"Come on."

"She wanted to leave some stuff behind and she's worried it's going to find her."

"What stuff?"

"Men."

"What's so bad about a picture?"

"They don't know her name but they know her face, somehow. I don't know." My mother lit a cigarette. Her fingers shook. "Beatrice had a different sort of upbringing than you or me. She was mistreated terribly. She wasn't loved right at all. It stays with you and governs you, they say, especially when you're young. She had no church or community, no real family apart from her brother—who sounds like a piece of work in his own right. Her brother is in some gang or was. I don't know. It's hard to piece it all together and real hard to imagine it from here in Monument." She tapped the ash from her cigarette, even though there wasn't any yet. "Bea smashed our phone."

"Yeah. I saw."

"You know how when a dog goes berserk and bites some kid they always say it's the owner's fault and not the dog?"

I hadn't heard anyone saying that, but I understood. "Yes."

"People aren't so different, maybe. Anyway." She kissed me on the cheek. "I don't want you to think about this, not when you have Simon in the hospital. Beatrice'll sort it out like she sorts everything out. It's going to be all right. Please don't worry."

It was another blue-sky day. There were fires in the mountains and though we could not see the smoke we could smell it. My mother lay back and squinted into the sun like she was trying to decipher a message. Marv and Beatrice were back in their house. Through their open windows we could hear doors slamming. Again Beatrice screamed.

My mother dressed entirely like Beatrice now, in dresses and shoes with heels. She spoke differently, even to Uncle Oscar on the phone.

"She didn't have to smash anything, Mom."

"We can replace it."

"How could someone only know her face? Not her name?"

My mother did not answer. After a long time her fingers shook less. She sighed out a cloud of smoke and her breath trembled with it. "Coach Jarvis called this afternoon."

"That's not what we're talking about, Mom. If someone wants to find Beatrice—"

"You quit the team, he said."

"He kicked me off the team."

"You've been skipping practices all summer. What have you been doing instead of going to practice?" Her cigarette trembled between her fingers.

I had an answer ready. After visiting Mr. Kinoro I'd sat in the park next to Big Red, where the Katies and Father Tim had protested against abortion, and I'd done some thinking. "It's like there was a dark cloud over me for a while. I was depressed, I guess. I couldn't get up. I'd try and the next thing I knew practice was over and there I was, still in bed."

"You couldn't talk to me?" She put her cigarette in the ashtray and took my hand in hers. She kissed it. "You see, I knew it. I knew something was up. All those weird scratches on you—"

"I did it to myself."

"What?"

"I'm sorry, Mom. You always know."

She kissed my hand some more. "No, no, no. We can fix this. We'll get you an appointment with Dr. Fischer."

"I'm feeling better. I think a big part of it was Phoebe being away."

"Don't you dare do this."

"Do what?"

"Dismiss it. This is big. It's real. I'm pulling back from Jefferson Gardens and I'm gonna help you." She looked toward Marv and Beatrice's house. "It might be for the best anyway."

"I'll get back on the team. Phoebe's plane lands tonight. School's starting and I'm excited about that."

"You're back on the team, Adam." She shook her head and smiled at her dying cigarette. "You honestly think they'd play a *game* without you? You just gotta call Coach Jarvis and talk to him. Tell him what you told me."

"Right now?"

"You'll have to use the downstairs phone."

I was going to ask if he was at home or at work but my mother was silently praying.

For an hour I pulled weeds from the haunted garden across the street to prepare it for the television cameras. News crews from KMGH and KCNC in Denver wanted to do a story on the lady property developer. The raspberries were on the branches but they were not yet red enough to eat.

"You could borrow our gardeners for an afternoon." Phoebe was less freckled than before she'd left because it had rained most of the time in Northern Europe. Her shorts and shirt were new, the shoes too. There was something just a little off about it, the colours and the stiffness of the fabric. European, I guessed. "My father wouldn't mind. I'm sure they could give you some good advice."

"I'll ask my mom."

"He said he'd be happy to give *her* some advice too. On developing the land. He had no idea! Why didn't you tell me your mom was planning this? Why didn't she? My dad knows all this stuff."

I did not want to tell her the truth about it being Beatrice's idea. She had said we were building a mythology. "She wanted to keep it a secret."

"My dad says almost everyone in the industry is men. Like: everyone. This is wonderful."

Now that Phoebe had been in Europe she said words like "wonderful" in normal conversations. She told me about the fjords and demonstrated all the accents she had learned in the United Kingdom: Scottish, Irish, Welsh, Posh. She'd never been a naïve or provincial girl but world travel had lent her a royal quality. Phoebe saw our town and its people anew, in all of our smallness. A guitarist on the ship had given her lessons, and with her background in piano she had learned the chords quickly. She strapped her acoustic guitar on and as I pulled weeds she sang a version of "Is This Love" by Bob Marley. She closed her eyes and crinkled her nose, like she really felt it, and since the song was about being in love and about building a home and a life together it made me sweat like a yogi.

At the end I clapped. There was so much to admire about Phoebe, but the lack of timidity in her was irresistible and infuriating. It seemed simple enough, just a firm decision: *I shall be confident and sure of myself. I will sing as loudly as I like, and make faces as I do it.*

"Blake taught me five songs. Do you want me to play 'Love Bites' by Def Lep?"

"Maybe not that one. The guitar teacher's name was Blake?"

"He wasn't a guitar teacher. He was just on the cruise too, with his parents. They're from Connecticut. He's seventeen and if you aren't eighteen there isn't much you can do. They're pretty strict about all that on the ship."

"So he sang love songs to you."

"He taught me how to play them."

I wanted to get on an airplane to Connecticut and look Blake up in the phone book and ask him to meet me in an empty park. "You didn't tell him about me?"

"Of course I did. He has a girlfriend too."

"Fuck him."

"Adam. Jeez. It's not like we did anything." She looked down at her new shoes and smiled at them, like they shared a *wonderful* secret. "Should I sing you another song?"

"Blake taught you this one too?"

"I learned it so I could sing it to you, you big redneck."

"You should tell him to come visit."

"Oh, he's not like you. He's an artist. He wouldn't even fight back."

She started to sing "Better Be Home Soon" by Crowded House. A gust threw her skirt up for a moment. She stopped the song to adjust it and started again. When she sang, "It would cause me pain if we were to end it," she leaned over me and squinted naughtily. Fucking Blake! I imagined he had hair that hung loosely over his forehead like River Phoenix's, not like my curly mess, and that his parents had stayed in a penthouse suite on the cruise ship like the Brandts. He drove a brand-new Saab and played tennis and led the debate team and wore pink shaker-knit Polo sweaters. A month was a long time to be playing love songs with Blake. They had kissed, I was sure of it, and when she smiled at her shoes she was telling me. They had kissed often as the sun went soft and low over the fjords—what the hell was a fjord?—and it had hurt them to leave one another. They had made promises. I wanted her to tell me I was wrong, that she had not fallen in love with Blake, but I knew even if she said she had not, that he was ugly and four-foot-seven, I would not believe her.

At the end of the song she stood with the guitar strap between her breasts. She looked away for a while. I could tell there was something she'd been wanting to say. "You didn't quit the team, did you? My dad heard it. How could they let a Lisinski quit the football team?"

"Who cares?"

"Don't be a baby, Adam. I'm here, aren't I? I just sang you a song."

"I'm back on it. You don't have to worry about that."

"It's your way into Stanford. Don't be dumb." She pulled off the guitar and slipped it into its case, looked around to be sure we were alone. "Why won't you kiss me?"

My face was dirty, so she tried to keep everything but my lips away. It was more than that. The kiss was tentative, like we were no longer sure about one another. She took my hands. There were remnants of scratches all over me.

"Did anything mental happen while I was gone?"

"I don't know what you mean."

"With Simon, maybe. Your art gallery parties."

I told her then about how my teammates had attacked him, and I made it seem that was why I had really quit. How could I be on a football team with boys who had broken my best friend's cheekbone because he was Kenyan or Black or poetic or Wendy?

"You know for sure who did it?"

"Simon won't say."

"Adam, you might hate me for saying this, but you can't fix something from the outside by quitting. Be a leader. If you think your teammates are assholes, there's only one person who can do something about it. You can't wait for someone else to do it for you. That's how failures think. You're not a failure. What would your brother say? Or your mom?"

"My brother would never be Simon's friend."

"Why not?"

"Simon's different."

"Why are you Simon's friend?"

"Simon's different."

Phoebe stared at me for a while without saying anything. She saw it or smelled it, tasted it in my kiss. She knew. She could not say what it was, not yet. I could not marry Beatrice and go to Stanford with her, kiss her on the streets of Manhattan. The wind eased from hot to merely warm, and it carried the first hint of rain. Phoebe's hands were soft and she smelled of the sort of moisturizer that costs fifty dollars a bottle.

That night, after practice, I showered and waited for Beatrice in the garage, reading Walt Whitman, but again she did not come.

———

My mother called the company Magpie Developments. She did not have money to pay a designer so she copied a drawing from *The Birds of America* for the logo. Men in suits stood on the sidewalk with her, in front of the haunted garden, and smoked cigarettes and talked about business. She seemed taller. The people who owned the *Denver Post* also owned the *Bee*, so they ran the newspaper story and the same photograph in Denver. It was also in the Boulder and Fort Morgan and Brush papers. Lots of people had seen my mother on television. Developers from Denver wanted to partner on other projects even though it was clear from the story that Magpie Developments hadn't actually built anything. They did have signed documents and deposits from people who wanted to live in Jefferson Gardens the moment it was ready, and a waiting list of thirty-seven other people.

During the day, when Marv was out, Beatrice did not invite me to visit. If she was home, she did not answer the door. One morning I came upstairs and she was standing in our kitchen in a bathrobe, holding a bottle of white wine. Her hair was unwashed. For a moment it seemed she didn't recognize me. I was about to ask her about Gord the Haberdasher, ask her why she'd dumped me, when my mother walked in with some documents. "Oh. Good morning, sunshine." My mother was wearing a new navy-blue dress. With her eyes she sent me back down the stairs.

I visited Simon in the hospital. He was not surprised Beatrice was obsessed with violent men on Harleys, and gave me ten examples of things she might have done to encourage a gang to come after her. He called her a viper and begged me to fall back in love with Phoebe. I told him about her guitar teacher by the pink-sunset fjords of Norway. He shook his head and called me a damn fool.

"It's a curse, Sye," I told him.

"What's a curse?"

"I cursed us. You and I both, and Beatrice. Maybe my mom too."

"There's no such thing."

"I wasn't supposed to tell anyone about Beatrice and I told you. That's why Squeak and those boys attacked you."

"Stop it."

"And it's why men on motorcycles are coming for her."

Simon waited a long time before he spoke. "I am worried about you, fella. You have inky handbags under your eyes. You need sleep. You're obsessed with a woman in her thirties who doesn't care one bit about you."

There was no point waiting for her in the garage but I did it anyway, every night. I watched her house through the filthy little window and imagined her there, on the porch, and with Nivea I imagined her coming to me. At practice I watched Squeak but he did and said nothing strange. I asked Coach Jarvis if he had seen Simon the day he was attacked and he had never heard of Simon. He said he could barely keep track of the kids on the football team. In our first pre-season game, against Cherry Creek, I had three interceptions and a touchdown.

Two days before school started Phoebe and I met in the town library and hunted the legal section for a case that resembled Simon's. Mr. Brandt was a lawyer and she wanted to be one too. Who else in Colorado had been hurt by a group of men? With no witnesses? The librarian, who looked like David Letterman dressed as a woman, had nothing much else to do so she helped us.

I took notes.

The library was half an hour from closing when I spotted Beatrice in the fiction section. There were only four people in there, apart from our table. It was not a big library—only one large room in a strip mall. Beatrice beckoned me with a wink. I walked over and pretended to be looking for something. She stumbled a bit, and through the dust of the Dickens shelf I could smell the wine on her breath.

"You have to go to the bathroom in a few minutes."

"I do?"

"You really do." She struggled to speak without slurring.

Back at the library table, Phoebe was already beginning to dictate. In the late seventies a woman was camping alone when four men, frat boys, attacked her. The men had claimed it was this woman's big plan to have a gangbang. All four of the men were convicted of rape when a police officer separated them and they started telling on one another. Phoebe lit up.

"It'd be so much easier to get a bunch of dense football players—sorry—to rat one another out. We separate them and the truth flows. All we have to do is convince Simon to press charges. Do you think he would?"

Simon said he would not, not ever. But Phoebe was so excited and Beatrice was waiting for me. "I have to go to the bathroom."

"Maybe we should chat with the police. We could pretend we're a couple of dopey kids working on a school project."

"But school hasn't started yet." I was already up and on my way to the bathroom.

The door did not lock. There was one cubicle and one urinal. I looked under the cubicle: no shoes.

"Hello?" I pushed opened the door and there she was, crouched on the toilet like an owl in a grey cotton dress.

"What's going on?"

She hopped off and crashed into me. "We gotta leave."

"Who does?"

"You and I. We gotta leave town."

"I don't understand. What about—"

"Helen will be fine. It's her ship."

"But you don't talk to me anymore."

"Only because Helen's too damn close."

"What about Gord at Modern You and . . ." I went for it. "And the other men?"

"Oh, that's nothing."

"What's nothing?"

"Focus, Adam." She lost her balance and slammed into the wall of the cubicle. Her armpits were bad fruit. "Here's what we do. We fly to Paris. We buy a castle in the valley of the River Loire. We have servants, like your prissy girl-friend does, and a retriever dog, and when it's cold we walk down our stone staircases—Jesus, imagine!—and drink wine by one of our massive fireplaces. Tapestries. We have tapestries."

"When?"

"We have to go soon—tomorrow or the next day."

"These men on motorcycles: who are they?"

"Business can be complicated sometimes. After a while they'll forget about me and we can come back. We can come back and really get into the property development game together. We're gonna change our names."

"I don't understand."

"New passports will be ready tomorrow. I'm Carol and you're my son Chris. We're from Boise."

"Why?"

"Why what?"

"The new names. Why are we going to France?"

She kissed my neck and unfastened my jeans. "Stop being so fucking stupid." It had been a long time since she'd bathed. "We'll work together and when the feeling strikes us you can fuck me on my French desk." Her deep voice went deeper when she said dirty words. All of the *Mousterpiece Theater* was gone.

I stopped her.

"Are you pushing me away?"

"Phoebe is here. I can't."

She reached down and pulled off her panties, threw them in the toilet. "In France we'll be aristocrats. Carol and Chris."

We were in the men's bathroom in the library of Monument, Colorado.

I turned to go and when she dug into my arm with her nails I yanked it away. "Not now."

She shoved me into the wall, face-first. She whispered in my ear, hard and wild things.

There was a knock on the door. "Adam?" It was Phoebe. "Are you all right?"

Beatrice reached for my hand and put it between her legs. "Now. While she's talking."

To get away I had to push her. She fell to the floor. "You'll pay for that."

I ran to the door without looking in the mirror. Phoebe was waiting for me, leaning with one arm on a short stack of encyclopedias. "What's going on?"

"Nothing. I'm not feeling the best."

"Oh my God, you're all red."

"Yeah. Did you find anything else out?"

Phoebe did not raise her voice. She took her arm off the books, standing very straight. The librarian who had been helping us was off in the distance, pulling a tray of cards from a cabinet.

"Someone was in there with you, Adam."

"A guy was in there."

"What guy? Doing what?"

"I don't know." I walked past her, to the table. "Using the bathroom."

"God, look at you." She did not follow me. "Are you doing drugs?"

"No."

"You and Simon do drugs?" She had not looked away. "Is that what this whole thing is about—Simon's smashed face, your strangeness? Some drug thing? I was on the cruise and you were . . . what drug is it?"

"No drug! I promise. Come sit down."

"I'm waiting to see."

"To see what?"

"You were speaking to someone in there. Some drug dealer?"

I was at the table with the thick law books, my notebook and my baseball cap, my pack of Dentyne. I was one decision away from being a normal boy, a football player, an honour student. I was one decision away from living in a castle in France. She looked down at me. "You're all gross and sweaty."

A million tiny needles poked the inside of my skin and my face turned hotter, redder. I wanted to shout at her to sit down and forget this, *forget this nonsense.*

I imagined what I might say when Beatrice walked out. We had a secret plan for my mother's birthday, or for Phoebe's birthday, and we were working on it. I had a mysterious illness and I did not want anyone to know, but Beatrice knew. She had trained as a nurse. Experimental treatments. No, she was selling me a fifth of rum. Since Phoebe had left for the fjords with Blake I had become a rum guy and I needed it hard. They were not good enough lies. Maybe Beatrice had a brilliant idea with this France thing. But we were the frat-boy rapists and Phoebe was too smart. She had supreme power. If she separated us and asked us what we'd been doing in the bathroom she would destroy us.

The library was too small to have a public address system. It was just something the librarian said: "I regret to inform you folks that in five minutes the library closes. If there's anything you want to check out bring it up now, please and thank you kindly."

Simon had taught me a wrestling trick. When someone bigger and stronger is on top of you the worst thing you can do is panic. You have to slow your heart and your breath. Then explode out of it. In the library I slowed my heart and my breath.

"Phoebe, come help me clean this up."

"I'm waiting."

"Come look in my eyes and you'll see I haven't done any drugs. Remember what the police chief said in the gymnasium. That's how they can tell when someone is high."

She walked to the table, pulled out a chair, and sat next to me. For a minute, maybe more, she looked at me—into my eyes. She hunted in her tough way.

Phoebe sighed. "All right. But I heard talking."

"I was talking to myself. I didn't want to say anything but I was throwing up."

"What? Why?"

"I don't know."

She slid her chair away.

"See. That's why I didn't want to tell you. I knew you wouldn't want to be around me."

"Don't be a goof." She touched my forehead. "Well, you're certainly hot."

We put our notes and water bottles and gum in my backpack. Out the open windows the parking lot was dark. A light wind blew in, with its new scent. I wanted to walk hand in hand with Phoebe. It was harvest time in the fields east of town, fields that went on forever, and the smell of ready fruit, the smell of relief, sweetened the cooler air.

The librarian came over to our table to announce that the library was now closed and would reopen in the morning. Phoebe stood and reached down to help me up. We were three steps away when the men's bathroom door opened with a squeak.

Phoebe stopped, stiffened, and turned around. "Oh, Adam."

PART THREE

nine

Phoebe walked out of the library as though she had washed her memory clean of me. I called out to her, over the empty pavement of the strip mall. A man watched me from inside the convenience store. I begged her to stop and listen and I chased her through the weeds and wildflowers on the way to the interstate. I stepped in swamp water. A cloud of vile bugs rose up and surrounded me.

I ran and tried to hop the barbwire fence, cut my hand and my leg. By the time I was halfway through the dusty and smelly grass east of the interstate Phoebe had already crossed both sides, north and south. I stopped hurrying. I didn't know what I would say if I did catch her.

On my way home I walked past Norm's. He was closed. On Third Street I noticed, for the first time, how many of the people in my part of town had cars and trucks on cement blocks in their driveways. They had been there, just like this, since I was born and I had never seen them.

I did not sleep that night. I wrote more than a dozen versions of a letter to Phoebe. The next day I expected a phone call, an angry visit, a group intervention. But no one said a word about the library bathroom and what had happened inside. On the first day of school, registration day, Phoebe avoided me and Beatrice did not come to our house or to the garage.

Again I did not sleep.

The following morning my mother had a meeting on Second Street with a man from Denver who wanted to see about a joint venture with Magpie Developments. She had not seen or heard from Beatrice, who had missed two appointments. The man from Denver, one of the state's top real estate developers, was fascinated by how my mother had secured so much free publicity for her little project. This whole lady developer thing was, he thought, a gold mine she had only picked at with her pretty painted fingernails. For the first time in my lifetime she had pretty painted fingernails.

The second day of school was a social day. Cheerleaders and actors and painters and yearbook people, 4-Hers and hunters and D&D nerds and athletes would be setting up tables and booths on the running track. They would put on demonstrations. A speaker, probably a politician or an industrialist, would seek to convince us that drugs and sex were no fun at all. I showered and put on jeans and a T-shirt, ate Cap'n Crunch. My mother kissed me and walked out into the dewy morning to drive downtown. I let the dogs out one final time and just as I was locking the door Beatrice walked up the stairs.

"School starts today. Doesn't it."

"Yesterday, actually."

"You going to push me away again? Throw me to the floor and go to school? Or are you coming with me? This is the day."

My stomach ached. I had never skipped a day of school, not even a social day. I still wanted to play for Stanford. I wanted to kiss Phoebe on the morning sidewalks of Manhattan. I wanted to be in Paris for dinner tonight.

"I'm coming."

Beatrice wore the prettiest dress I had seen on her, soft red with polka dots and a matching handbag. She spun on the deck like a little girl and the skirt came up, but then she lost her balance and nearly fell and laughed too hard. "I bought this dress yesterday for our trip, our new life together. I bought it with hope."

"You can wear it on the airplane tonight."

"Yes." There was wine in her breath. "Has Phoebe been going around telling?"

"No. And I don't think she will."

"These rich kids, judging from on high. Her, your Simon."

I did not want to hear her say anything about Simon, who had just moved back into his own bedroom in his own home to convalesce. "I have more than one thousand dollars in the bank. You have Marv's credit card. Let's go right now."

"One whole thousand?"

"I can get more."

She looked around and shoved me into the door.

I opened it and we went inside. The dogs jumped at me. Beatrice closed the curtains all the way. Gary hyperventilated and I shushed him. I led her downstairs. "Who are these bikers?"

"Bad men are everywhere. Nothing to worry about."

"What did you do? Your brother is a biker and you stole his money or something? Someone's money?"

"Who told you that?"

"No one."

"It's a fucking lie. I am Beatrice Cyr of the Oglala Lakota."

"Mom said people hurt you."

"What else did she say?"

"Let's go right now. I can pack in ten minutes."

"What did she say?"

I told her, and added some things I'd figured out, some of what Simon said. She stared at me a while, like I was far away and moving farther.

"You think I'm a liar?"

"No."

"Here's what matters. I am standing right here in front of you. I am. Me. Whatever you want to call me or say about me, I am here. Nothing else matters. Does it?"

"No, Miss Beatrice. Let's go to Paris right now and stay there forever. I don't care."

"You don't care." Her face was red. She poked me. "Nothing else matters."

"Let's go!"

"I have some administrative duties to take care of, my Chris. Our passports won't be ready until two. There's the bank." She shoved her fingers into the waist of my jeans. "I can help you pack." Then she stepped away and winked and slapped me in the face, harder than ever before. "Now get down on your fucking knees. You think you can push me away?"

In the bedroom she pulled the baby oil out of her purse.

"I want you to call me Carol."

"Carol."

"Say, 'Fuck me, Carol.'"

I said it, and everything else she wanted me to say. To punish me for the library she had me lie down and she rode hard on my face, so hard that I got a bloody nose. When I tried to stop her, to get some tissues, she just rubbed it on herself and put me inside her and moved on me and called me Chris and slapped the right side of my face and told me what we would do, on a day like this, in our castle along the River Loire. The servants would bring coffee and bread to us in the mornings, fresh jam. Had I heard of quince? I closed my eyes as she spoke of it, as my nose bled all over, as she put blood on her breasts. In my imagination we were Carol and Chris making love without hurting on our French bed with a stone fireplace in the room.

The plan was to meet at two in the morning. We would sneak out and call for a taxi at the site of our humiliation, in front of the library. By then I would have a bit more money. At the airport we would buy business class tickets on the six a.m. flight to Paris. Then we would sit in the departure lounge like a couple of newlyweds. Or, according to our new

223

passports, like a mother and her son. I told her how I had
been feeling, that she had abandoned me.

"Never!"

"Really never?"

There was a bang upstairs. She was on top of me, a bloody
mess. There was even some on her face and neck. "What
was that?"

"Maybe one of the dogs."

"It sounded big for a dog."

"Gary only has three legs. He's clumsy."

She waited in the silence and started again. "Helen won't
be back until noon. I'm sure of that. We locked the door."

I could see Beatrice pink in the mirror, the blood and
sweat smeared about her, slashes of baby oil on her ass, the
new heaviness around her eyes.

The door opened with a creak. I had been meaning to
put WD-40 in the hinges. The bass of Marv's breath came in
under it, the breath of panic. "Oh."

Beatrice did not scream and jump off. She reached for her
dress, moved on me five more times. It made a wet sound
that normally excited me but now made me feel sick. I did
not want to push her off but I needed her to stop. The instant
she slid back I dove off the bed and hid my nakedness on the
far side. My bare feet crushed the tracks of my model train.

There was a sheet of paper in Marv's hands, folded to fit
in an envelope, and our house key. Of course he had a key.

"Is one of you hurt?"

I figured it was my question to answer. "No, sir."

"Adam." He covered his eyes with the paper. "My boy."

Beatrice wiped the blood off herself with one of my Ocean Pacific T-shirts and stepped into her new dress. It had a zipper in the back. She turned so Marv could zip it and he actually did.

"I just never . . ." Marv's hand lingered on the zipper and then he touched the top of his head and leaned back heavily against the wall. "What am I supposed to do now?"

Beatrice looked down at me. I shrank from her. They took a long, careful look at one another. Then he moved his big hands gently on her shoulders, as though she were a robin that had flown into the window, and he touched her face. He made a sound like he had been stabbed and life was draining from him, a final sound. He released her and Beatrice walked slowly out of the room.

"At the library." She spoke without turning around.

I watched Marv. "Yes, ma'am."

"Pardon me?"

"Yes, Miss Beatrice."

She climbed the stairs like this was just a regular morning in Colorado.

It was the two of us now. There was a pair of pyjama bottoms on the carpet so I gathered them up but they were sticky because I had masturbated into them a few times. There were cat heads on them. I was just disgusting.

"Adam, I read the note." He was breathing deeply, like he had just finished a set of wind-sprints. He still had not looked at me. "I couldn't believe it was true."

I wanted to say something to make Marv feel better but there was nothing. If there was a note I knew what was in the note, and who had written it. There was not even a lie I could tell.

He looked. "Why are you all bloody?"

"Miss Beatrice hurt my nose."

"Shouldn't you be in school?"

"Yes, sir."

"Stand up, please."

I did.

"All the way, son." He watched me for a moment in my awful nudity and he sighed, and then he turned to my dresser and inspected things. There were Teenage Mutant Ninja Turtles on it, from when I was twelve, and a Black, bald Cabbage Patch Kid with a birth certificate that announced his name as Alphonse Ramón Garner. I had always meant to change it to something cool like Jeff. Marv picked up one of the turtles—Donatello, I think. "You're a little boy. You're my boy. I love you so damn much, since you were a sprout. And you do this."

A lawn mower pumped three times and hummed to life down the street. It was the sound of normal people doing normal things and it shook us out of the moment. Marv put down Donatello and looked at me again, naked as a baboon before him.

Marv reached down without looking and that is when I spotted the holster. It was on his belt, like in the movies. He lifted a heavy silver handgun and looked at it the way he had looked at the ninja turtle.

"Mr. Walker."

"You know, in Korea." He pointed the gun at the far wall, past me. "No matter what they tell you, you don't forget it after. Using these things."

"I didn't mean to—"

"But in the moment, there's nothing else like it. When you think: It's me or him. You have all these long thoughts in the shortest amount of time. You think about how it was when your parents tucked you into bed. Songs you were sure you forgot. Pictures on the wall that meant so much, torn from magazines that don't exist anymore, whatnot. Where do they all go, things like that? Raspberries, when they're first good enough to eat. Eating them with your mom. The damnedest things."

"I didn't mean to hurt you, Mr. Walker."

He seemed to have a question to ask. Then his body convulsed and he threw up on the carpet at the corner of my bed. He did it one more time and then slammed back into the dresser and I thought he was going to shoot his gun by accident but then he righted himself and it was quiet for a moment. My turtles and my deodorant fell to the floor. The smell of his vomit roared up in the room.

He put the gun back in its holster, opened the door, and walked out of my bedroom. At the bottom of the stairs he looked up. "Yeah, I got my Visa bill. You owe me eight hundred dollars. I guess you can pay me back in monthly installments or whatever, if you don't got it right now." It took him a long time because the railing was loose and untrustworthy. I had tried to tighten it but the screws were stripped.

I jumped over the pond of yellow vomit and put on my robe and walked to the base of the stairs, to help him in case he fell. His breath whistled and rattled all the way up.

Alone in my bedroom I wondered who would clean up the vomit. My mother would not be home until noon. The letter on the dresser was a computer print-out in a swirly font.

Dear Mr. Walker,

It is my special horror to inform you that your wife, Beatrice Walker, is having a love affair with your fourteen year old next-door neighbour Adam Lisinski, son of Helen Lisinski. This is a vile accusation, I know, but I imagine the truth will not be difficult to discover if you are inconspicuous. I did not want to send this letter to your place of work but Adam is clever and it especially concerned me that if I placed it in the mailbox of your home he would discover this letter and dispose of it before you had a chance to peruse its wretched contents.

Yours truly,

Anonymous

The font gave her away. I could imagine Phoebe's blue Roget's Thesaurus with her name written on the top right-hand corner on a blotch of white-out. Upstairs, under the sink, there was a roll of paper towel and a spray bottle of stain remover we used when Maggie and Gary messed the carpet.

I did not feel old enough or strong enough to clean a man's vomit but no one would do this for me.

It was mine.

All I had missed were the speeches in the gymnasium, by a regional vice-president of Bank of the West and a deacon of First Presbyterian Church. His theme was "Succeeding in Business While Living a Moral Life." It made me think of Phoebe's "special horror." Marv's sweet acid and peppery vomit returned to my blood-clogged nose every few minutes.

There were just about five hundred kids at Lewis-Palmer, from all over the county. It was a sunny day with a murmur of autumn cool about it, so all of them were out in their brand-new denim and bright T-shirts, their shorts and skirts and cowboy hats. They were all tanned from a summer without rain. I was officially a sophomore now and I could tell there was something different about us. Freshmen were terrified and juniors walked around like social day was an insult to their taste and intelligence. Seniors were behind the booths organizing the show or, more likely, skipping the social day to drink beer and smoke. Everyone wore too much Obsession by Calvin Klein and Drakkar Noir. The students in my grade—the kids I'd known since kindergarten, the ones who had invited me to their movies-and-bowling birthday parties—gathered in the middle of the field, studying how to take ownership of the school.

A few of my teammates sat around the goalposts with
Slurpees. I was on my way to meet them, aware that kids were
watching me, more than usual.

They knew.

Where was Phoebe? I stopped and turned and walked back
toward the school. Antoine, a senior who played cornerback
and special teams with me, ran and caught up. He lived on a
farm and had four brothers who looked just like him, with
short legs and long torsos and one long eyebrow. He wore a
sun-stained John Deere cap every day of the year and when we
weren't playing football he always had a plug of Copenhagen
in his lip.

"Is it true?"

"Tell me what you heard."

He looked around, to make sure no one was listening, but
of course everyone had already heard. "You've been fucking
a *mom* all summer? Some ugly crazy woman?"

"People are saying that?"

"Is that why you were off the team for a bit? Because of
the mom-fucking?"

"I don't know."

"You get kicked off the team for being a *stud*? While
you're dating Phoebe Brandt? Lisinski! You fucking guy."
He lifted his hand, to high-five me, and I did not have it in
me to leave him hanging so we high-fived and I hated myself
for it.

At the wall of the school I leaned against the red brick and
looked back, to where I had been, and now all the kids were
looking at me.

"You all right, Homes?" Antoine spit his tobacco juice into a Coke can. It was usually fine, the idea of all that spit in a can, but not today. I wanted to crawl under a dumpster. When had I last slept? Why did Antoine, a white farm kid, talk like Ice Cube? "Walk proud. Unless she's a gimp or something, or fat. Is she? Even if she is! Fuck 'em. I'd fuck a fat gimp. I'd fuck anything! Oh hey, what happened to Simon Kinoro? There's a bunch of shit going around."

I rode my father's ten-speed back to town. On Second Street the woman at the used bookstore leaned on her door jamb and watched me. Some old men in suits that were too big for them watched me from the front of the empty Italian restaurant that had only lasted eight months. Everyone watched me. They all knew. I was going to stop in at my mother's little office to warn her but I decided I could not say the words.

France.

The Kinoro house was usually perfect in the summertime: blooming, freshly painted, and weedless. Simon's father did calculations before he trimmed hedges, in search of geometric truth. It was at first a shock to see bags and clothes in front, a milk crate full of cassette tapes, and a few plastic bags filled with knick-knacks. It was the sort of mess you might see every day on Jefferson Street but never here. Simon's mother stood among the chaos with her arms crossed. She peeked at her watch. "Good morning, Adam."

Simon appeared in the door, his left cheek one massive bruise. He dragged a suitcase down the stairs like a hunchback. I ran up and took it from him and he exhaled in thanks, leaned against the railing. He had only been out of the hospital for one day.

"What's going on?"

"My father can't take it, so I am out of here."

"Wait, wait. Can't take what?"

Simon looked over at his mother and for a long time they stared at one another. She put up her hands in surrender and walked up the stairs.

"My father signed me up for a special school in Montana."

"What sort of school?"

"A very religious school."

This was common among kids who misbehaved. "You're packing to go?"

"I should go, now that everyone in school thinks I'm gay as Pegasus. Thanks to Charlene and her eye makeup. But I'm packing to move in with you again. Is that all right?"

"Yeah, man."

"If you ask my father, you will understand none of this is my fault. It's the special turpitude of America, a permissive culture."

"What's turpitude?"

"It isn't good."

"Let's go to the cops right now, turn Squeak and those guys in."

I carried the rest of his clothes and the boxes from his room to the front yard. I helped him load the front trunk and the back seat of the Beetle. When we were finished Simon wanted to leave without saying goodbye. I went inside and asked Mrs. Kinoro to come and speak to him. The house was close enough to Monument Lake that a cottonwood tree survived on the front lawn. I leaned on it and watched the house.

Mr. Kinoro moved the big mustard curtain and watched me. I smiled and waved and flipped him a thumbs-up and he closed the curtain.

It was careful work, easing Simon into the driver's seat of the Beetle. He wiped his eyes and drove along the railroad tracks. "Thanks again for this, fella."

"I'm sorry about your dad. He'll come around."

"On his deathbed—or mine." He slapped his steering wheel and called out in pain, touched his ribs, laughed maniacally. "How was your day?"

We passed the ugly fourplex on the gravel road, with broken toys and bicycles and mattresses and other items too big for garbage pickup strewn about the brown grass. These were the only people in town poorer than us, if you didn't count the trailer park on the way to Palmer Lake. They were so poor they didn't have cars on blocks. Two men in wifebeaters sat in lawn chairs in the middle of Trash Island and watched us pass. They were surrounded by empty Old Milwaukee cans and it wasn't yet noon. Had they done something foolish in high school that had led them to this? Had they said yes to a woman like Beatrice when they should have said no?

I told Simon about Phoebe catching us at the library; about the letter, Marv, and the gun. I told about leaving for France. He pulled into the ditch along the railroad tracks.

"You're Chris?"

"And she's Carol. We're from Boise."

"Why do you need new names?"

"So we can hide, maybe."

"From her brother and the gangsters on Harleys. If she even has a brother. This is crazy, Adam. And everyone knows about you and her?"

"I was at school today. *Everyone.*"

"What does she do now?" He looked ahead, at the dust and weeds that went on forever along the railroad tracks, not at me. This was not a question for me. He was a student of her mysteries. "What does she want?"

"Me."

"Fella, she doesn't want you. You're just a . . ."

Simon did not finish. He put the Beetle back in gear and drove in silence. We parked in front of our house and he leaned on the car and smoked while I unpacked. "I suppose all Phoebe had to do was tell one person, swear them to secrecy forever. Ten minutes later, it's out."

Geraldine was on her front veranda, fussing with a planter. She waved at us. Did she know?

"Deny it. You have to. Just say it's a disgusting rumour."

I carried the first load to the back deck. "At an assembly, maybe? So I reach everyone? Write an article in the *Bee*?"

"Beatrice can deny it too." Simon followed me with his cigarette. "Only one person caught you in the act and he won't tell."

"It hurts so much that I hurt Marv."

The house next door was quiet. Their windows were open to the screens but I heard no voices, no music, no television. I was relieved when in the distance a chainsaw revved. The social day must have finished early. A few kids cut down Jefferson Street and walked slowly as they passed our place, which was really on the way to nowhere. Now *we* were the haunted family.

Simon watched them go. "We're doomed here."

I stood close to him. "We're going to be rich in France. Everything's different there. We'll have *staff*, like the Brandts. You can come visit."

"Fella."

"It's true!"

"I am afraid not."

"She's been rich before. She has fur coats and this jewellery that belongs in a palace. If you saw all the stuff she has. And that way of hers." There was a word I wanted to say but I could not think of it. My finger was up, to stop him. "Courtly."

"And she lives on Jefferson Street in Monument, Colorado, with Marv Walker. And hurts your body. Promise you won't get mad."

"Why?"

"Just promise." Sometimes the gulf between us, between almost fifteen and newly sixteen, seemed an actual gulf. "You promise?"

"I promise."

"The word is *hustler*."

"People hurt her, Simon. We hurt her ancestors. All she wants is to get what she's owed."

"She is a good saleswoman, that is true. You're convinced. But who fakes a passport? I'm sorry, but who has an affair with a fourteen-year-old boy?"

"It's not an affair. We fell in love."

"Please."

"It's true, Sye, all right?"

"I'm just saying."

"I get what you're *saying*. You've been trying to split us up from the beginning because you're jealous."

He laughed.

"You smoke like Wendy."

He looked at his cigarette. "What?"

"That night at the goth party. It wasn't just the makeup, was it?"

"We're talking about you, fella." He pointed to his temple. "She's using you."

I wanted to make him tell me he was Wendy but I wanted him to tell me he was not. We were standing next to a pile of his things on our messed-up gravel driveway. A magpie watched us from the brown grass between Marv's house and ours. I didn't want to talk anymore. "No, she isn't."

"To feel . . . better than she is. I get that part of her. I understand."

"Just stop it."

"You asked! There's a scary part too, and it isn't even the scratches and bruises all over you. She's a liar, but she's telling the truth about one thing. Men are after her. I think it's another reason she's using you, why she wants to run. New names, new passports. Who does that? If she actually loved you—*insane*—why would she want to put you in danger?"

"It's my fault, not hers, because I broke the vow. I told you when I wasn't supposed to tell. It's why you got hurt. It's why everything. I can help her, once we get to Paris."

Simon stared at me.

Once I was finished bringing in his bags Simon went to work arranging his clothes in Jason's closets and drawers. I made lemonade from scratch. Alone in the kitchen, my chest hurt with worry and I leaned over the sink. I wanted someone to clean my mess, undo the curse. I had broken Phoebe's heart and Marv's heart and I had put Beatrice in danger with my carelessness and I had let my mother and brother down. I'd never get the blood out of my sheets and the bedroom would always smell like vomit. There was no life for me here. Maybe I would never see this house, or Colorado, or anyone in my family again. My favourite cup was in the drying rack, a Captain America glass that could hold almost a can of soda. I threw it in the sink and it exploded up and onto the counter, on the floor. Then I laughed. I was going to Paris!

My mother stood on the deck, looking in through the screen door. There was an envelope in her hand, opened at the top. How long had she been there, watching me? Had she seen me ruin the glass?

"Mom."

She lifted her chin at me.

"The meeting was good? With the man from Denver?"

An airplane passed overhead. Maybe, I thought, it's ours. It will land and they will fuel it up and clean it for us. The dogs sensed her quiet arrival and jumped at the door.

"Let me see the letter. I know who sent it. It's lies, Mom."

"'Depressed?' 'A dark cloud'?"

I went back to the sink to clean up the broken glass. A few minutes later my mother came in and hugged me, the back of me.

"Adam, I'm so sorry."

"For what? Nothing's wrong, Mom."

"I didn't see it. I was so caught up in my own . . ." She squeezed hard and screamed hot into my shoulder. "My baby. You're just my baby."

For a while she held on and mumbled into my shirt. It was too embarrassing so I had to look outside and think about the train that was coming. I wanted to break more glasses. Simon had said deny it. "It didn't happen. None of it did."

"I already spoke to her."

"What did she say?"

My mother hugged me harder.

"What did she say about me, Mom? Because—"

"I'll get you someone to talk with." She turned me around. Her eyes were a mess and she was stooped over like she had to sleep or pee. She spoke in bursts, like there wasn't quite enough breath in her lungs to finish a thought. "The right kinds of books. Maybe there's a group. A group of boys like you who can share and help one another. At St. Peter . . . I know you're not much for it. When your dad left it helped. It helped me! It did. To know other women ruined by men like him. It helps to know you're not the only one. It's not too late. We'll turn back the clock on this. Get you started right."

"I'm fine, Mom."

Gently she moved me out of the way. "Let me. You'll cut yourself."

My mother's suitcase was stiff and rectangular, old-fashioned, so I emptied my football bag in the garage. A police car pulled into the driveway as I was opening the garage door. I recognized the chief from two presentations in the gymnasium, one about stealing car stereos and the other about drinking and driving.

He waved at me. His window was open. "Excuse me, boy."

I wanted to sprint through the yard and over the fence. "Yes, sir?"

His hands were enormous. The notebook was tiny in his palm. "You Jason Lisinski's kin? Adam?"

"I am."

He stepped out of the car, a tall and thin man with a mess of white hair. At each of his joints it looked like he might just break and tumble to the ground. He lifted his glasses to read something in his notebook. Officer Jiminy Cricket. "Can I call you Adam?"

"Sure."

"I'm Chief Dunn, in case we ain't met. Maybe we could sit down." He grunted as he reached inside the car and then he put a dark hat on. His accent was like my father's, with a strong hint of the south about it. "Maybe get a glass of water or two into us?"

My mother was in the basement, talking to Simon. Everyone in Monument was talking about me and I was not in the room for any of it. This man, who smelled of ferny aftershave and cigars, could not stop me from going to Paris.

"We could just chat out here."

"It's so dang hot's the thing, Adam. And I could really use some water if you can spare it."

While I drew water from the tap he watched me in a cautious way, like I might splash it in his face and run. We sat in the living room and the smell of him filled it up. I wanted us to whisper so my mother would not hear from downstairs. The dogs rubbed against the chief's shins and he did not like it.

"How old are you, boy?"

"Fourteen."

"Okeedoke." His voice sounded like he'd just finished a pack of cigarettes as he pulled up. "When's your birthday?"

"November."

"So you're the youngest in your class, I bet."

"Yes, sir."

"My daughter was a November baby. Same problem. She saved a bundle on gasoline because all her friends turned sixteen first." He looked down at his notepad. "Where's your mom?"

"Lying down."

"Your pop ain't in the picture, is he?"

"He's on the west coast, I surmise." This was the first time I had ever used the word "surmise" and I was not sure I had said it correctly. It was a Simon word. "We haven't seen him since I was a kid."

"You're still a kid, Adam, you ask me."

"Yes, sir."

"Now when we're done I'll ask you to rouse your mom. I got a few questions for her, too. Okay? She's been in the news some. A couple of women in my office are keen on living across the street there, when it's finished. Divorcées. She's a big celebrity all of a sudden, your mom. Front page news."

I pet the dogs. Chief Dunn had removed his hat. It was stained yellow on the inside, along the brim where he perspired. I imagined it would not smell good inside that hat.

"Here's what I'm curious about, young man. Here's the nature of my visit. Have you been . . . encouraged into doing anything you did not want to do?"

"Like what?"

"By an adult, say, into doing something only adults do?"

I desperately hoped for a moment he meant drinking. Dana at the liquor store had gone to Jesus and had phoned the police to relate her sins. "No."

"Of a sexual nature?"

"I haven't done nothing. I mean, done anything . . . anything I don't want." I spoke slowly, to avoid stuttering.

The chief closed his notepad and looked at me in a way that stirred all the regretful and sinful feelings in my gut. A career's worth of looking at people like me had made him a master of it. His squinty eyes were surrounded by lines and grooves. If it were not for his hat, I might have confessed everything. The ridiculousness of the chief's hat was my courage.

"Maybe it's time to rouse your mama."

I realized I had not been the model of nonchalance. I had not eaten since Cap'n Crunch at breakfast. The glass of water looked scrumptious all of a sudden so I took a sip. My sip transformed into a long gulp. I was so tired I nearly forgot what had just happened moments ago. I glanced away, at panting Maggie. She seemed to understand everything was going to hell.

The chief sat back and crossed his legs, as though he were tucking into a steaming mug of coffee and Southern Comfort. "Can you tell me about Beatrice Cyr?"

"Who?"

"What kind of contact you had with her? With Beatrice Cyr, your mom's partner in the apartment complex."

"Can I be right back, sir?"

"You bet, Adam."

I tried to walk at a composed pace to the bathroom. When the door was closed I wanted to bawl it out, the whole summer. The window was too small to crawl out of, and if I did sneak away I had nowhere to go until my rendezvous with Beatrice at two in the morning. I had not even started packing for Paris. I ran the water and stared at my red eyes in the mirror. All of my tan had drained away in one afternoon. I splashed water on my face, to rinse the pale worry away, and dried myself and focused on the boulevards of Paris. The airplane would land and I would look out the window at those pretty stone apartments and people would look back at me but they would not *see* me. Not the way the kids did now, and the chief.

In health class, the teacher had made us listen to a meditation cassette. Whale song played and a woman with a tranquil, breathy voice told us to repeat affirmations. *I am intelligence.*

I am abundance. I am happiness. For a whole minute in the bathroom, maybe more, I stared in the sincerest way and said these phrases to myself.

Back in the living room I decided it was smarter for me to stand.

"All better?"

"Yes, sir."

"Now, before we were interrupted by the forces of nature, I was asking about your neighbour, Beatrice Cyr."

"Right."

"Can you describe your contact with her?"

"Describe it, sir?"

The chief leaned back on the couch, opened his arms. He was abundance. "Yes, Adam."

"She's my mom's business partner."

"Got that."

"She comes over most Thursday nights. My mom has neighbours over, for beer. Sometimes pizza too. They all sit on the deck."

"That's civilized."

"I'm worried about her because her husband, Marv, was acting strange this morning."

"Was he?"

"Yes sir."

"What kind of strange?"

Now that he was asking me I realized I did not want to say anything about Marv and the gun, what I worried he might do to Beatrice if he drank too many Millers. "I don't know."

"How do you know it's strange?"

I shrugged.

"Here's the thing. I spoke to a couple of the administrators over at Lewis-Palmer and they directed me to your coach. He says you were off the team, a recent thing. Seemed odd, right before the first real game of the season, homecoming. Then you told him, you said . . ." The chief pulled a pair of reading glasses from his shirt pocket, put them on, and looked down at his notes. This took forever. "You said you wanted to be back on the team because your emotional crisis was over. Ain't you a bit young for an emotional crisis, Adam?"

"That's private."

"Is it?"

"Yes sir. It's a private matter."

"You're taking the Fifth."

"Yes. No." I had to think, for a moment, about what that meant. "I'm not hiding anything."

"You aren't?"

"Sir, can I ask you something?"

"You bet."

"Why are you asking me about this?"

The basement door opened and closed and the dogs barked and ran to it. Gary started hyperventilating when my mother emerged; it was not a pretty sound. The seventy-year-old grasshopper removed his hat and opened his arms like this was the grandest surprise.

"Mrs. Lisinski? I'm Chief Dunn. I'm a little star-struck. You've been in the papers, on the TV."

"Is everything all right?"

244

"That's a darn good question, Mrs. Lisinski. Adam and I were just going over a few matters, private and not, talking about the summer and your terrific new business and your neighbours here on Jefferson Street. He's a good boy, this one, with lots of curiosity about police work. A curious boy and a handsome boy."

This last thing, *handsome boy*, had a sinister quality. It was as though I had chosen to become handsome to cause trouble. The dogs jumped at my mother's legs because she had not yet kneeled down to give them loving. Through the chief's eyes I saw Gary anew: a three-legged hyperventilating white mutt with an ass discoloured by shitting. If my family were on an English exam, it would be simple to write a paragraph about Gary as a symbol of the Lisinskis.

"Will you sit?" The chief pointed at my mother's recliner with his hat and put it back on his head.

She sat and stopped the chair from rocking. Maggie jumped up and my mother pushed her off.

"How about me? Can I go, sir?"

"Actually, Adam, would you mind joining us?"

I sat in the other recliner and reached up my shirt and pulled at my chest hairs.

"First of all, congratulations, Mrs. Lisinski, on your new business."

"Thank you, Chief."

"It's real exciting for us all."

"It's a big change for me, for Adam and me."

"Now Mrs. Lisinski, it's the strangest thing. I received an anonymous tip, a darn specific one, about young Adam here."

The chief reached into the inside pocket of his jacket and pulled out an envelope. "The writer claims your son was sexually assaulted. *Raped* is the word the writer uses."

"My goodness." She turned to me.

"We don't get accusations much more serious than that, here in Monument."

"Is this true, Adam?" My mother placed her hands on the sides of her recliner, lifted herself up, and turned to me. "Could this be true?"

I was in a bit of a daze. It took me some time to realize what my mother was doing. "No. No ma'am, it isn't. That sure never happened to me."

The chief waited for my mother to turn back to him. He fussed with the arms of his reading glasses. "Have you heard of *statutory* rape, Mrs. Lisinski?"

"I've heard of it, Chief, but I won't pretend to know what it means."

"Even if relations seem consensual between an adult and a young person, it's oftentimes considered rape. Do you know what 'consensual' means? It means agreement. Now here's the thing: boys and girls of Adam's age, they aren't capable of true consent. He doesn't understand, is the court's reasoning."

"Okay."

"If an adult has sexual relations with a fourteen-year-old, that adult is committing a serious crime in the state of Colorado."

"And a good thing it is." My mother turned to me again. "Have you had sexual relations with an adult, Adam?"

"No, Mom."

"Chief, may I read your anonymous letter?"

He did not say no. He just returned it to his pocket and rubbed his hands together. "I want to thank you both for your hospitality. This has been an informative visit."

"Can I get you anything else, Chief?"

"No, no, Mrs. Lisinski, you've done your part." He stood up and placed his hands on his lower back, stretched again, vocalized.

Simon appeared in the doorway between the kitchen and the living room. "Good afternoon."

The chief pointed at his face. "I heard about your accident, boy. How are you recovering?"

When he'd called me boy it had sounded different. Simon looked away from him. "Very well. Thank you for asking, sir."

"Ready to tell me who did it to you?"

"Did it to myself, sir. I fell pretty hard on that concrete embankment."

The chief looked around like he had just walked into the room and we were brand-new museum exhibits. "I'm relieved y'all are doing so good here. It's rewarding to be in such a happy and prosperous home."

After some handshakes and unnecessary gratitude for his glass of water the chief walked out onto the deck. I followed him. On the driveway he stood looking over at Marv and Beatrice's house with his arms crossed, as though it were the hard part in a crossword puzzle. He went around and knocked on the front door. When it opened he went inside.

My mother asked me sweetly, through the screen door, to turn on the barbecue. She was a jack-in-the-box near the end of its crank, stirring to pop.

ten

all three of our lakes were swamps, really. No river ran through Monument and all the proper water was deep in the Rockies. Palmer Lake was the fancy one, but it also had a tendency to dry up in the toughest years and drain the spirit of the place. O'Grady's was the only real tavern in the whole area and that was because you could sit on the patio of the converted house and look out over Palmer Lake, where the railroad used to go, over the Harleys that were always parked in front. And you could be as loud as you liked.

Kids were permitted at O'Grady's. I parked my father's ten-speed out front, among the motorcycles, and ordered my last American milkshake. Chocolate, why not, but there was nothing chocolatey about it so I mooned in regret. I wore my wedding suit because I did not want to pack it and have it wrinkled when I arrived in Paris. Steppenwolf was playing too loud for the speakers to handle. People I recognized from football games, from the farmers' market, from Eugene's Gas Stop, from the Coffee Cup Café, and from the grocery store watched me from the other tables. This was not new. But tonight they did not smile. No one asked about Jason or the Rangers. The suit did not help me fit in. Steppenwolf distorted in the speakers and all those eyes on me turned the milkshake into a grey-tasting thing so I gave up halfway, paid my bill, threw on my football bag, and rode back to Monument on the El Paso Trail, though not to go home.

It had felt final, leaving the house. My mother had already been in bed. I'd let the dogs lick my face and told them to watch over her. Then I'd hugged Simon, who was dreamy and distracted. He whispered an apology.

"For what?"

"I don't know."

"Sye. Come on."

"I'm sorry. That's all. And I mean it. I hope someday you understand."

"Understand what?"

He'd been about to say something but instead he'd turned away and lifted his hand, went downstairs. I figured it was because he did not like goodbyes. I did not want to think it was because of anything Beatrice had said about him loving me and resenting her. It would have spoiled things.

There was no way to say goodbye to my mother, either. She had said nothing specific about Beatrice and me after the chief left, but after dinner she'd sat with me on the couch for the first time in as long as I could remember, holding my hand as we watched *Stripes*—starring Bill Murray, my favourite. She'd rubbed my arm, tracing the scratches softly with her fingers. Two police officers I did not recognize, a man and a woman, spent some time over at Marv's house. They poked around in his backyard and smoked. Then another cop came, with a different uniform, maybe from Denver, and I hoped it was not all for me. At one time there were three police cars. My mother and Simon looked at one another a lot. We ate our hamburgers in front of *Stripes* and then my mother hugged me for a long time and told me this was day one of the rest of my life and she went to bed at nine-thirty like most work nights.

She would understand someday. She would visit Beatrice and me at the castle in the valley of the River Loire.

When I got back to Monument I walked my bike up and down Jefferson and Washington Streets with my football bag on the seat, looking in the windows where the televisions were on. They were on everywhere. It opened up a new world when you wondered what folks had done before televisions. I guessed they played pianos and read books, like Phoebe. She was the richest girl in town, and the Brandts could have bought the biggest television in the world, but she hardly watched TV at all. We poor kids knew way more about shows than she did.

Some people walked their dogs on the road. When my neighbours looked at me I looked at their dogs. By eleven, the people of my town were in their homes. I rode my bicycle down to Monument Lake and skipped some rocks, said goodbye to it. Pike came to the surface, hunting for air or bugs. I knew why my parents had chosen this town. It was this quiet at eleven. No one hurt anyone else and nothing bad ever happened here.

Mount Herman, stupid name, was part of the Rampart Range, cool name. I knew that ramparts had something to do with battle, but whenever I heard the word in the national anthem I imagined myself up on Mount Herman, looking down on my own little house by the railroad tracks on the road without a sidewalk.

Only a few trucks rolled down Second Street. Everything on Old Denver Road was closed. I left my bag in the darkness around the corner and, when I could hear no cars or trucks, I put on our dishwashing gloves and opened the back door of the Gas Stop with a nail from home. I crawled on the white-tile floor, hidden by the racks of oil and filters and batteries and booster cables. The safe was under a gluey black-rubber mat and the combination was Hailey's birthday. It went year, month, day, and then the tricky one: current age. There were three thousand, five hundred dollars in the sack. It had been a good but not great day on the pumps. Gene was the worst bookkeeper. I took seven hundred and returned the sack, locked the safe, and went out the back door. Any moron could break into the Gas Stop, as we only locked the back door with a button on the handle. I left it open.

I arrived early at the library with my football bag filled with clothes and comics. I sat on the bag and read a pile of *X-Men*, even though it meant I'd have fewer to read on the airplane. Beatrice had said they give you a bunch of magazines in business class anyway.

At two o'clock in the morning I was still alone. My mother was often late for appointments, running around the house looking for her wallet and her keys, and this was a big trip, so I decided not to worry about Beatrice. I did not want to fall asleep but my body did, so to keep myself awake I strolled along the front of the library, reading the titles on the shelves through the window. In the first week of our love affair Beatrice and I met at a stand of scrub oaks on the burnt-yellow hill behind the library and we did it standing up. She forgot her oil so I had to use spit. She tore a branch off and hit me for a while. Something in it left my back and shoulders sore and itchy for a few days. Every time I scratched I thought of her. I went where we had gone, to see if I could smell her in the darkness. Maybe she had forgotten her panties here. One of her black hairs might have fallen in the dust, a drop of her saliva. I would have eaten it if I had found it.

Through the branches I could see my football bag out there in the floodlights, my pile of *X-Men* on top. At three o'clock I unfastened my suit pants and closed my eyes and imagined I could smell her in the scrub oaks, white wine in her breath, and cigarettes, cinnamon Dentyne. I imagined Beatrice, an old-fashioned version of her on horseback, dressed in pale leather, her face painted for war, her hands and arms bloody from scalping some dumb cowboy, throwing me to the ground and shouting horror in my face. In Cherokee: "*Hold him down!*" I remembered us here, the shine of the moonlight on her spine when she bent over and put her hands on the ground, like that drawing in *The Joy of Sex*. Whipping me with the branch of oak. In a big hotel room in Paris, overlooking fountains and bakeries and bicycles, and in the distance there is the Eiffel Tower. Against the window we make love not in a huffing, angry, hurting American way but French this time, classy and soft. I am allowed to drink wine in the bistros with her and stay up as late as I want before the first day of school.

I finished on some pine needles and all the hope drained from me. I tried to make it funny, a joke to tell. I would tell her about it when she arrived, how I had lost utter control of myself between our seven oaks. It would honour her to know! In front of the library, on a small island of watered grass in the parking lot, I lay on my bag looking up at the stars and for the first time I tested a possibility: Beatrice had chosen someone else, another future, another young traveller who did not make mistakes. A property developer from Denver. Gord the Haberdasher had sold everything to be with her.

No matter what she had chosen instead of me: she had chosen. It made me cold despite the heat and I forced myself to believe she would come. I prayed to the stars. My stomach ached, poisoned with the truth. Then the sun came up pink and lit up a hint of fog, erased the stars.

I heard someone approach and I closed my eyes, pretended to be asleep, so she could wake me with kisses. There were no kisses, just the nudge of a soft black shoe.

"Hey there. Hey." An Indian man stood over me, the one who owned the sandwich shop next to the library. He squinted. "I know you. Football guy?"

"Yes, sir." We came in some days after practice.

"How about a coffee." He pointed at his shop in a really obvious way, like I was either drunk or stupid. "Are you old enough for coffee?"

"Thanks for the offer, sir, but I should head on home. My mom will be worried."

"Can I ask why you are sleeping here, in this remarkable suit, covered in dew?"

"I was waiting for a friend."

"And your friend did not arrive?"

I shook my head.

"Pity." He offered me a hand and I took it and stood up. His skin was unusually soft for a man's.

I had planned to abandon my father's garbage bicycle when Beatrice arrived. I put the bag on my back and cycled over the bridge. There was not much action on the interstate. It took less than ten minutes to bike home, normally, but I took my time. Not sleeping for three nights made everything slower—unless it was faster and *I* was slower. Marv's truck was in the driveway. The Cadillac was gone. I walked close enough to the fence to hear, through the screen, the fan in their bedroom. After everything that had happened, the fan was ludicrous. Our social studies teacher had said Hitler talked to his generals about dog breeding the night he killed himself. Ludicrous. I hopped the fence and peeked through the window. Marv was in the bed but I could not see Beatrice. The sun lit the dewy car parts in all the backyards of Jefferson Street. There was no sneaking up to our house. My feet on the back deck alerted Maggie and Gary and they barked and jumped at the door until I opened it and quieted them. Gary hyperventilated.

It was not yet six. There was no sign anyone had noticed I was gone. The kitchen was cleaner than usual. No jackets or sweatshirts hung from the chairs, and apart from a shopping list on a pink sticky pad—*milk, bread, 2 lh lean ground beef, tomatoes, C. Crunch*—the table was clear.

During the school year I normally woke at seven. I went downstairs and closed my door and punched the Acapulco poster Uncle Oscar had given me and I punched it again and hollered into my pillow. I listened to R.E.M. The ceiling squeaked above and the shower came on: my mother was preparing for her day. She had slept through everything. I unpacked my bag and took off my suit and hung it up and sat on my bed in my newest Fruit of the Looms, which I had worn especially for my love. Then I put on jeans and my *Chicks dig me 'cause I surf* T-shirt and I waited outside Marv Walker's door.

eleven

"Where is she?"

Marv leaned on his cane. His hair was ridiculous and he had not bathed. The stubble on his chin was uneven, like he had shaved in random patches. His overalls, from the medical devices plant, had grease stains on the front. "Please get out of my way, Adam."

I had planned to be tough, to use cuss words, to threaten him with violence. There was a paring knife in my back pocket, the only knife in our drawer that was not dull. It had an olive wood handle. Uncle Oscar had brought it back from a trip to Japan. When I'd heard Marv in the kitchen, nearing the door, the rubber thump of his cane, my heart beat so fast I could actually feel it in there. I had practiced saying the words. *I'll kill you. You tell me what you did with her or I'll kill you.* "Did you hurt her?"

The whites of his eyes were as rusted as the car parts. He stared at me until I moved to let him pass, and he paused as he stepped around me. Something happened with his mouth. I thought he was maybe trying to pick something out of his teeth. Then he spit a gob in my face. He stayed there and admired his work, as I reached up to wipe if off with the sleeve of my shirt, and then he put a hand in his hair and pulled at it and stepped down from the deck onto his gravel driveway.

It was painful and awkward for him to step up into his truck. He did not pretend to be agile, like he had done in front of Beatrice. I took a couple of steps toward him, so he would not know how I felt. He had not yet closed his truck door. He looked at the steering wheel.

"It's awful what you did, Adam."

I pretended not to hear him.

"What you did to me and your mom." Then he stepped back out of the truck with a handkerchief and he gave it to me and said sorry and something else too quiet to understand. Maybe, "You're my boy."

I did not know what to do or where to go when he was gone, so I took the key he had given us for emergencies, our version of the one he'd used to discover me and Beatrice. I rinsed my face in his kitchen sink to make sure I got all the spit off. The clean towels were in the pantry. When I dried my face I thought the towel might smell like Beatrice but it did not smell like anything but Tide.

Her dresses were gone, and her boxes of special things. The nine-dollar coffee table was in its place but the sticker was gone. Beer bottles and tissues were everywhere, and the dishes were piled unwashed in the sink. I did not know what a clue would be, but nothing I found told me where she had gone. There was a picture in a frame on the dresser, lying face down. I turned it upright and there I was, my freshman-year picture. My mother had only ordered two big ones, for her and for Marv.

I went to school, hoping Beatrice would be home at the end of the day. Denver had a big airport; planes left for Paris all the time. It was not too late. There would be a simple explanation for why she had abandoned me at the library: a sudden illness, a concussion.

Phoebe and I were in the academic stream, the same English, math, and social studies classes. She would not look at me. When I tried to speak to her she pretended she could not hear. I could tell she was on the verge of crying a couple of times, and I was, too. It didn't matter what sport I played or who my brother was: there was no way I could cry at school. So I did not harass her with my apologies or worries or explanations. They weren't any good anyway. I stole off to the locker-room toilet and in the mirror my eyes were ghoulish. Everyone watched me and whispered. I had lit up their imaginations.

Right after school I ran home and knocked on Marv's door. I went inside. Nothing had changed but the smell in the kitchen, which was worse. The game was not until six so I fetched my father's appalling ten-speed and rode it downtown. I looked through the glass door of the Magpie Developments office on Main Street and saw my mother on the telephone. The second desk was empty. I pedalled to Modern You and asked Gord the Haberdasher if he had seen Beatrice. There were two women and a man in the store, and they were not together. Gord the Haberdasher watched them instead of me.

"Not in more than a week. Why?"

"She's gone."

"What do you mean *gone*? Since when?"

"Since yesterday."

"Ah, she ain't gone. She wouldn't leave me." He went over to help one of the women find a pink dress in the right size. For a while I waited for him. My plan was to take him by the hair and smash his face against my knee a few times. I didn't care if the shoppers saw or even if one of them called Chief Dunn. But the woman had nothing but questions so I left.

That night we played the Palmer Terrors and they beat us but it was still the pre-season and my lack of sleep gave me a special focus. I thought maybe she was there watching somehow, from behind a pole. I had three interceptions. At the end of every game, in the locker room, the coaches shouted at us, to shame us and to inspire us. Our team is named after a kind of horse, from right here in Colorado, and now Coach Jarvis was going on about how much people hated rangers, hated even their colouring. To them we weren't real horses; we were unnatural and dangerous, disgusting. We were their nightmare.

If we did not run faster, if we were not hungrier, more focused, more vicious, more ravenous for winning, the rest of the league would be right about us. We were shit horses! Coach Jarvis had the biggest voice and he always led the call-and-answer part of the talk. "Why are we Rangers? Rangers no matter what they say?"

None of this made any sense. No one cared about ranger horses. Once I'd asked a fat-necked ranch hand Marv brought over for Thursday-night beer what made a ranger a ranger, but all he said was they had good "cow sense." What does that even mean? But in the moment these talks always seemed crucial and we did want to stomp all the other teams, even if they had no idea what horse we represented.

At the end of all this we would huddle in even closer, like loving families, close enough to smell one another's dinner on our breaths. If a kid's parent was sick or if a grandmother died, Coach would make a speech out of it. If any of us were to pick on a member of our team who was suffering he would *make an example*. That meant wind-sprints in full gear at the next practice until someone barfed.

I could tell Coach had made a speech about me to some of the seniors because they were too complimentary about my sticky hands and my wheels. They voted me the game star. All the boys wanted to say something about Beatrice but no one did.

After the game I set myself up on the back deck with a blanket and *Leaves of Grass* and I watched Marv's house. No one was home. The wind had come from the northwest and it had autumn in it, more than autumn: a hint of snow. The crickets and toads were too chilled to sing. I was afraid if I read more than a line or two at a time I would miss something:

a revealing movement on Marv's part or, much better, Beatrice returning from an unplanned trip to the home of the Oglala Lakota where one of her parents or a special auntie had taken ill.

My mother arrived home, late, with a new briefcase. It startled her to see me on the deck. "What are you doing, sweetheart?"

"Watching Marv's."

"Why?"

"In case he did something to her. In case she comes back." Even one day earlier I could not have imagined speaking about her in this way, but I had not slept and my mother knew everything.

"He would never hurt anyone, Adam." She took my hand. "You know that."

I did not know that.

For a while she talked about a discussion group she had found for me, in The Springs: a group of boys who had been abused. All the rest of them had been abused by men but it's all the same thing, she said. This made me feel sick. I had not been abused. After a while I stopped listening to her.

"I'll make us grilled cheese sandwiches and tomato soup. Come inside."

After dinner, just to do something, I searched Marv's yard with a flashlight, under the tarps and in the piles of scrap where the police had crept. When I found only a muskrat I went to bed with my door open and my underwear off. Beatrice had a key to the house. I would sleep naked to make it easy when she slipped next to me in the middle of the night with her finger on her lips, *shhh*, the wine in her breath and the cigarettes, her body on mine, her whispers in my ear, her black hair in my face. She would slap me, pinch me, dig her loving fingernails into my chest. Every noise in town, every footstep and passing car, was Beatrice Cyr. I would not pleasure myself again, not until she came to me, and I would not think impure thoughts about any other girls or entertain the possibility that she would not come. I would not sleep. A man has to believe.

In the morning, as I prepared for school, there were two police cars in Marv's driveway. I ran out onto the deck, without a shirt on, and watched Chief Dunn walk out the back door with a box. He looked over. By this time Simon had silently joined me.

"Boys."

I lifted a hand.

"Nothing to worry about. You two head on off to school."

Two hours later, a stout policewoman stood at the door of my Spanish class. I closed my book and binder the moment I saw her. She took off her hat and nodded at my teacher. "*Lo siento mucho, señor.*"

My teacher, Señor Rodriguez, had a deep voice and a beard. "*Sí?*"

The policewoman pointed at me. "Adam Lisinski. *Por favor.*"

On the way to the chief's office we talked about football. The officer would not say why she had pulled me out of class and there was nothing she could say about the attack on

Simon. In the waiting room it smelled of burnt coffee. Two women behind the counter, both of them with teased-up blonde hair, talked about white zinfandel. They liked to put sliced-up fruit in it. The talk-radio station played on a little ghetto blaster in the corner. There was electrical tape on the antenna. The printer was going.

I went into the bathroom, where Lysol danced with old cigarettes, and stood over the toilet. I tried to make myself puke, because I was sure it would be an improvement. I just gagged myself.

There was a knock on the cubicle.

"You all right in there, son?"

"Yes, sir."

"Chief Dunn here."

I knew his voice. He did not have to tell me. "I'll be right out."

"Nauseated, are you?"

I took the Fifth.

When I was done in there, Chief Dunn led me through a security door and down a corridor, into a small conference room. He closed the blinds against the sun and offered me a chair. There was a dusty ficus in the corner and a laminated poster outlining the levels of government in America. We had the same one in our social studies class. I was standing in a small outpost of the judiciary with a thin carpet and a particle-board table, chairs that belonged in the garbage. I thought it would be helpful for Phoebe's father to see this room, since he worried quite a lot about the wasted resources of government. The chief wore a white shirt this time, still official, and a pair of jeans that did not quite make it to his waist. Without a hat he was a less silly figure.

He sat with a grunt and he stared at me with his hands clasped over the table. "Now, Adam. Why do you think you're here?"

"Beatrice Cyr, the woman next door—something's happened to her."

"I appreciate candour in a boy."

"Yes, sir."

"How would you know this?"

"From being her neighbour. You and the other police are taking stuff out of Marv's house. Investigating, I guess."

"Couple days ago you had nothing to say to me about Mrs. Walker, Ms. Cyr, what have you. Were you telling me the whole truth, Adam?"

I shrugged again. "That stuff doesn't matter."

"What stuff?"

"You know."

"I came over to talk to you and your mama about a letter I'd received here at the station, about a fourteen-year-old boy and a thirty-seven-year-old woman. An accusation of statutory rape."

It was best not to talk about that. "She isn't thirty-seven."

The chief crossed his arms and looked at me awhile, with the start of a smile in his eyes. "When did you last sleep?"

"A while ago."

"You'll make yourself sick."

"Yeah."

"You drink coffee?"

"No, sir."

"A child doesn't do adult stuff like drink coffee, right?"
He winked. "I'll be right back."

The chief closed the door behind him and then I could
hear muffled voices in the hall. One of the voices was his. I
waited five minutes and then five minutes more. If I did not
leave soon I would be late for practice. There was only one
door into and out of the little conference room. I had convinced myself that Chief Dunn had run into a more serious
problem and he had forgotten to release me. I was just about
to sneak out when the door opened and he returned with two
mugs, one in each hand, and a folder under his arm. Steam
rose from his mug as he placed it on the table. He slid a dark
blue mug to me, an Aries mug. I was a Scorpio. It had water
inside. "Figured I'd return the favour."

"I have to get to practice."

"Of course you do. I'll take you, when we're done here.
I'll walk you right to the field. It's a real good excuse, that
you were with the chief."

The folder was beige and new and full of paper, letter-sized
and longer, and on the tab someone had written *Cyr / Marrane
/ Matathias / Smith / Ahasver / Laquedem.*

I did not want to hear this. I stood up. "If I leave right now
it'll be okay."

The chief did not tell me to sit. He just watched me until
I did it. "You're nervous."

"Yes, sir."

"Tell me why."

My voice broke. I could not help it. "I'm in the chief's
office and my coaches are already mad at me."

265

"On account of your emotional crisis?" The chief stood up and opened the blinds and looked outside. He was half turned to me, like he wanted to show me something. There was a box of Kleenex on his side of the table. He slid it over. Outside there was nothing to look at but weeds and a parking lot in the sunshine. Nothing grew in this awful place. "Maybe you could fill me in on that."

Sweat fell from my armpit and slid down my side. This had never happened to me before. I could not move. If I opened my mouth to answer I feared I would cry more but it was not my house so I could not escape to the bathroom.

"Did Beatrice Cyr ever say anything about ditching town?"

"Yes, sir."

The chief took his seat again and opened his notepad. "She did?"

"To France, sir."

"Did she say *where* in France?"

"No sir, but she was flying to Paris."

"How do you know?"

"Because she was going with me."

"You and this neighbour lady you hardly knew. That's funny. Why?"

"We're in love, that's why!" Now I cried in the chief's office. I told him I had not slept more than a couple of hours in a bunch of nights, which was true, and that was why I was crying. It took me a long time to say so. The chief did not move or change his expression. Though I cannot say he *enjoyed* watching me blubber away, it meant something to him.

"Did she decide, in the last while, that she maybe wasn't in love with you the way you figured? She *does* have a husband, after all. And I had a chance to speak to a few other men who enjoyed dalliances with her." He opened the folder in a way that blocked my view of the papers. I could see, by the thinness of them, the sheets on top were from a fax machine. "And what a colourful past. Sometimes a person just has to go. Right?"

"No."

"No what?"

"She didn't decide anything without me. We were going to live in France together. In a castle in the valley of the Loire River."

"Until the day you got caught. Then she changed her plans, your plans." He made a fist and snarled at it. "And you were gonna stop her."

I had a hard time catching up to what the chief was saying. I started, got lost, and started again.

"You remember the day I visited you and your mom? What did you do in between my nice visit and the evening hours?"

"I packed a bag. I made hamburgers."

"What else?"

"We watched TV. Then my mom went to bed and I went for a milkshake at Palmer Lake."

"Anyone see you there?"

"Plenty of people. Drunks, mostly. It was at O'Grady's."

"You speak to Beatrice?"

"No, sir."

He made some notes. "She say much about her life before she arrived here?"

I took my time. "Her family was descended from Red Cloud of the Oglala Lakota, chief of all chiefs, and leader of the Cheyenne and Arapaho."

His eyebrows were up. Rather than look at him I studied the levels of government.

"Why did you tell me that steaming pile of shit when I visited? What were you hiding?"

I shrugged. "It was private."

"What was private?"

"Our love affair."

"Your mom and I chatted this morning too. I visited her at the office there, on Second Street. I sat in Mrs. Walker-Cyr's desk. She's worried about you, your mom. She needs some guidance. I put her in touch with a few organizations. There's a lot of precedent for what happened to you."

"I don't know what you mean."

"Rape, son. It can be traumatic."

"No one got raped, sir."

"You say that now. Then you're forty-six and you're on *Oprah* to talk about why you yank your own eyelashes out."

I had no idea what that meant.

"Did your Beatrice ever mention past associates? Husbands? Business partners? Errors? Entanglements?"

"Just the usual stuff."

"What usual stuff?"

"Boyfriends and whatnot. Her brother was in the property development business with her. Men were not always nice. She was mistreated. *Never again*, she figured. She turned tough. There were people who couldn't know she was here. She didn't want her picture in the paper, or to be on TV. And when she was—"

"What people, specifically?"

I shrugged. "There were motorcycle men. Mean ones. Associates of her brother, or maybe enemies of him."

"Don't see no brother here in any of this. And nothing remotely about being Cheyenne or Arapaho." The chief flipped through his pages and read some notes on one of the faxed sheets. I could not answer any of his questions about the motorcycle men. He seemed to know a thing or two about them. He closed his folder and exhaled out his nose. It had been so hot and now the weather could break. There were tornado warnings. But there was an equally strong chance it could all blow north of us, wallop Fort Collins, and amount to nothing. The chief stared at me some more. It was so quiet in the room I could hear the distant click of an electric typewriter. I knew what it meant, the other names beside *Cyr* on his folder.

"Sir? You figure one of the men on motorcycles captured her up?" I thought of what James Bond would do in a situation like this. "Or hurt her?"

The chief did not say anything for a long time. He crossed his arms and waited in the silence for something important to happen, some truth to reveal itself. It did not.

"Chief Dunn. Is Beatrice gone?"

———

269

My mother was there when I got home after practice, chopping green peppers. She talked about workers coming with earthmovers in the morning to prepare the ground for Jefferson Gardens. You have to keep an eye on contractors, she said, as though she had often hired movers of earth. "You gotta watch them, someone has to. If not, they'll find a million ways to charge you extra."

"Who told you that?"

She said a man's name: one of the men from the city who had signed joint ventures with Magpie Developments.

"This all still happens, without Beatrice?"

"We have a shotgun clause."

She explained, but I did not pay attention, really. If one partner wants to buy the company, or takes off to France, the other gets a chance at it. Beatrice had signed it all over to her.

"I talked to the chief today."

"Me too." She kept chopping.

"He wanted to know where I was the day Beatrice disappeared."

"I already told him . . ." She stabbed the knife into the cutting board and put on a fake smile. "I found a counsellor who will speak to you. To us, about what's happened here. Why does he have to hurt you all over again, making you go through it? You're the victim here." She went back to chopping but her hands shook and so did her voice. "We have an appointment next Wednesday. None of this will affect your future. None. Zero. It will make you stronger."

"But I love her, Mom."

My mother took a step toward me with the knife, remembered it, placed it on the counter, and hugged me. She half-kissed the top of my ear and held me so long the sun moved below the houses on the other side of the alley and the kitchen went dark. I did not try to wriggle away, even when she growled for a bit like Gary when he sees a bird outside and knows he'll never get it.

I did not want to speak to a counsellor. And I did not want Beatrice's raspberries to be destroyed by earthmovers; so in the dark, with a flashlight, I filled three ice-cream pails. We did not live in a neighbourhood of flowerbeds and well-tended gardens. We were poor people—I remembered Jason saying it, when I was angry with him for leaving, when he might have played closer to home for the Colorado Buffaloes with less scholarship money. "It's a humiliation to be poor in this country and if I can stop it, at least for me, I will. I'll do anything."

When I was sure I had picked all her raspberries I stood under the yellow streetlights. I could not understand or abide it, the big lack of her, so I ripped out the bushes. The thorns tore open the skin of my palms but I kept pulling the canes until there was nothing left. The smell of it was green. I was wrong about having found all the berries. Bits of ripe fruit mushed in my hands and stung where I was bleeding. It did not take long and when I was finished I did not know what to destroy next. I was dizzy from lack of sleep. My mother arrived in her silky pyjamas and bare feet. Geraldine and Don were on their porch, watching me, and the Doberman pinschers barked wildly from the pile-of-junk backyard of

Shirley and Brother H. Why "Brother H"? Why couldn't he just live with Hubert? What did they all want?

Marv's front porch light popped on and then it went off again. Murderer. I realized I had been shouting *murderer* as I pulled out the raspberries.

Then my mother was out there with me, singing in my ear. *You are my sunshine.* The dogs stopped barking and Don and Geraldine went back inside. My mother and I walked across the street with the buckets of raspberries and she washed the blood from my hands and bandaged them. Simon worked the scissors. We did not turn on the television. The airplanes and dogs were finished for the night and the dark and quiet of the house made me feel stupid for believing Beatrice, the real Beatrice, was still in town. Our town was a town of ghosts.

That night, my palms and fingers burning, I took the dogs for a late-night walk and I stood in front of his house. There Marv sat like a regular man, drinking a Miller in his living room. His massive head, just *there*. How could he be watching television? When they tried to piss on the flowers Beatrice had planted on his front lawn I pulled the dogs away. It hurt my hands to do just about everything.

I had never stayed awake for so long. It was hilarious to me that Marv was probably watching *Mr. Belvedere*. I shared this observation with the dogs, who looked up at me. As quickly as *Mr. Belvedere* had seemed hilarious it was now sad.

Marv's lights went out at half past twelve. My mother and Simon were asleep. Every drop of me wanted to crawl into bed but I needed to know. If Marv had killed her he would tell me.

His back door creaked when I opened and closed it but the fans were on, turned to high. It smelled worse. I took off my shoes and Sho Kosugi—sneaked through the kitchen sideways so I could see in front of me and behind without turning around.

His snore was irregular, loud and then quiet, long and then short. I moved through the hallway, where Beatrice and I had done it on the floor one morning, a painful morning, and into his bedroom. Miller beer, cycled through his body and snored out, had built a sweet-and-sour fog in the darkness. It said 12:51 on the clock radio. His shutters were open and light from the street entered the room, enough for me to see his clothes piled on the floor. Marv lay on his side, facing the light. He did not wear pyjamas to bed and what I could see of his bare skin was yellow, his beard greyer than in sunshine. Under the blue sheet his knees were up near his saggy chest. He was a sixty-year-old baby in a crib. I thought of him taking me fishing and to the game, to the state fair and rodeo in Pueblo because my mother could not stand that sort of thing.

I walked over the mound of his clothes and I kneeled beside his bed. Now that I was here I did not know what I had snuck inside to do. To force the truth out of him, sure, but what if he confessed? The knife was not in my back pocket this time.

I waited for the right moment to wake him. I touched and pulled gently at his beard, the dry curls of it. Something about his beer breath and his snoring comforted me. For just a few seconds I closed my eyes. Then I crawled onto the bed, her side of the bed, while I worked on my plan. He could either tell me or I would look for clues in every drawer and under every rug, behind every VHS tape on every shelf, and I would not be tidy about it. Things were going to be knocked over. With all that Miller in him he would have forgotten something—some crumb on some trail that would lead me to her. My hands throbbed in their bandages and the smell of the raspberries was stained on my arms, in the back of my raw throat. I needed a glass of water. I dozed and woke up and realized where I was and then I fell asleep.

The birds woke me the same as they did every morning across the gravel driveway. I opened my eyes and Marv was already watching me, his brow furrowed.

"What are you doing, son?"

Everything that had made beautiful sense the night before now seemed difficult to bring together in the light of the morning. "I had to know."

"Know what?"

"Where she is. What you did to her."

"You really think I could?"

"If you were mad enough."

"I was plenty mad. I don't remember being as mad as I was in your basement. I brought a gun, for lord's sake! Adam. Adam, I threw up on your floor, I was so angry. Well, heartsick more than angry, I guess. Betrayed by her. By *you*, my own boy. I guess you're just a kid, though. Chief Dunn's helped me see it that way." He sat up, with a series of grunts, and reached over for his cigarettes. "Not that it's easy. I've half a mind to knock your block off."

He smoked for a while and looked at the opposite wall.

"How did you get in here, son?"

"A key."

"What was your big plan? Come here in the night and . . . what?"

"You really don't know where she is?"

"Hell, I don't even know *who* she is. Did the chief share that dossier of his?"

"Dossier?"

"The folder with all her aliases. We weren't even legally married. She was already married to a fella in Edmonton."

"Are you lying?"

"Lying about what?"

"Hurting her. Knowing things."

He sighed out some cigarette smoke. "Here's what I know." His eyes were glassy now. He started to talk and then he stopped. Started again and stopped. He dabbed at his eyes with a handkerchief on the side of his bed. The morning sun brought all the dust about him to swirling life. "Men can be pretty damn awful to women. You read about it every day. Men were awful to her, right from when she was little. Maybe she told you all about it. I kinda hope not. There's stuff I know I'll never forget. But I fear deep down she came here just to wound me. It's like she was sent just to make me think I could have a final love and then to . . ." He did something with his arms, some demonstration of mechanics. Then he gave up on it. "You know what, Adam, I'm genuine sorry but get the fuck out of my house."

The yellow tractors arrived at seven in the morning, on the backs of two massive muddy trucks. Men with hard lunch-boxes and blue jeans thwarted by what had happened to their bellies smoked cigarettes. I went out and stood on the gravel road next to my mother. She looked at me for a moment, like she wasn't sure of me anymore, and then she put her arm in mine like we were army buddies.

Even over the beeping and growling tractors, the men shouting at one another, I heard Marv approach from behind. He walked heavy on his cane. His hair was swirled from sleep and he had not shaved. Before Beatrice arrived, even when he was lonely or despairing for himself in a jokey fashion on a Thursday night, Marv had smiled.

I had come to know his schedule. By now he was supposed to be in his overalls, climbing up into his truck for a country-music commute to the medical device factory. "Morning, Helen. Adam."

"Thanks for coming." My mother put her other arm around him and I could hear him swallow, even over the machines. Then she let him go and pulled a Kleenex from her purse and wiped her nose with it, watched the tractors. Marv asked for one and he wiped his own nose. They looked for a moment like a mismatched but loving wife and husband at the burial of a beloved pet.

I thought they were here to talk about what had happened last night. I prepared to explain to my mother why I had crawled into bed with Marv.

"It's not that I didn't understand your message, Helen."

"It's pretty simple, Marv. A good chunk of our money is missing. Bea and I were the only two with access to it. It wasn't even our money, not really. You know how it is. It's the bank's money." She pointed to the earthmovers. "It's their money."

"The chief asked about that. She didn't take any of mine, apart from what we spent on the car and her clothes. The boy's suit."

"Well, there's that at least."

"I'm so sorry, Helen." He started to walk away. "This is all my doing."

"Wait!"

Marv kept walking. He did not turn around or wave or apologize or commiserate with us. My mother went to him and they hugged and said things to one another I could not hear. I turned back to the machines and the men in hardhats.

There were clouds on the eastern horizon but they were thin and unserious, daunted by the sun. My mother returned after a while. "It's hard to imagine what it was like two months ago, before she came. Isn't it?" Her dress was another new one, a dark brown that I remembered the writers of GQ being pretty excited about this season. She looked elegant and a bit old-fashioned, as though she could be summoned at any moment to New York.

"Mom. Are you in trouble? Are we in trouble?"

Over the beep of a tractor she sighed. I was six years old and I had just asked where babies come from. This part embarrassed her. For a while we watched the tractors. "Magpie Developments is all mine now, the good and the bad."

"You're in trouble."

"Big trouble."

"Beatrice stole the money?"

"Yes."

"But it's not your money."

"It's my company. One hundred percent mine now. So the debt is mine too."

"That means she's still alive. No one hurt her, then. Did you tell the chief?"

"Yesterday."

"Where did she go? Did Marv hurt her? Or the gangsters? Do you know, Mom?"

The pink morning sun was on her face and she squinted into it and took my arm again. There was nothing to look at, really: two yellow tractors and a lot of dirt. I had never seen my mother make a fist. She made two of them and a muscle flared along her jawline.

twelve

On the side of our refrigerator I noticed what had been invisible to me for months: a bunny magnet. Easter magnets came out in March; Christmas magnets, in December. I still insisted on putting the magnets up, even though they were for little tykes. Somehow we had forgotten to put the Easter bunny away along with the eggs and tulips, the baby chick, and the basket dangerously overflowing with eggs and greenery. On that morning the bunny's smile made me feel like Marv had made me feel. I had abandoned the bunny and all the other seasonal magnets when I abused myself behind the fridge door. That choice had made all other choices possible. Inevitable. I repacked the gym bag and called a taxi, asking that the driver meet me a block from home.

Simon stumbled out of Jason's room as I carried the gym bag upstairs. "What are you doing?"

"Heading to the airport."

"Come on, brother."

"I have to try."

Simon reached into his hair to scratch. Normally he kept it short, like his father's. It was better for wrestling. Since he'd begun his new life as a poet, though, he had abandoned the electric razor and his hair was blooming into a sweet Afro. "Let me drive you at least."

"Mom will see us leave. Besides, you'll just try to talk me out of it."

"Yes I will. This is crazy."

"It's a leap of faith."

"What do you know about faith?"

"Walt Whitman would do it. Gwendolyn Brooks would, too. What's the worst that can happen? I spend a week in France."

"You can't speak French. And what is the population of Paris? Ten, fifteen million?"

"I believe."

"You believe what?"

"I believe if I go, I will find her."

"Just by going. Just by being in Paris."

"Some people, my mom—your parents—believe in Jesus and coming back from the dead and turning water to wine. All I believe is when you love someone enough you will *feel* where she is and you will go there, to her." I had seen plenty enough of Paris in the movies to know it would be a bistro or café with all the wicker chairs turned toward the street. From her balcony on Rue Something she was looking up at the same sky as me, wishing.

"You've blinded yourself. She could have gone a lot of places."

"But all she ever talked about was France."

"Why didn't she tell you? Why didn't you go with her?"

"She stole money from the company."

"You can't go to Paris, alone, to find a forty-year-old woman. You don't even know her!"

"She's thirty-two. I know her better than anyone."

"Her body, maybe. And she's thirty-seven. I saw her driver's licence. Which, by the way, did not have the name—"

"Stop."

"Why don't you ask Helen where she went?"

"She doesn't know."

We went upstairs and Simon pulled a pail of raspberries from the fridge, started eating. "Let me tell you something. The day you quit the team I went to the field to speak to your coach. A car was following me, a blue Ford car."

"Squeak. And I know why he did it. Squeak's a racist. And he thinks—"

"It was not Squeak." The seeds were already stuck in his teeth. "It wasn't boys who beat me up. It was men."

"What men?"

He shrugged. "Friends of Emory's. They told me to keep my mouth shut about his party, about what I saw, what I did,

I guess, and I have kept it shut. I memorized the licence plate of the car."

"What did you see? What did you do?"

"Fella. Come on."

"Anyone could tell on him. Anyone at the party! Why you?"

"Why *you*, Adam?"

At the airport a grandmotherly woman in a cowboy hat showed me where to go and what to do. I was six hours early for the first flight to Paris. It enchanted the flamboyant man at the Delta desk that I had just decided to *go*. I had never used my passport. Jason and I had applied for them because Uncle Oscar always promised to take us to his place in Acapulco, but he was always tied up with business. I had never been on an airplane. The flamboyant man waved his fellow agents over and they called me adorable. One of the Delta women walked me to the security line and showed me what to do. She gave me a voucher for a free lunch at José's Mexican Grill. I ordered a chimichanga with rice but I was too nervous to finish it. There was a little bookstore with guidebooks for sale. I bought a fat one for all of France and it had a long section about Paris. There were directions for getting into the central part of the city from the airport, but I worried the signs would be in French. Everyone said French was easy if you knew Spanish but when I flipped through a French novel in the little bookstore I could not understand a thing.

Two hours before my flight was set to depart, I was reading through my guidebook and underlining the cafés and gardens I would visit, to find Beatrice, when my mother sat down in the seat across from me.

"Goddamn Simon."

"Don't blame him."

There was a bird in the rafters of the airport. It was above us somewhere, calling out. I was so angry and so embarrassed I could not speak. For a long time neither of us said much at all. We looked up when they made announcements about gate changes and departures, though they had nothing to do with us.

"Adam, sweetheart." My mother wore her navy-blue dress with a scarf. She sat up straight in the hard chair. If this woman had walked past me two months ago I might not have recognized her. Yet here she was. "Beatrice isn't in Paris."

"How do you know?"

A golf cart whizzed past, driven by that same grandmother in a cowboy hat. In the back, an obese couple. My first thought was I would end up sitting next to the big people on the airplane. My second thought was I was not going on an airplane.

"You know the word *alias*."

"I watch movies."

"Chief Dunn visited me again today. Beatrice is in his system, with her other names, because law enforcement agencies are looking for her. And not only them."

"She was already married, Marv said."

"There's a word for it: bigamy."

283

"Why are the men on motorcycles looking for her?"

My mother shrugged. "She never told me. Money, I expect. Some bad betrayal somewhere. Sort of like she did with me. With us."

There was a hole in me and it was growing. I wished I had eaten more of the chimichanga. "How do you know she isn't in Paris?"

My mother looked in her purse but she didn't take anything out. I feared she was going to tell me a story about her own childhood or about the birds and the bees, the perils of travel. "She isn't the great-granddaughter of the chief of all chiefs. You don't have to make many calls to check that out, I guess, if you're a policeman. The Lakota have a phone number and an office, a fax machine."

"You don't know, do you? She could be in Paris."

"She doesn't have a passport."

"Yes, she does."

"Not in any of the names Chief Dunn knows."

I did not tell her about Carol and Chris because I still intended to follow Beatrice to Paris somehow. My mother stood up and sat next to me, put her arm around me. I could have finished my chimichanga and ten more and still I would have been hungry.

"All the kids know. It must be awful. You wanted to escape it all, escape from Monument and from me. Find her in Paris."

I looked up at the bird. A sparrow, I figured, that had flown in when someone opened the doors. You forget to listen to sparrows. You allow them to be background noise. Now that

I was listening to the sparrow, I understood it was not chirping just to chirp. The sparrow was trapped and knew it would die in this place if something did not change.

"You know, I spoke to the nice people at Delta Airlines."

"Aw, for Christ's sake, Mom." The sparrow would have enough to eat, but it would not have other birds.

"Don't blaspheme, please. They can't refund your money, it's too late for that, but they'll give you a credit to fly somewhere else. You and I could go see Jason in a game."

A young couple was sitting across from us, both of them wearing Broncos caps. They looked like they were from East India. The man had fallen asleep on the woman's shoulder and she watched us. She did not know a thing about me but she pitied me. I could see it in her little smile and her soft, exhausted eyes. There was no Carol and Chris Laquedem from Boise, Idaho. There never was.

"They're pulling your luggage from the system. Let's get you home."

I didn't say much on the way back. My mother talked about Magpie Developments and her new debts, her new fears. But there was no fear in her voice. It was the middle of the afternoon but the clouds had come for the first time in months. They were so thick and so low it felt like dusk. We pulled off the interstate and I could not see Mount Herman or any other hills or mountains of the Front Range. Autumn was here. Soon the leaves would turn and we would stop going outside. The wind would come up and blow all the dust up from the gravel roads. We would watch television and go to school and drive cars just about everywhere. I went downstairs and called for Simon the traitor. He didn't answer. All of his clothes were gone from my brother's closets and so were his books of Black poetry and his Darth Vader statue and his briefcases full of cassettes. *Leaves of Grass* lay on the middle of the bed with a sticky note on the front that said, "These words are yours."

thirteen

there was a home game the following night, against
Pomona, and since they had won the state championships
everyone was sure the college scouts would come. I hated it
when my teammates thought scouts were coming. They
were so nervous they forgot our formations and dropped the
ball and threw tantrums, even the seniors. We had to wear
shirts and ties on home game days so I dressed smart casual
for school: an ironed white shirt, a tie, blue jeans, and my
suit jacket.

It took more than half an hour to walk to Lewis-Palmer,
but I felt like walking so I did. The skin under my right eye
twitched like always when I had been sleeping poorly. Clouds
were still upon us and the air was cool. "Wishing Well" by
Terence Trent D'Arby had been on the radio while I ironed

my shirt, and now I could not get it out of my head—but at least, for the first time in a long time, it wasn't just Beatrice in there.

In the parking lot I saw Phoebe and Mrs. Brandt speaking to one another on the edge of the yellow flowerbeds, both of them in shiny new back-to-school jeans and sweaters. Mrs. Brandt's Mercedes was parked next to them, far from all the other cars. She waved me over.

I pretended I didn't understand, that I thought she was waving to say hello, and I waved back. *Hello, good morning,* half a smile, *I'm sorry.* Everyone knew more than I did. I walked between the cars in the parking lot, and the boys were saying *fuck* to one another and *pussy* and *piss* and *faggot* like always. They stopped talking as I passed. *Hey man. Hey.*

In class I was too tired to concentrate on the holy documents that had informed the creation of our great republic. I caught Phoebe looking at me.

In one of her books about personal power she had read the phrase "impulse control." One evening at Monument Lake, as we sat on the rocks and kissed, she told me it is what separates successful and unsuccessful people, the sophisticate and the brute. I lived in our neighbourhood of misfits and drunks because my parents had lacked impulse control. My father ran off because he did not have it. In the end Phoebe caught me in a library men's room with Beatrice because I did not have it either. All of our most enchanting American ideas, like the ones from these holy documents of the republic that I could not concentrate on, are stripped and undone by a lack of impulse control.

Before Beatrice moved in next door I was not Jason, not a national football star, not special, not yet, but my sophomore year had still carried the promise of thrill and grace. I had seen Phoebe in a bikini and if I was careful and patient I might see the way her freckles covered the rest of her. Now that her sister had moved out I could sneak in without Gabriela or Lorenzo seeing me and I could kiss the hard perfume off other parts of her body when her parents were at their place in Vail.

I stayed in my desk for a few minutes after social studies as everyone else left class. That way I could walk out alone and avoid answering questions or looking at people—I'd been doing that for a while. My teacher, Mr. Chan, leaned back on his desk and watched me as I sat there but he did not say anything. I thanked him for the lesson about the holy documents and he wished me good luck against Pomona in a funereal tone.

Phoebe was waiting for me outside the classroom. She leaned against some lockers, hugging her books.

"Hey, Adam."

I leaned against the lockers opposite. "Hey."

"My mom wanted to talk to you."

"She did?"

Phoebe reached up with one of her long fingers and traced under her eyes. "You need some sleep."

"Yeah."

"I'm supposed to apologize for everything."

"Supposed to?"

"It wasn't my place to do what I did. Maybe I didn't understand." Some kids passed close by, so Phoebe looked away and stopped talking for a moment. When they were gone she breathed slowly, like she had a stomach ache and wanted it to go away. "My mom has a therapist. This woman from The Springs. She made me speak to her about you. She thought I was suffering trauma, my mom, but the therapist didn't think so."

"No?"

"She thinks *you are*." Phoebe considered her shoes: shiny new ones from drizzling Europe. "I never considered what happened to you was against your wishes. It's true what I wrote the chief. That woman raped you and it isn't fair for me to blame *you* for it."

"The chief's been nice."

Phoebe took a small step forward. She met me in the middle of the hallway and bent forward the way ballet dancers do, with straight legs, and we hugged. She kept her pelvis far from mine, like I had a disease there. She whispered something so low I did not hear it. We're just kids. Let's be kids. We can kiss.

There was a new smell in her hair, of hot herbs.

"She hurt you, didn't she?"

"I didn't do anything with her, in the library bathroom. We just talked. She was drunk."

She squeezed me a little harder.

"I'm sorry, Phoebe."

"Where is she?"

"She ran off."

"Good. I mean, she's super fucked up. You need to get better, that's all. I can help."

"It wasn't all bad."

Phoebe whispered. "What wasn't?"

"I learned things I didn't know before. I know how to do it now."

"Do what?"

Beatrice talked about Phoebe all the time. Do this to her. Have you tried?

"She was teaching me."

Phoebe tried to get away, to end our hug, but I pulled her closer. I said into her ear what Beatrice had taught me to do to her, with my fingers and my mouth. She squirmed so I let her go and she tripped over her books and fell against the lockers with a bang.

Mr. Chan stepped out into the hall and saw Phoebe holding her skirt in place.

"Everything all right, Phoebe?"

She looked at him, at me, at him again. "Yes, Mr. Chan. Thank you."

He lingered for a moment and returned to his classroom. Then neither of us spoke. We stood so silently in the hall I could hear the buzz of the fluorescent lights above us.

I picked up Phoebe's books for her and she took them from me and walked away, the heels of her new shoes echoing through the hall. She looked back at me as she rounded the corner.

In the game against Pomona one of our starting wide receivers, Tyson Smith, jumped for the ball and landed wrong and broke his ankle. I went in for Tyson and played both ends of the field. The stands are always full on warm nights in September, especially for homecoming, which is an idea I never really understood. Does anyone actually come home? My mother was in the second row with a group of men I did not yet recognize. They would come to be familiar to me as her business partners from the city, my partners. I scored three touchdowns and intercepted four passes. We beat the reigning champs 41-36. Something started that night and did not stop: my teammates were happy we won but they watched me in the locker room as though I had stolen something from them. I'd stolen something and they had to pretend I had not.

Afterward, Phoebe and her parents waved from in front of their Mercedes, where they stood eating ice cream cones. Mr. Brandt shouted across the parking lot at me, "That was amazing."

A new cloud blocked the setting sun and hid the mountaintops again. The thunder began as a murmur.

Gene had phoned to say I could pick up my final cheque. On my way home I stopped at the station. Simon was putting gas in a K-Car. I waited until he was finished and asked why he had left without saying goodbye.

"I wrote a note."

"And the book, yeah—thanks."

"I just decided it's best for me to go." He gestured toward the mountains.

"Go where?"

"That special school in Montana."

"Why the hell would you do that, Sye? Just move back in with us."

"I have my books. My music."

"Your dad can't make you. Don't let him."

He walked toward the shack as the K-Car took off. The driver was listening to one of those radio shows about Jesus and how disappointed and angry He is about how we've turned out.

"Sye, wait."

"Just let me go."

"Is this about Beatrice?"

He stopped. "Adam—"

"Do you know where she went? Did she tell you or something?"

"Ask your mom."

In the shack Gene slid the envelope across the counter without looking at me. I told him to keep it. I told him to spend it on a trip with Hailey, to take her to Disneyland, because she always talked about it and she had never gone. It insulted Gene that I did not want his money, and he was so insistent I nearly told him about the seven hundred dollars I had taken from the safe. Gene insisted because he knew he was wrong about the shitty twenty, knew he had mistreated me, and in his heart I had made a sinner of him. But he was not strong enough to say sorry and hire me back.

I was so angry with Simon I shouted cuss words at him on the way out of the shack, and my voice was cracking like I was about to cry. I guess I was. When we were kids Jason and I fought like any two brothers, but we were not allowed to scream at one another or wrestle in the house. My mother forced us to go outside, even in the winter, for our arguments and fistfights. By the time we put our shoes and jackets on we had usually slowed our hearts. We either forced calm on ourselves or, if we made it outside, we forgot why we had been so furious. A few minutes later I was miserable about what I had shouted at Simon so at home I wrote him an apology letter and sealed it in an envelope and walked it to his mailbox as the storm arrived.

No lights were on in our living room so when the lightning flashed it lit up the photographs on the mantel, the dusty bronze candlesticks, the football trophies. Gary and Maggie hid behind the toilet.

I could not stand the quiet so I turned on the television. A rerun of *The Wonder Years* was on. I had seen this episode. Kevin, who was about my age on the show, was in love with a girl named Winnie. In this one she was dating an asshole named Kirk and somewhat lording it over Kevin because deep down she really liked him but he was too timid to get his shit together. While I had posters of older, blonder women on the walls of my bedroom, Winnie was my true crush.

The things Beatrice and I had done in many rooms of our house hung in the air like the not-quite-shit Gary sprayed out his ass when he was startled. The power went out before the episode ended. My mother was not yet home.

I made some cheese and crackers and ate them in front of the picture window. The men had already dug the hole for Jefferson Gardens and they had stacked wood and rebar in the alley. These items did not yet excite me. Tarps flapped in the new wind. I did not want to read *Leaves of Grass* because I thought it would make me sad so I read an *Archie* by flashlight until I fell asleep.

In my dream, it was a truck smashing into a house—our house, any house. I braced myself against the wall and the dream faded. I could hear footsteps. I crept up the stairs and into the kitchen. My mother sneaked in front of me, from behind a chair, shielding me as though I were the president. "Did you lock the door when you got home?"

"No."

No one stood looking in through the kitchen window at us, no wet face, no clown smile. The power was still out. It was dark and pouring rain for the first time in months. This is how it was in our town. No rain and then so much rain basements filled with water, news trucks came from Denver and shot footage of people crying in their yards like this had never happened before. I had not cleaned the gutters so the water fell heavily along the perimeter of our little house. My glow watch said it was a few minutes after four. I was sore from playing both sides of the field and thirsty from eating cheese, no longer sleepy. I asked my mother what was happening.

"You didn't hear it?"

"I heard something. A smash."

"It was a gunshot, real close."

"Beatrice."

I stood up and she pulled me back down. "Don't move." My mother adjusted her pyjama pants. She opened the knife drawer and took out a big one. "Anything could happen."

I followed her. "I'll go to her. You stay here."

"Get back downstairs."

"No. Mom, I don't think—"

"Now!"

I ran to the open door that led to the basement and my mother slammed it closed after me. I lay on my bed and hugged my pillow, half wanting to listen and half wanting to cover my ears. I could hear her talking to herself as she fussed in the hall closet. Our back door needed grease so it squeaked when it opened. I was ashamed I obeyed her with such relief.

A few minutes later she came back inside and closed the door behind her. I ran upstairs. She was already on the phone.

I went out in my bare feet and T-shirt and my mother shouted after me to stop but she could not abandon the phone. The rain carried mountain cold in it. Marv was in his back-yard. He wore his short-sleeved white dress shirt and a tie, and sat in an easy chair he must have dragged with awful effort from his living room. It was too dark to see from the deck so I walked down the stairs and across the driveway and I could hear my mother screaming at me through the door. The big chrome gun was on his lap, still in his hand. There was a giant bottle of Southern Comfort in the other. Above his jaw there was not much left. His bottom teeth. The rain had washed the gore into the mud. I am sure the notes in his last will and testament have coloured my memory of that night but the way he was sitting, what remained of him, he seemed something like happy.

PART FOUR

fourteen

marv left everything to my mother: the house and its furniture and secrets, his truck, the benefits of his insurance policy, and almost six hundred thousand dollars in savings. He did not have a family. His first divorce was final, his second marriage was fraudulent, and his sister had died years ago. In the letter he left on the kitchen table he wrote that he had never in his life felt special, never really felt loved, not until these last months, and now that his blessed time had come to an end he saw no point in burdening himself, his community, or the doctors and nurses who had better things to do with their time and expertise than care for a failing man.

I went to Stanford—on a football scholarship, but by the time I graduated high school my mother could have paid the tuition many times over. In her obituary last week a business reporter in the *Denver Post* called her "our Cinderella, our Horatio Alger story." I have never read a Horatio Alger story but I am up on my Cinderella, and if anyone was her Prince Charming it was Beatrice.

I stayed obsessed with Beatrice throughout high school and she remained with me in my university years, a spook in the room whenever I was alone with a woman. I had to learn what to do and say, how fast to go, how to be gentle. Things I thought were normal were not normal and could hurt and frighten people. There was no way to tell a girl why I did the things I did.

When I was forced to meet with therapists I could tell they worried for me when I told them about what we'd done together. Since it was their job, I told them a truth I could admit to no one else: I was still in something-like-love with Beatrice. I could tell by their eyes that I sounded like those shaky women on talk shows who sympathize with the husbands who knock them out. *He's really sweet when you get to know him.*

My mother had just turned seventy. Once that had sounded old, but now I understand it is young. She was killed by the one part of her past she could not transcend—her Marlboro Lights. No matter how successful she became, my mother always saw Jefferson Street as a holy place, Jefferson Gardens the first of her triumphs, and whenever she had business in the suburbs between Denver and The Springs she came back to our town and parked between our old house and the haunted ground across the street.

We had to work around two christenings and a wedding, but there was only one place to celebrate her life and the

turn it took: St. Peter. It had once seemed too big for her, for
any of the Lisinskis. Now she filled every hotel in the county,
and we had to set up a projection screen in the high school
gymnasium for the overflow crowd. Men and women came
from all over the country, from Canada and the United
Kingdom, from Belgium, from Dubai. Simon came from
London. My ex-wife—Phoebe—lived in her parents' house
in Monument with her third husband, Carlos, now that Steve
and Laverne had retired and moved away. They came, too,
flying in from Maui.

I do not know where Beatrice came from.

She stood in the back of the church in a tight-fitting black
silk dress. Her chin was up, like it was the day she first arrived.
Maya, our thirty-two-year-old director of marketing, a
University of Chicago woman, stood next to me at the base
of the sanctuary.

"You see her?"

"Who?"

I stood on my toes to point her out. By then, she was gone.
"No one."

"You need some fucking sleep, boss."

"Maybe don't say 'fucking' in here."

"Really?"

I began to describe Beatrice. She would have been in her
late sixties by then, but in the strange light of the woody
church she was thirty-seven. I stopped because there wasn't
much I could say. I had only seen her for a moment. The

carpet in the church was new. It seemed wrong, carpet in a church. Jesus was bigger and fancier than when I was a kid, more thoughtful than anguished in front of a blue stained-glass window. My mother had given the church a million dollars in the early 2000s and there was a picture of her on the wall. That morning my phone had rung and I was sure it was my mother on the line, saying my name the way she said it, before the call dropped.

"I'll keep an eye out."

"Would you? It's crucial I speak to her."

"Friend of Helen's?" Maya watched me a while, in the silence, and patted me on the arm like we had just lost the game. She liked our usual comic banter and didn't seem to recognize the look on my face. "No one trains us for this moment. Do they, boss?"

The service began with a rather long speech from Father Alexander, a Polish man I had come to know since the diagnosis. It was mostly about Jesus, not my mother, but I could not blame him because they hardly knew each other. My mother had allowed her Christianity to lapse over the years, but as the disease flowered she returned to her faith, blending it with some Qi Gong from the holistic medicine centre around the corner from her house in Cherry Creek. Father Alexander did not like the Chinese spirituality and he did not like me, especially when I insisted that a woman named Kaitlyn Yee could come in during the funeral and play a sound bowl and lead us in some breathing exercises. A couple of my mother's business associates told stories, and so did Uncle Oscar. It was my job to deliver the eulogy.

My mother was next to me, in a casket, and Phoebe was in the fourth row with Carlos and with Simon, who had never married a woman or a man. I did need some fucking sleep. I broke down reading what I had written the night before, quotations from the book of memories we had placed in my mother's room in palliative care. I was forty-one years old, the CEO of the company my mother had built. I made speeches and presentations all the time but I could not read a few quotations aloud.

Shortly after my marriage ended I paid a man in New York a lot of money to find Beatrice and he failed. The Internet seemed to make this sort of thing easier but she was not on it, at least not as Beatrice Cyr or any of the aliases she had brought to Jefferson Street. Before he died Chief Dunn, who had become a friend, gave me his box of information on Beatrice, official and unofficial. There were files on her from her life before us, from cities and towns across this country and in Canada. In the end, like me, the chief had come to see her arrival in our town as both simpler and more complicated than we had ever imagined, as magic and chaos. The chief believed there were plenty of kinds of justice.

My boys were six and eight, too young for their grandmother's funeral. It was Phoebe's week with them, which meant they were with Nikki the nanny. As I returned to my seat, after the weepy eulogy, I felt the warmth of my mother's friends and mine, and while it was a comfort I did not want to sit in the front row with their eyes on me. I wanted to go to the back of the church, to stand with Beatrice and ask if she had been in Paris all these years as Father Alexander made sure to get some digs in at abortion and gay marriage.

At the end, as my mother had requested, we walked across the street to the park next to Big Red for a glass of sparkling wine. She had wanted champagne, but we saved twenty dollars a bottle by choosing a delicious Crémant de Bourgogne. Business acquaintances shook my hand to congratulate me for the eulogy—as though it had been a performance.

A man named Mike, who owns a construction company in The Springs, wanted to tell me a funny story about my mother. I knew it would not be funny. It would be about how my mother was tough, unwilling to compromise, sneaky as a Manhattan lawyer, but—get this—*a lady*. There was already a lot of whiskey in his breath. Mike told me my mother would not budge, never, not once, and I scanned the crowd for the small woman in a black silk dress. After his first story Mike launched into a second one even as his wife, who possessed all the social awareness in the family, pulled him away.

My sedan was parked on Second Street, which had hardly changed since high school. I climbed onto the hood for a better look at the mourners and dented it a little. She was not here. Jason and his wife Kate and I led the toast and a few hundred people lifted flutes and said, "To Helen," and we all drank and then, as we had hoped, it felt like the party was over. Some of the out-of-town guests were staying at the Overland, which Simon's parents had lost to creditors in 2010. It was now a Best Western. The bar in the Overland was still the closest thing to fancy in town, with frontier signs and brass poles and red cushions on the banquettes. We had booked it for the small "wake" portion of the funeral, also at my mother's urging. Despite what she had achieved, she never stopped seeing herself as the hostess of the Thursday-night drinking party.

Before I drove to the Overland I walked down Jefferson Street. Some of the houses had been renovated, but most were still victims of the train and, frankly, what I did for a living. I developed neighbourhoods and built new houses far from here, with new appliances and front garages.

Back when I was still in high school my mother had bought Shirley and Brother H's house and the one next door to build phase two of Jefferson Gardens. Three or four of the balconies nearly overflowed with broken chairs and cases of empty beer, but most had planters and pots, small tables and chairs, decorative lights. These were, as my mother had always hoped, the simple homes of honourable people who did not see a way out of their jobs at the Humane Society.

We still own Jefferson Gardens, but our property managers take care of everything. Unlike my mother, I almost never come out here. It stirs no triumph or pride, no spiritual obstacles overcome. The town owns our house now, and Marv's. Both houses are part of a women's recovery program my mother endowed in her name. When they leave their abusive boyfriends and husbands, women can come here. One of them had set up an easel in front of Marv's house. She painted in a white smock and a Rockies baseball cap backwards. The brilliant town gardeners had figured out how to grow flowers at the front of our house—begonias, not sweet williams. I waited, leaning on my car, watching the houses and the woman with the easel, the fading taste of crémant on my tongue, because I thought maybe Beatrice had come here to feel some species of what I felt.

Before I started at Stanford, when I was not yet eighteen, I flew to Paris with Phoebe for two weeks. She didn't know that I hoped to find Beatrice there, to at least see her from afar in the Café de Flore or the Luxembourg Gardens. I had planned to leave Phoebe, to sneak behind some plane trees and keep walking. In the hope that she would one day summon me, I had studied the city in guidebooks and novels. I had grown anxious about it, giddy. But I did not find her. Phoebe crowded her out, stood between us, and I drank too much wine. I would caution anyone with a penchant for shameful thoughts who seeks a meaningful career as a residential property developer in the western half of the United States to stay as far away from Paris as possible. On a bus trip to the Loire Valley I discovered you cannot buy those castles.

I'd booked us rooms at the Overland, too, so we would not have to worry about driving home after the wake. My brother and Simon and I sat at a table in the corner with our jackets off, top two buttons undone, our ties in our pockets. Folks came by, shook our hands, hugged us, talked about Helen, assured us she was looking down with a pint of her own, and walked back to wherever they had been sitting or standing and drinking. More than a few of them hinted at business arrangements we might consider. Father Alexander asked for another donation and it gave me immense pleasure to refer him to the woman in my office who says no to people.

After a decade in New York making video installations I only pretended to understand, Simon had moved to London and become an art dealer. Jason had spent one year in the NFL, in Baltimore, but he hardly played so he went to law school, dropped out, gave it another shot, and finished the second time. He's our senior vice-president of business development, but to be honest he doesn't much like it. More than I did, he inherited our mother's tendency to dreaminess and depression; but unlike her, he has not found a way to punch through it. He plays a lot of first-person shooters with his sons and watches footage of himself in college games.

Marijuana is legal now in Colorado, which explained Maya's absence. I had booked a room for her too. Maya was married, with a two-year-old, but she was stricken with the seeker's gene. When she finally made it to the bar with Barry, one of our consulting architects, her eyes were small and glassy. I waved at her and she walked over. I did not want to speak to her in front of Jason and Simon so I met her in the middle of what would transform into the dance floor at ten o'clock.

Maya looked at her phone. "I'm sorry I was flip, in the church."

"It doesn't matter."

"I could tell it bothered you."

"Nah."

"I have trouble believing things, in sincerity, in nice moments. It makes a real asshole out of me, boss. I don't know why I'm like this. School, maybe? New England? Twitter?"

"It's why we love you."

"Do you? Do you love me?"

Barry watched us. There were two pints in front of him. One was for Maya. Her shirt was crooked, from whatever she had been doing with Barry.

"Did you ever see the woman in the black silk dress, the one I told you about?"

"No."

"You looked?"

"In the church and outside. I'm sorry."

I pulled out my phone. "You think I could take a week?"

"Fuck, yeah. Take a week. Take two."

Even high, she was faster on a phone than me. It took her less than five minutes to book me a flight to Paris, leaving just after midnight. She slapped the phone and my credit card back into my hand and swanned to the bar, to Barry's great relief. I pointed at Barry and dished him a look of warning. He lifted his hands in mock-surrender.

At another banquette, Phoebe nodded as Carlos told a mystical story. He was from Santa Fe. When I was ungenerous about Carlos he was a poor, lazy, untalented artist-of-all-sorts who sought a woman like Phoebe so she could rescue him from dry-walling and hedge trimming. I did not want to interrupt him so I began with Jason. He was shocked by what I asked him but quietly honoured, too, that I trusted him to step in as CEO for a week. His voice went a bit deeper. Carlos insisted on being present as I spoke to Phoebe, and by *being present* he meant something I did not fully understand. He put his hand on my shoulder and closed his eyes and told me to take as much healing time as I needed. "Seek the waters, Adam. Seek the waters."

I took Phoebe's hand for a moment, asked her without asking, because I was not looking for another answer from Carlos.

"The boys will be fine, Adam. It's our week. But why Paris?"

Carlos chuckled. "Why Paris? Kitten: *Why Paris?* This time of year it's absolutely glorious."

Phoebe ignored Carlos as he explained about the city of love, my love for my mother, and the love that is all around us like webs connecting the molecules of the air we breathe. Simon joined us, listening in.

I could have explained about Beatrice but it would have hurt and confused Phoebe for no good reason. "Maybe I'll end up in Lourdes."

"Because you're such a major Catholic."

Simon pulled at one of my sleeves. "I'm going out for a fag. Care to join me?"

"Fag."

"Yes, I know, Adam. You're secretly eleven years old."

If anything, the summer had been even drier than the summer of 1989. People didn't cheat anymore, watering their lawns during killer droughts, though not because of any moral improvements. Political signs and stupid elections had encouraged neighbours to distrust and resent one another. They ratted one another out to bylaw officers in vengeance.

We sat on the ledge of the new Best Western sign. Cigarette butts and snack wrappers lay in every crevice. Simon moved the butts and trash into a small pile with his black shoe, shined to un-American perfection. "My father's heart would break to see this."

"How are your mom and dad?"

"I'll see them tomorrow. Absolutely miserable, I think."

When the hotel veered toward bankruptcy I phoned Simon in London and asked if I ought to buy it. His father could continue to manage the place. His mother could book weddings and banquets like always. Without a moment of hesitation he said no. The humiliation, he said, would be unbearable for them.

We sat in the closest thing to silence the town offered and Simon smoked. Some juiced trucks revved in the distance. There was not much left of the Old Denver Road we knew. There was a Safeway now and a Starbucks and a Walgreen's, like everywhere. Norm's was long gone and the Gas Stop had become a Conoco. The town had fanned out into subdivisions with borrowed and nonsense names like The Hamptons and River Wynde and Falconridge and Glenbrook and The Grange. I had developed them. I had named them. Nearly all these people shopped at power centres between here and The Springs or south of Denver, where you could worship at the temple Costco. Also my fault.

I had not been unhappy. Maybe in love. Yes, I had been unhappy. But everyone was unhappy. I drank too much, even though it was good wine, and I ate too much salt and bad fat even though it was pink Himalayan salt and local, free-range bad fat. I did not have to worry about money anymore but I did anyway.

"Why not come see me in London instead of smelly Paris?"

"Paris is prettier."

"Come on." He seemed to dread asking it, because he knew and preferred to simply know. "You don't have business in Paris. No one does."

"I saw Beatrice today."

"What?" He tilted his head at me. Shortly after he'd arrived in the UK, his Kenyan accent had taken on a veneer of posh. "Did you ever talk about her, with Helen?"

"Not really."

"What does that mean, Adam? *Not really.* One discusses Beatrice or one does not."

"Our time with her ended with a man shooting his face off. It was never something I could enjoy discussing with my mother. With anyone, really. I thought about it, about her, constantly. Mom did too, I think. But—"

"What do you mean you *saw her?*"

"She was in the church today, at the back."

"The narthex."

"What?"

"The back of a church is called the narthex."

"You made that up."

"And you, brother, saw a ghost."

"Probably."

The smirk that attended our conversations, even at the grimmest of occasions, departed from him. He looked away. Thousands and thousands of times I had returned to the day Marv caught us making love—the day she disappeared. When the chief was with me in the living room, my mother was in the basement with Simon. My mother was not furious that day,

311

not distraught. She seemed to be daydreaming. "You know what, Adam? I take it back. If you feel she's alive, she's alive."

"Wait."

"Just go to Paris. In fact, I'll go with you. There's a restaurant on the Place des Vosges."

"Please."

"You could not have seen Beatrice in the church."

"Why not?

Simon put out his cigarette even though it was not finished. He waved me along and I followed him through the parking lot. The setting sun shone on a spotless red Audi surrounded by filthy pickup trucks. I was going to make a joke about him renting the Simon of Automobiles when he popped the trunk and the hot new plastic off-gassed into our faces. He pulled out a shiny Harrods jewellery bag and handed it to me.

I opened the bag and there were two passports inside. "What are these?"

"Look at them."

Before I opened the first one I knew what it was. There was a photograph of Beatrice with the name "Carol Laquedem." The other was mine: "Chris Laquedem."

"Helen gave them to me the day you were supposed to meet Beatrice at the library."

"Where did she get them?"

"The plan was to send Beatrice away with a promise of money from your company. Remember, Beatrice was said to have stolen it?"

"'Was *said to have*'? It might have bankrupted us if Marv hadn't put mom in his will."

"No. Helen pulled out that money, not Beatrice. I think she really was going to wire it, to get rid of her. Your uncle had a cabin on some mountain lake in Idaho."

"Redfish Lake."

"Beatrice was supposed to drive that white Cadillac to Idaho. She was going to stay at the lake for a month or so and then make her way to—yes, maybe—France. We would never see her again. Helen went next door one final time that afternoon, when Beatrice was packing, to settle things."

"And she found these."

"Beatrice planned to come back for you, planned to take you away. Helen was sure of it."

"And I would have gone."

"You're still going."

I imagined my mother at the veterinary clinic, in her blood-stained scrubs, apologizing and whispering a silent prayer before injecting Beatrice with too much tranquilizer. *All I do is kill, every day. I'm a genuine killer. Shhh. Close your eyes.*

"What did she do, Simon?"

"I'll tell you on the airplane."

"Jesus Christ. No one's going to Paris."

"I'm terrible at secrets. This is the only one I ever kept. It's been heavy."

"Can I have the passports?"

"It's why I brought them." He grabbed my arm as I took the bag. "You're a dad now. You understand why. Where would you be now if you had gone?"

She was there, all this time, tangled in garbage at the bottom of Monument Lake. Wherever murderers put people. I practiced saying it in my mind before I said it, before I whispered in the parking lot: *murderer*.

"These . . . gangsters looking for Beatrice were not men of dignity and honour and compassion."

"Just say it, Sye."

"Beatrice had told Helen all about them. They were easy to find. They owned restaurants, tattoo parlours, even pharmacies. Helen just phoned. A man phoned her back and she told him where to find her in Idaho—whatever her real name was. Helen made the calls that same day, from the basement. I was with her. She finished the last call maybe ten minutes before the police chief showed up."

Uncle Oscar's cabin had always smelled of cedar logs and of the fireplace and the pipe tobacco he smoked. There was a red rug on the floor, and a blown-up version of the photo of us—my mother and Jason and me—above the mantel. When you first arrived at Redfish Lake you had to pull back the bedsheets to be sure mice hadn't built nests inside.

"You were her confessional."

"I just happened to be there. No, that's not correct. I encouraged her." He closed the trunk of his glittering car and lit another skinny Davidoff cigarette and looked at it, like it had surprised him somehow. "I didn't go to my parents' bible camp because I wanted to go to my parents' bible camp. My plan was never to speak to you again, none of you cursed Lisinskis. Over time I forgave Helen, and you, and myself. What would you do for your boys? This whole country, the world, it's full of . . . we're all killers in our hearts."

"I'm sorry."

"I felt I had done it too, just by knowing."

"Just by knowing. But do you know? Do you know what happened to her?"

"No. But Helen did."

In 2009, Steve and Laverne Brandt turned off the water to save money. They trucked in some dirt, transformed the mermaid fountain into a circular mound of untended shrubbery and weeds, and moved to a condo in Hawaii. Theirs is now the oldest mansion in Sage Landing, a gated neighbourhood of twisting roads, multi-million-dollar homes, and carefully planted boulders and pines. My mother and I developed almost one hundred and fifty acres into luxury villas and collected our fees before the crash in 2008. Phoebe's parents lost a good piece of their wealth when they sold many of the properties for an enormous loss. Citibank seized twenty of them. That did not cause our divorce, but it fuelled grievances and conspiracies that helped it along.

I had a key to the house but I did not want to startle Nikki, the last remaining domestic staff member. It was fifteen minutes after the boys' bedtime, and I knew what that meant. I rang the doorbell. Nikki opened it, her black hair pulled into a hasty ponytail. The air conditioning was still broken. I had offered to take care of it but Carlos had read *Zen and the Art of Motorcycle Maintenance* and felt he was obliged. The hot air was heavy with cooked pasta. "Mr. Adam, thank heaven."

"Is it bad?"

"They are monsters tonight."

Nikki, who supported her own family in a suburb of Manila by working here, flopped into a decorative wing chair in the foyer. She looked as though she had spent the evening breaking up a prison riot. My oldest, Henry, was afraid of the dark, so even though they lived in a house with nine bedrooms they shared one. I climbed the stairs and ran into the boys' room barking like a baboon. We bounced on the beds together.

I read *If I Ran the Zoo* and alternated between answering their questions about Grandma's funeral and shushing them in the dark for half an hour until they were asleep. An acre of land separated Phoebe's house from the adjacent one in Sage Landing, so when it was quiet it was quiet. The boys breathed and shifted on their sheets, mumbling nonsense to themselves. I looked at photos of my mother on my phone, a bunch I had gathered for the slideshow in the church, and lay on the floor of my sons' bedroom. In one of the photographs she stands in front of her first subdivision in Denver. The day she made it. She always wore dresses after the summer of 1989, and carried matching purses. An alert popped on my screen: it was time to leave for the airport. I pulled down Henry's extra pillow and closed my eyes.

By the time the police dismissed us on the night Marv blew his face off, the storm had passed and the rain had nearly stopped. Neither of us was ready to sleep, and the lights of the emergency vehicles flashed on our walls. I did not want to be alone in the basement and my mother did not want to be alone either. It was 1989, so no one had thought to dispatch a psychologist to Jefferson Street. We didn't know what else to do so we walked the dogs.

I was wearing a T-shirt. The rain had cooled the town. My mother took off her cardigan and handed it to me.

"It's way too small."

"Please."

"You'll be cold, Mom. I'll just go back and grab one."

"Just this one thing." She started to put it on me. "I need you to put it on."

The sweater smelled like Marlboro Lights and Imari by Avon, which she wore her whole life: I sprayed it on her tiny wrist in palliative care. My mother and I walked the dogs every day but we were not dog walkers. There were too few real trees to make a walk feel like leisure or even a thing in itself. But on the night Marv died it seemed right and pure, much better than watching a James Bond movie.

At the end of our block, beyond where the Katies lived, the street curved naturally into Santa Fe Avenue. There was an old playground beyond the ugly parking lot where the school buses spent the night. It was my playground and Jason's, next to a basketball court without nets. All of it lay steaming from the rain, in the sea-foam glow of a distant streetlight. There was no other destination in our neighbourhood and nowhere to explore, so we sat on the swings, two slabs of hard plastic attached to chains. My mother took off her shoes and socks. I had been desperate to ask for all her secrets about Beatrice but now, on the swings, in her soft and fragrant cardigan whose sleeves came up to my elbows, I decided not to do it. I would never do it. The chains had rusted and the whole contraption flexed and squeaked when I pumped forward and back. When I was little the swing set had seemed massive; but now it was small and fragile and untrustworthy. Swings made me dizzy when I was a boy and they made me dizzy when I was fourteen but I went as high as I could go and then higher. My mother did not swing. She looked down at the wet and dirty sand, moved it with her toes. She was forty-one. The stars were out, the dogs were sniffing for other dogs, and we could hear the cars on the interstate. Somewhere in the distance they were frying chicken two hours before sunrise.

We are six and eight, fourteen and forty-one forever. We are underdressed for the cold and we are sick with love, what feels like love, and we know we must stop and we try, we say we try, but we just can't stop. I pumped as high as I could go and for an instant I was too high. The old chains of the swing set cried out. I looked down and my mother reached for me.

discussion questions

1. How did reading this story from Adam's perspective influence the way you view this community of people?

2. "The woman lowered herself from Marv's pickup truck wearing the first pair of high-heeled shoes I'd ever seen touch Jefferson Street. At contact she lifted one from the gravel like she had stepped into a colony of snails and looked up the sunburned lawn at me." (p. 3) What does this first description of Beatrice tell you about her? How does your understanding of her character evolve?

3. "Marv Walker of the—what?—New York bloody Yankees? Yet here you are, a fat American labourer like all the millions of other fat American labourers. You do something—what

do you do?—in a medical devices factory that—if my sources are correct—could shut down any time and move to Mexico if not China. This is a particularly American disease, wishing upon a star, and frankly it's below even you."(p. 18) How does this outburst from Don set the tone of the novel?

4. Are there several possible meanings to the title, *The Empress of Idaho*, or does the title only refer to the way that Adam sees Beatrice? Why or why not?

5. "Every year at Christmastime our insurance agent stapled a pouch of flower seeds to a desk calendar and hired a girl to put it in the mailbox. With a shaky hand he wrote a passage from the Bible, the same one every year, and included it in the envelope. I remember how it ended: *the time of the singing of birds is come, and the voice of the turtledove is heard in our land.* In 1988, his gift had been a packet of sweet williams."(p. 3) What's the significance of this quote from the Bible and the imagery of the sweet williams?

6. *The Empress of Idaho* is as much about the power of human relationships as it is about betrayal. Discuss the novel's portrayal of fundamental relationships. What is Adam's relationship with his mother like? What do you think of Adam's friendship with Simon?

7. "Men can be pretty damn awful to women. You read about it every day. Men were awful to her, right from when she

was little. Maybe she told you all about it. I kinda hope not. There's stuff I know I'll never forget. But I fear deep down she came here just to wound me." (p. 275) This passage from Marv describes Beatrice as a victim and a culprit. Do you think it's as simple as labelling her one or the other? In which ways does her character make you ask challenging questions about the cycle of sexual abuse?

8. ". . . if we are refugees our children will be refugees, even our children's children. They may not know it."(p. 193) What is Mr. Kinoro trying to say about the experience of being a refugee in this passage?

9. The characters in this novel provide a range of views on the ways that sexual assault is addressed in society, from the victim trying to disassociate from the trauma to the mother of the victim trying to help her child get past the trauma. What does Chief Dunn's point of view bring to the narrative? What did you make of the interaction between Chief Dunn and Adam?

10. How does this novel explore the idea of masculinity? And how does Adam's understanding of it change over time?"

11. There are a multitude of experiences being unpacked in this novel. What did you learn about coming of age, racism, and socioeconomic status? Has reading this novel influenced the way you look at these complicated experiences?

12. Helen observes, "You never get it back. They take it away from you, that feeling *it's all yours, this is your town, your state, this is your country, your life to build*. And it's gone. For the rest of Simon's life . . ." (p. 187) How did you react to what happened to Simon?

13. At the end of the novel, did you get the sense that Adam has come to terms with his past and with the trauma of what he experienced?

14. Through characters like Helen, the author weaves together the harsh realities and the beauty in this town, in this story. What is your opinion of Helen? Did your opinion of her change when you found out about her thriving businesses?

15. Discuss the ending of *The Empress of Idaho*. How did you react to the truth about what happened to Beatrice?

TODD BABIAK'S most recent novels are *Son of France* and *Come Barbarians*, which was a *Globe and Mail* book of the year and a number one bestseller. His earlier work includes *The Garneau Block*, which was a national bestseller, a longlisted title for the Scotiabank Giller Prize, and the winner of the City of Edmonton Book Prize; *The Book of Stanley*; and *Toby: A Man*, which was shortlisted for the Stephen Leacock Medal and won the Alberta Book Award for Best Novel. Todd Babiak is the co-founder of Story Engine, a consulting company based in Edmonton and Vancouver.